Space Magic

Space Magic

Stories by
David D. Levine

With an Introduction by
Bruce Holland Rogers

 **Wheatland Press**
http://www.wheatlandpress.com

Wheatland Press

http://www.wheatlandpress.com

Library of Congress Cataloging-in-Publication data is available upon request.
ISBN **978-0-9794054-3-3**
Printed in the United States of America
Interior design by Deborah Layne.
Cover art and design by Darin Bradley.

Contents

Some Guy Talking About Some Other Guy's Stories

Short story collections are notoriously hard to sell, particularly for a writer whose name is not already well known, even if the stories that make up the book are really good and have won awards. Hence the need for an introduction. The publisher hopes that at least a few readers who don't know David Levine's name will have heard of Bruce Holland Rogers and will read the introduction to see what I have to say. My job is to snag those readers in the book store (Buy this book!) or the library (Borrow this book!) thanks to my name and my enthusiasm for Mr. Levine's stories.

However, like Levine, I am a short story writer. Novels build name recognition. Stories generally don't. I've been in this game a bit longer than Mr. Levine, but to the average book browser, I'm unknown. To the average book browser, this introduction is Some Guy writing to introduce the stories of Some Other Guy. The average book browser should be thinking right about now, Why don't I just skip the introduction and read a story?

By all means, do!

I suggest that you begin with the story with the least pronounceable title, "Tk'Tk'Tk." Members of the World Science Fiction Convention for 2006, meeting in Anaheim, California, voted it the best English-language science-fiction short story of the year, adding Levine's name to an impressive list of past winners such as Neil Gaiman, Mike Resnick, Michael Swanwick, and Connie Willis. "Tk'Tk'Tk" is the story of a salesman who is trying to work what must be the least promising sales territory in the galaxy, and his frustration at dealing with the complex customs and language of his prospective clients will remind some readers of classic alien encounters such as Jack Vance's "The Moon Moth." It's not just the aliens and their wonderful money that make this story memorable, though. "Tk'Tk'Tk" comes to an apt yet surprising ending.

So, average book browser, off you go! There's nothing to see here. Go read that story!

Now, for the compulsive who has to read every word of a book, and in order, let me see if I can tempt you into giving up that practice here and now. If I couldn't get you to go read "Tk'tk'tk" immediately, maybe I can tempt you with "Love in the Balance," a story set in a city floating in the sky, where the chief mode of transportation is zeppelins.

Or how about a teen love story, a contemporary fantasy with a lovely twist or two? "Falling off the Unicorn" is where the Western Quarter Horse Association national horse show meets Faerie, complete with stage mothers and snippy pre-teen competitors. It is likely to be the only story you ever read where one character is described as "a barracuda in a double-A bra."

What, you're still here?

Instead of continuing with this introduction, wouldn't you rather read a story about a man whose father has decided to become a dog? Or the story about a junk yard where things that never existed in this universe are scattered among the broken washing machines, rusting away? How about a fairy story written from an ecological perspective? Or a story demonstrating what it's like to live inside a comic book as one of its characters? Go read the stories!

Yet here you still are, in spite of my best efforts.

I might as well tell you, then, that is is a particular pleasure for me to introduce this collection because I had the honor of buying Levine's story "Wind From a Dying Star" years ago when I was editing an original anthology. It was his first sale. I'm sure that selling the story made him very happy, but finding his story made me very happy, too. Every writer should spend some time in the editor's chair, learning how many hopeless manuscripts come in response to a call for submissions, discovering for himself what it feels like, while reading one mediocre first page after another, to read a first page that pulls him right in and transports him. I knew from the first lines of this story that I was in good hands, and I'm pleased to say that I still like "Wind From a Dying Star," from first words to last, as much as I did years ago.

One of the best things about writing short stories instead of novels is that no one cares if you cross or blend genres, writing heroic fantasy, contemporary fantasy, science fiction, or expressionism. Novelists are expected to specialize. Short story writers can work in a variety of different traditions, as Levine demonstrates.

As much as Levine's work is varied, it also demonstrates a consistency. This is science fiction and fantasy where they have come to be written in the post-industrial age. The borders between the genres have blurred, and the agenda has changed. At one time, science fiction was propelled by the dream of humanity's leap into interstellar space. I grew up thinking that I might have a life among the stars. The goal of humanity was, I once thought, to spread ourselves beyond this ball of dirt circling this one sun.

Increasingly, the dreams of science fiction have bumped against the realities of the physical world. Gravity wells are deep. The biosphere is a web that supports us but also, like a spider web, holds us. We are this little ball of dirt. It's likely that the only planet humans will ever know is this one. Although science fiction is the literature of what is possible, much of what is possible is also highly unlikely.

For many readers and writers, science fiction has changed from being a brochure for the future to being, like fairy tales, another way of telling stories that engage our imaginations with a purely invented reality, an exclusively literary reality. Some readers who first encountered science fiction when I did look at our current realities and despair. Where are our moon colonies? Our flying cars? Our terraformed Mars? We thought SF was more than just art.

But writers like David Levine remind us that we can still go to flying cities, the far reaches of deep space, and planets inhabited by exceedingly polite chitinous aliens. Better yet, our destinations don't have to be limited by what's actually possible or can be made—by science-fictional sleight of hand— to seem possible. We can go to a present time that's only a little different from the time we know, one populated with creatures of myth or with 1950's model-year nuclear cars. Outer space or faerie, an alternate medieval China or a haunted 1930's America, we can visit right now.

Just turn the page.

Bruce Holland Rogers
London, England
February, 2008

Acknowledgements

The author gratefully acknowledges everyone who has helped to make these stories possible, including but not limited to: the staff and students of Clarion West class of 2000 (especially Patrick Weekes, Pat Murphy and Candas Jane Dorsey), the members of the Lucky Lab Rats critique group (especially Sara Mueller, M.K. Hobson, and John C. Bunnell), the editors who bought them (especially Gordon Van Gelder, Gardner Dozois, Deborah Layne, and Bruce Holland Rogers—who not only bought my very first story, he also wrote the Introduction), and all the fans and writers who have offered their support and encouragement over the years (especially Jay Lake, Karen Berry, Paul Wrigley and Debbie Cross). But first and fundamentally, this my first published book is dedicated to Kate Yule—my love, my flying partner, and my best friend forever.

Wind From a Dying Star

GUNAI SEETHED WITH SORROW and rage as she helped to prepare Kula's corpse for its final journey.

Kula had always delighted in her body, its warm and golden glow, the way it flowed into a thousand useful and expressive shapes. She had explored the universe with its senses and reached out with its fields. Now it was nothing but a senseless lump of flesh and brain and polymer, a cold mockery of what she had been. Kula the person was gone. Taken by a wolf.

The torn and ravaged corpse floated between Gunai and Old John, barely visible in the dim starlight. The other members of the tribe were gathered in a sphere around them, their glowing forms held in angular shapes of grief as Old John spoke the words of Kula's eulogy.

More than Kula's life had been lost in the attack. Kula had carried a child, conceived at their recent meeting with the tribe of Yeoshi. Gone now, along with whatever fraction of the father's memories it had carried. Even Kula's intuition, one of the best in the tribe, was gone. A compound tragedy.

"We mourn and remember Kula," Old John concluded. "For as long as we remember her, in a very real way she still lives."

"We mourn and remember Kula," they all said, and paused for silent reflection.

Unwillingly, Gunai's mind returned to the moment when Kula's screams had been their first notice. She blamed herself. Kula should not have strayed so far from the tribe, she knew; Enaji and Huss should have kept a better lookout; Yaeri should have called a warning. But Gunai, as tribe leader, was ultimately responsible. She should have recognized the danger, should have prevented it somehow. That knowledge pained her, burned from the inside like the hunger that chewed at her belly.

Old John caught Gunai's attention. His form did not show emotion like a normal person's; it was fixed in an archaic five-lobed shape. But through long acquaintance Gunai had learned to read his attitudes and intentions. Without a word, Gunai and Old John grasped Kula's body with their fields and accelerated it toward the nearest star.

The cold and lifeless thing quickly faded from view—just another bit of dark matter in a cooling universe. The tribe stared after it long after it had vanished, then gathered together in a group embrace of sorrow and reassurance. They held each other for a long time, but eventually, one by one, they drifted away to forage for food. Not even grief was stronger than hunger.

Gunai made sure all four lookouts were at their stations before she allowed herself to begin foraging.

After a time she found a small patch of zeren. She spread across it, taking a little solace from its sparkling sweetness. "Zero-point energy" was what Old John called it, but to Gunai and the rest of her tribe it was zeren, delicious and rare. Gunai recalled a time when zeren was something you could almost ignore—a constant crackling thrum beneath the surface of perception—but now there were just a few thin patches here and there. These days the tribe subsisted mostly on a thin diet of starlight, and even that was growing cold. Soon they would be forced to move on again. Yeoshi had told her the foraging was better in the direction of the galactic core, but it was so far...

A sudden motion caught Gunai's nervous eye, but it was just her daughter Teda. She had bumped Old John with her fields, sending his blocky form tumbling for a moment. "Teda!" Gunai scolded privately.

"But Mother, he's so *slow!*"

"He's doing the best he can. You should apologize."

Teda turned to Old John, forming herself into a flattened oval of contrition, and said "I'm sorry I bumped you." Gunai was pleased that it seemed sincere, but he replied only with a curt gesture of acknowledgement.

Old John's silence troubled Gunai. Apart from necessities, he had barely said anything since their meeting with the tribe of Yeoshi. This was unlike him. Usually he loved to share stories from his many years—though some derided them as mere legends—and Gunai was surprised he hadn't picked up anything new at the gathering. Until now she had left him alone, thinking he might spring back by himself, but after Teda moved away she asked him privately what was bothering him.

"You know there was another of my... cohort, in the other tribe. One nearly as old as I. Shala was her name."

"Yes, I know. I saw you with her." It had been strange to see another with Old John's stiff and blocky shape. She had thought he was unique. "Did she have any new stories for you?"

"She had new information. But not stories I would like to tell."

"Go on."

"She told me... she told me Earth's sun is dying." There was a sadness in his voice Gunai had never heard before. "Ballooning into a red giant. Much sooner than anyone had expected."

"I'm sorry." The words seemed so tiny.

"Given the velocities we use, I suppose I should have expected to outlive my birth planet. But still, the news hurt."

"I thought Earth was gone already?"

"No. Dead, yes. Emptied, wasted, ruined, picked over. But still there. Massive with history. No other planet holds the stones where Shakespeare and Caesar walked. No other planet has that year, that gravity, that... that place in the sky." His awkward form curled into a ball. "Soon even the headstone of Humanity will be gone."

"It is a shame," Gunai said, though many of his words meant nothing to her.

"My own bones are there," the old man sobbed.

"What are bones?"

"Parts of me I threw away to become what I am today. Parts you never even had. They are buried with my parents."

"I'm sorry, I don't understand."

"No," he sighed, relaxing. "No, you wouldn't. And you aren't going to understand this either, but I want... no, I *need* to visit Earth again. To see it one more time before we both are gone."

"You can't be serious." Gunai's intuition told her where Earth was — over a thousand light-years away, in the very center of the deadest, most used-up area of the galaxy. "There's nothing there."

"I am serious. I will go by myself if I have to."

Part of Gunai sneered that the tribe would be better off without the old man slowing them down. She beat that part down. "I'm afraid I can't allow that. We need your wisdom."

Old John's body never showed emotion, but his voice now held a mixture of pleasure and regret. "Thank you. But... I feel I've taught you all I know already. Let an old man go to visit his dying homeworld. Please."

"It would be different if you could have children to carry on your memories." Old John looked away at that, and Gunai chided herself for raising the awkward issue. "I will consult with Enaji."

Enaji was one of Gunai's most trusted advisers. He was old — nearly half as old as Old John — but he had been born in space in the usual way, and upgraded his body and intuition regularly.

"Let him go," he said. "Drain on the tribe."

4

Gunai felt herself contracting in denial at his words. "How can you say that? Remember how he saved Rael and Kanna from the wolves? How he found a way out of the poison nebula? How his stories kept Jori alive?"

"Long time ago." He furled his edges at her. "These are new times. Perilous. Universe is changing, and he is too old to change with it. Remember, I offered to share my intuition with him. He refused."

"I can't believe you could be so ungrateful."

"Gunai... don't you see?" He stroked her with his fields, his tone softening. "His time is past. He knows it. Let him go. Let him keep his dignity."

She turned away, presenting Enaji with a blind surface. "If I let him attempt that journey alone he would die. I could never live with myself."

"Hard times call for hard decisions."

The stars were tiny shards of light, scattered thinly on a dark background. Cold and heartless. They stared in at Gunai as she thought. How could she jeopardize her tribe for one old man's insane whim? But how could she abandon the tribe's eldest, wisest member — possibly the oldest human of all?

Gunai's intuiton told her there were trillions of humans, but space was so vast that even in her long life she'd encountered other tribes less than a hundred times. To leave a person alone, to cast them into the depths of time and space where they might never meet another human being again, was the greatest sin. Would a person who could convince herself to commit that sin be worthy of leadership? Would a tribe that could condone such a sin be worth leading?

No. She had lost Kula; she would not lose Old John.

"I will not abandon him," she said to Enaji, "and I will not deny his request. We will all go to Earth."

He pulled into a tight little ball. "We will regret this."

5

"We may. But we would be less than human if we did not make the attempt."

She sent out a call to the rest of the tribe. They gathered in a loose sphere with Gunai at the center.

She told them that Earth, ancestral home of humanity, was dying. She reminded them of Old John's stories, which they all knew from their earliest days—fables of trees and mountains, castles and whales. She raised the spectre of isolation. She recalled the tragedy of Kula's loss, and reminded them of regrets at things left undone until too late.

She called to their hearts.

There was debate. There was anger and acrimony. But in the end Gunai prevailed, for no one—not even Enaji—was cold-hearted enough to leave Old John to die of loneliness. Even if it meant risking their own lives.

The tribe scattered to forage. They would need all the energy they could muster for the journey.

Old John had been silent the whole time, sitting alone just outside the sphere of the meeting. Listening. After the last of the tribe had left, he came to Gunai.

"Thank you," he said. The words were tiny, but they filled Gunai's heart.

Some time later, the tribe gathered together to begin the journey. Rubbing and jostling, they pulled into a single mass -- a teardrop shape with a hard, smooth outer surface. Intuition told them it was the best shape for this task. Then they channeled their energies together and pushed.

The motion was not immediately apparent, but they kept on, straining and huffing, pouring energy into acceleration. From time to time one or another member would relax for a moment, borne along by the others, then would resume the effort. But frail Old John never rested—he kept up a constant, steady thread of power.

As their velocity increased, they began to be peppered with

particles of dust. Matter was thin here, but each particle stung, and they encountered more and more as they went faster. Soon they had to divert some of their energy to shielding the tribe from the impacts, and they all stared forward with eyes and intuition for larger masses that could do more than hurt.

The stars ahead appeared to brighten, their color changing from red to yellow and then to blue, and they seemed to smear out to the sides. As the eye swept to the side and back it could see a spectrum of colors, fading to red and finally to black behind them. The starbow.

"You told us about something called a 'rainbow,'" Teda said to Old John. "Did it look like this?"

"Something like it," he said, "but brighter, not so diffuse." He paused, panting, for a moment, then said "I think that the eyes I had then would not even be able to see the starbow. I wonder what a rainbow would look like to the eyes I have now?"

On and on they pushed, watching the universe flatten from a sphere into a ring of stars around them, fending off a rain of stinging impacts, feeling their motivators burn from unaccustomed effort and their bellies ache from hunger.

Finally they could push no more. They relaxed and coasted, though they still had to expend energy on shielding and course corrections. They coasted for a long time—fourteen years by their intuition, a thousand years or more by the stars. Most of them spent most of the time asleep, conserving energy. Gunai made sure there was always someone awake to maintain the shields and watch out for obstacles.

At last the time arrived to turn about. Guided by their intuition, they reformed themselves into a flaring saucer shape, catching the hail of dust they had been avoiding before. Even with shields, the dust burned their skins, but it helped them to slow. They began to push again, motivators aching. The universe expanded to a sphere, fading from a starbow back to a simple background of stars.

One star was much larger than the rest. They had come to a halt only a few hundred light-minutes away from it.

More than half the tribe had never been this close to a star before.

None but Old John had ever been so close to this particular star. Sol.

The mother star looked sick. Its disk was turgid, yellow mottled with red, and its magnetic field roiled like their starving bellies. The wind of charged particles flowing from it battered the tribe as they separated from a traveling mass into a tribe of individuals. They took a little nourishment from the solar wind, but it was barely worth the effort. Old John said it was "like trying to drink from a hailstorm," whatever that meant.

Gunai took on a streamlined shape, to resist the wind as best she could. She sent Enaji, Huss, and the rest of the best foragers out to look for zeren, and guided the rest of the tribe to the shadow of a nearby comet. Molecules of water and methane, burned from the comet by Sol's angry heat, chilled their skins, but the comet's rocky body shielded them from the wind.

After a time Enaji returned. "There's nothing here," he said, visibly shaken. "No zeren. Not a trace."

"That's impossible," said Gunai. "Zeren forms from the energy of space itself. There's always *something*."

"The theory says zero-point energy cannot be consumed," said Old John, "but there's no denying it's getting scarce. Apparently, around here, humanity managed to find a way to use it all up." He went quiet for a moment. "This might explain why Sol is dying young."

Gunai fought the urge to contract in fear. She needed to present a confident facade. "Perhaps one of the other foragers will find something."

But as they came back, each had the same story: Nothing.

Nothing. Nothing.

Gunai's heart tore as Huss, the last to return, came in sight. She was glad to see him safe, hopeful that he might have found forage, but after so much disappointment she was certain he would bring more of the same.

"Bad news," Huss called. "Just one patch of zeren. Very thin."

Gunai felt her edges flare in relief.

The tribe gathered together and left the comet's tail, pushing into the battering solar wind. The stronger individuals shielded the weaker as much as they could, but all were pummeled. Gunai moved at the head of the tribe, taking the wind's full force.

"You're pushing yourself too hard," said Enaji privately. "You should rest. Let me lead the tribe for a time."

"No. I made the decision to come here. I should live with the consequences." She tightened her leading edge and shoved herself forward, spreading wide to give Teda and Old John a little protection.

The chill wind rasped her skin. She gnawed on the pain, a bitter taste that deepened her martyred mood. How could she have been so foolish? She should have listened to Enaji before. She should listen to Enaji now. But to rest would spoil her self-punishment.

Finally a field of zeren appeared at the edges of perception. It was small, and thin, but it was here and it was what they needed. They spread over it eagerly, reveling in the zeren's sweetness. Gunai was too tired to protest when Enaji channeled some of the energy he'd gathered to her; too tired to compliment Teda when she did the same for Old John.

They were all too tired, too hungry, to notice the wolves that circled the field.

They came knifing in from the dark of space, three hard black needles that cut through the tribe with inhuman screams. They lacked intelligence and intuition, but their natural abilities and instincts had been honed by eons of competition with the humans who had copied their bodies, and their hunger was sharp.

The first took Rael, piercing her through the center and carrying her away in one piece. Her cries were cut short before she was out of range. The second came at Gunai, but she dodged and lost only a few percent of her mass to the wolf's raking fields.

The third hit Teda. Hit her hard, tearing away a huge part of her substance. She pinweeled, screaming in agony, fields and mass spewing into the vacuum.

The shock of the impact ran through Gunai, hurting her more than the injury she herself had just suffered. She hurried to Teda's side, shielding her from the wind with her body, soothing her with strokes and healing energies. Teda's screams became whimpers, then began to fade.

"Here they come again!" cried Enaji.

Gunai whipped around to face the threat. Enaji and several of the others had firmed into needles, matching the wolves' forms — hard to spot, hard to hit. Most of the rest were tightened into balls. "Make yourselves thin, like Enaji!" Gunai called to the tribe. "Enaji, Duna, Huss! Defend!" She moved out with the three she'd named, positioning herself between the tribe and the incoming wolves, making her skin as hard as she could. Prepared to sacrifice herself to save the others.

Thrashed by the wind, her attention focused on the wolves, Gunai did not see Old John moving up until he was already past.

"John!" Gunai screamed. "Get back behind me!"

Old John's voice was determined as he accelerated away from Gunai, toward the wolves. "No," he said. "*You* get back. This old body still has a few surprises in it."

Then three bolts of energy sprang from Old John, three ragged lines of force that touched the wolves and tore them into pieces. Their death screams were briefer than Rael's.

When Gunai and Enaji reached Old John, his awkward form was glowing red. "Stay back," he called weakly. "I'm too hot to touch."

"What *was* that?" said Gunai.

"Gravitic cannon. A weapon built for a war that was fought and lost a million years ago. Right here at Sol System."

Enaji asked "Why have you never done this thing before?"

"I have, but never where you could see."

"Why?" cried Gunai.

"I didn't want to burden you with the knowledge of what I am."

Gunai was taken aback. "You are Old John. You are the oldest and wisest human I have ever met."

"I am a *weapon!*" His body, now cooled almost to black, trembled. "I gave up my humanity a long time ago. I let myself be turned into a copy of those wolves we just met—but better, faster, more deadly." He sighed. "For love of God and country."

What were God and country? "You are as human as any of us."

"You aren't..." He bit off his words, started again. "You were born this way. You are full and valid individuals, on your own terms. But I cannot forget that I was something else before this. I maintain a familiar shape"—he gestured at his five-lobed form—"but sometimes I feel I am only a parody of what I used to be."

Old John was now cool enough to approach. "Let us take you back to the tribe," Enaji said. "You need food, and rest."

"I am tired," he acknowledged, and closed his eyes.

The rest of the tribe was badly shaken from their encounter with the wolves. They mourned Rael, and Teda was still leaking substance, despite Kanna's ministrations. "She cannot heal properly without food," Kanna said.

"Gather zeren," said Gunai. "All you can find. She can have my share."

"I have already given her your share, and mine, and everyone's who could spare any. This field is too thin."

"We must find another field, then."

"Yes. But we don't know how far that might be. She might die on the journey."

"It's all we can do." She called to the tribe. Wearily the foragers prepared for another search.

Old John moved close to Gunai and whispered hoarsely. "There may be another way," he said.

"Go on."

"My intuition isn't as good as yours, but its memory is unsurpassed. The war for which I was... built, it was a long and brutal one. We had caches of energy and supplies all over the Inner System. Some of them may still be there."

"You said it was a million years ago!"

"We knew it would be a long war. Those caches were well-preserved, and well-defended. Only one who knows the old codes could open them."

Gunai thought hard. It seemed a thin chance, but Old John's wisdom had proven itself many times. The alternative was even thinner. "Very well. Take Enaji and Huss. Travel quickly and find one of these caches. I will follow with the rest of the tribe. Good luck."

"I'll do my best."

Old John, Enaji, and Huss formed into a single needle and moved off, while Gunai explained the plan to the tribe. She had expected protests, but her explanation met only weary stares; the tribe was too tired, too demoralized. She was ashamed, knowing her poor decisions had led them to this point.

The tribe grouped into a streamlined shape, with unconscious Teda cradled in its center and Gunai at the leading edge. She stroked Teda with a field as they melded together.

Gunai's motivators screamed in protest as she helped to accelerate the tribe into the oncoming wind. There was no starbow this time—they lacked the energy for those velocities. There was just a steady, slogging push, and the moans of exhausted tribe members.

The solar wind gusted and keened, battering them harder and harder as they came closer to the dying star. Old John's signal was a steady, unmoving point ahead of them. The weary tribe passed a gas giant, its surface roiled and its ring system pushed off-center by the wind's unnatural pressure. They entered a region scattered with chewed-up planetoids and worthless, abandoned hardware.

Finally they came in sight of Earth itself.

None of them had ever seen it before, but Old John's many stories had taught them what it had been. A delicate ball of white and blue, he'd said, clad in the thinnest gossamer of atmosphere, the subtle breath of life.

No longer.

The atmosphere had been stripped away—by the war, by the wind, or by human action, there was no telling. What remained was a picked-over skull of a world, a gray mottled thing pocked with craters and circled by belts of detritus. Old John was in one of those belts, in synchronous orbit over the night side of the planet.

The tribe passed gratefully into the Earth's shadow, relaxing as they left the pummeling solar wind. The dying star's corona flared wildly as it fell behind the horizon.

They found Old John, Enaji, and Huss orbiting near a battered lump of aluminum and titanium. Old John's relative position was steady; the other two flailed and fluttered, now falling back, now catching up. They had no experience with orbital mechanics this close to a primary.

Gunai came up to Old John, who steadied her with a field. Weary though she was, Gunai could see Old John was wearier still—tired as the ruined world below, from which his gaze did not stray. "I'm a million years old, Gunai," he said. "I don't think I ever really felt the... *depth* of that before."

"Only as the planets measure time, John."

"I think that's the only way that really matters."

They were silent for a time.

"I'm sorry," Gunai said at last, "but Teda needs help. We will be passing into the solar wind again soon. What have you found?"

"It's not a cache, I'm afraid. It's a cascade bomb. But it's still alive, and it responds to my codes. I think I can get it to give up its energies in a form we can use."

"This is all you found?"

"Yes. I'm sorry."

"How much energy?"

"A lot. More than we've seen in one place in... generations."

"That's wonderful!"

But he did not seem pleased. At last he spoke again. "The bomb's brain is very old, and not working well. I'm going to have to perform some of its functions myself."

"I don't understand."

"I'm going to have to go inside the bomb. I have to be in there to release the energies."

The ancient bomb was nothing but a shapeless lump of metal, cracked and dented. Yet it seemed to stare malevolently.

"You'll die."

"Probably."

"I can't let you do that."

"You have to. This is the only known source of usable energy for parsecs. Without it, the tribe will starve here. And Teda will die."

"Let me do it. It was my decision to come here. The tribe needs your wisdom."

"You can't. The codes are keyed to my neurotype. And it was my foolish whim that brought us all here."

The dying sun's corona began to lick over the horizon. Its light made the stiff planes of Old John's body seem to dance and flow like a modern person's.

"You won't be talked out of this," said Gunai. It was not a

question.

"No."

She fought to keep her form steady. "What can I do to help?"

"Form the tribe into a hemisphere around the bomb. Maybe a tenth of a light-second in diameter. Spread yourselves out as thin as you can. Be prepared to let some of the energy through; if you try to catch it all, it may be more than you can take."

"Very well."

"And one more thing." He stared at the dead planet for a long time. "Will you carry my child?"

Gunai was speechless. Finally she sputtered out "It would be an honor. I thought you could not, or I would have asked long ago."

"I can. But I never wanted to, because..." He paused, then began again. "I think of *all* of you as my children. With my tales, I have given you the good memories and kept the bad to myself. But a true child could receive *any* of my memories."

"Don't be ashamed of your memories. They are what make you what you are."

"There are parts of what I am that I don't like." He glanced at the flaring corona. The star's disk would be over the horizon soon. "No more time." He pinched off a bit of himself, a packet of mass and memory, and Gunai took it into her body. "Go now. Remember what I told you."

"I will remember everything."

They entwined their fields briefly, then Gunai departed to instruct the tribe.

Soon the flaring sun, mottled and spotted, appeared over the horizon. Its wind followed immediately, battering the loose hemisphere the tribe had formed. The members were spread out to molecule thinness, barely visible except edge-on. The open side of the hemisphere was toward the wasted planet below.

There was a click in Gunai's ears, then Old John's voice came as though he were right next to her. "I'm connected to the bomb's systems now. I can see everything. The whole system." The battered old bomb began to turn, slowly. "I can even see inside of you. Fields and mechanisms. You are so beautiful... Of all humanity's creations, you—our children—are the finest of all. We can be proud of you." The bomb was spinning faster now, panels opening on its scarred surface. "Take good care of the universe."

A rush of energy came from the bomb, reducing the light and wind from the old sun to insignificance. A colorless torrent of power, an overwhelming sweetness, rich and savory... a flavor Gunai had nearly forgotten. Zeren! Zeren as it once had flowed! But a thousandfold more powerful. Too powerful! She tried to drink it all in, absorb all the energy for the sake of the new life that stirred within her, but finally, sated to bursting, she had to let it go. Her whole body ruffled as the last of the energy passed through her.

The bomb spun, glowing white-hot but cooling rapidly. The tribe tumbled, overwhelmed, their hemispherical formation torn asunder by the bomb's power, the solar wind, and their differing orbits. Their senses rang; their eyes were deafened and their motivators dumb.

Eventually they gathered together in the planet's shadow. Several had tried to take in too much energy and had been burnt or torn. But they all surged with life. Vibrant and shimmering, they danced a pinwheel of sheer glee in the corona light. Even Teda danced, her mass reduced but the pain banished, the torn parts healed.

They gathered the carbonized remains of Old John's body from the bomb housing, and placed them gently in an orbit that would intersect the planet's surface. Gunai wept, but she wept from joy as well as sadness. Her tribe was strong and healthy, and John's child flourished within her, bearing an unknown fraction of the old man's memories.

Finally they drew together into an elegant shape, a majestic, streamlined thing out of one of Old John's tales. With a mere fraction of their energies, they leapt into the starbow.

A whale swam the stars, heading for the untapped regions of the galactic core.

Nucleon

"TATYRCZINSKI," HE SAID, extending his hand. "Karel Tatyrczinski." His blue eyes sparkled under bushy white eyebrows, set in a round pink face. Wispy white hair tried, and failed, to cover a shiny pink scalp. That clean pink and white head emerged from the world's grimiest coverall. It was a fascinating contrast; I thought he'd make a great colored-pencil sketch. I liked him immediately.

I took the hand and shook it. "Pleased to meet you, Mr. Tat... um..."

"Tatter-zin-ski," he repeated. "Call me Carl. What are you looking for, Mr....?"

"James. Phil James. It's kind of difficult to explain. I'll know it when I see it."

"Well," he said, extending his hands to encompass the piles of objects all around him, "whatever it is, I've got it." I was inclined to believe him.

STUFF FOR SALE read the sign above the gate, matching the one-line listing in the Yellow Pages that had led me to this place. It was way, *way* off the beaten path; I was glad I'd called ahead for directions.

The name was apt. A stolid 1920's Craftsman-style house, with an unfortunate skin condition of yellow 1970's asphalt shingles, sat in the middle of piles and piles of... stuff. Heaps of sinks. Stacks of televisions. Three barrels of shoes. File cabinets labeled CHAINS, DOORKNOBS, ALTERNATORS. A haphazard-looking structure of pipes and blue plastic sheeting kept the rain off the more fragile pieces, but a row of toilets standing by the fence wore beards of moss. The piles went on and on... he must have had at least a couple of acres. Through a window I saw that the house was just as crowded inside.

"I'm a commercial artist," I explained. "I'm doing a series of illustrations I call 'junklets' — gadgets made of junk. It's for a new ad campaign. The company wants to show how innovative and inventive it is. So what I need is stuff that *looks* interesting, things I can put together with other things in my pictures. It doesn't matter what it is, or whether or not it works." I pulled my digital camera out of my coat pocket. "Actually, all I need is reference photos. But I can pay you for your time."

"No need. I'm always glad to help an artist." He rubbed his chin with a grime-encrusted hand. The work-hardened skin scratched against his beard stubble. "Lessee. I think I had some old dentist equipment..." Suddenly he burst into motion and I had to scramble to keep up.

Down an alley of refrigerators, right turn at an old monitor-top Frigidaire, hard left at an ancient glass-fronted Coke machine, and there we were at a barrel of dental drills from the early 1900's. All joints and cables and black crinkle-finish metal struts, it looked like a family reunion of daddy-longlegs. "This is great!" I said. I snapped a dozen pictures of the barrel just as it stood, then asked him to haul out a few choice pieces for closer examination. I wanted dozens of jointed arms for my Shoe-Tying Machine, and these would be perfect. "What else have you got that's like this? Mechanical. Early Twentieth Century stuff."

"Hmm. Follow me." And he was off again, past racks of doors and windows, with me trailing in his wake. A moment later he was lifting a blue tarp from a huge shelving unit, revealing ranks of radios: streamlined Bakelite Emersons, shiny chrome Bendixes, squat, blocky Motorolas. A harvest of design from the 20's to the 50's.

"These are phenomenal! I love old radios!"

"Most of 'em don't work any more, I'm afraid..."

"I don't care." I picked up a sleek Emerson from the 30's. The original ivory finish had yellowed, but it was in gorgeous shape. "They just don't design things like this any more. How much do you want for it?"

"Twenty-five. Naah, make it twenty-two fifty."

"I'll take it." I tucked the radio under my arm. "But. These are too... unitary. For my junklets I need parts. Moving parts."

"I know just the thing." He zipped through a gap between two piles of tires. Juggling the radio and my camera, I followed as best I could.

The entire afternoon went like that. I filled the camera's memory—over three hundred images—and wound up taking home two boxes of stuff as well. Not that I needed any of it, not that I had room for any of it, but it was all just fabulous. How could I leave this keen little eggbeater behind? I'd never seen another one like it. I put most of my finds on my knickknack shelves as soon as I got home.

After dinner I transferred the pictures into my computer, then started sorting, organizing, and cogitating. The hydraulic cylinder from the old forklift could support the seat of that office chair, and I could pull in the control panel from the red generator as well. By the time I reluctantly shut down at 3 AM I had images for a dozen junklets sorted into folders.

Bright and early the next day—by which I mean noon—I booted up my computer again and put a big newsprint pad on my drawing board. All afternoon I sketched, popping up images on the monitor whenever I needed reference or inspiration. Most of my friends think I'm weird, using paper and pencil to draw images from a computer screen, but it works for me. I've never been comfortable drawing with a mouse or a stylus, but managing reference photos with a computer beats shuffling piles of prints.

Three days later I was back at STUFF FOR SALE again. "Carl, the pictures I got last time were great. I need some more. What have you got that's big and flat and heavy and goes around?"

"What, like an old record player?"

"Yeah, but bigger."

"I think I might have something for you." He took me to a huge rotating platform, must have weighed a ton, made of rusty waffle-patterned iron. Neither of us could figure out what it had originally been used for, but it would be a perfect base for my Plastering Machine. While we were clearing some mannequins out of the way so I could get far enough back for a good photo, the bell on the front gate rang. "'Scuse me while I tend to a paying customer," Carl said.

"Take your time," I replied. "I can look around on my own." Carl vanished down a row of bookcases.

After I finished up with the platform, I wandered around. I needed a big, tubby body for the Automated Barber, some tubes and pipes for the Plant Waterer, and a whole lot of irons for the Ironing Machine. But everywhere I went, all I found was... junk. Boxy, boring washing machines. Cracked water bottles. Hundreds of olive-drab ammo cases. Rusty metal shelving. I took a picture of a row of vending machines because I thought it was a nice composition, but I didn't see anything remotely useful for my project. I was getting pretty frustrated when Carl returned.

"I haven't found anything. Where's the good stuff?"

"It's all good stuff, to the right person. What are you looking for?"

"Well, first off, something with a round, tubby body. Person-sized."

"I know just the thing." He jogged down the row of washing machines, took a left turn. "How's this?" he asked, gesturing to a bulbous chrome 1950's water cooler.

"It's perfect!" I started snapping pictures, but something nagged at me. "Wait a minute. I was just here a minute ago. I stood on this very spot and took a picture of those vending machines over there. See?" I paged back through my stored pictures, showed him the vending machines on the camera's screen. "This water cooler is just what I was looking for. Why didn't I see it before?"

"I dunno. It hasn't moved lately." Indeed, there was grass growing through the holes in its base. How could I have missed it? "Sometimes folks can't find what they're looking for even if it's right in front of them. Sometimes they need a little help. Speaking of which, can I help you find anything else?"

"Uh, yeah. Some irons. Clothes irons."

"Right over here." But as I followed, I couldn't help but look back over my shoulder at the water cooler. I would have sworn there was nothing interesting in this whole area.

I visited STUFF FOR SALE two more times in the next three weeks. Carl never failed to find just the gizmo, gewgaw, or whatchamacallit I needed to complete my drawings, and I never failed to buy something. I spent over two hundred dollars on old radios alone. But it was worth it. I had all the reference images I needed; I had inspiration; I was happy. I turned out more and better work in less time than I ever had since art school.

That was just the beginning. The agency loved my junklets. The client loved my junklets. The industry loved my junklets; I even got my name in *Advertising Age*. The client ordered a second series of junklets, then another. They used my Automated Barber as the background image on their corporate stationery.

With all that publicity, I was inundated with new clients. I soon found myself with more work than I could handle and more money than I'd ever imagined. But I knew I was just the flavor of the month; I'd seen other artists rise meteorically and then vanish just as quickly. So I got myself a financial adviser, kept my frugal lifestyle (well, mostly), and put the extra cash into mutual funds.

Everyone wanted junklets, or something like junklets. I was constantly in need of more mechanical images, more inspirations. I sometimes visited Carl three times in a week. We got to be pals.

One day we were sitting in Carl's kitchen, sharing a beer after a long hot afternoon tramping around the junkyard. "Tell me, Phil," he said, "how did you get into this crazy advertising business anyway?"

I thought about it for a moment. "I suppose you'd have to blame my dad. He was an automotive designer at Ford. When I was a kid I'd visit him at his office during the summer; he'd always let me play with his colored pencils. I guess that's where I caught the art bug."

"Ford, eh? Did your dad design anything I might have seen?"

"He was on the team that did the '66 Fairlane. But mostly he did conceptual designs. It was exciting for him to be out beyond the cutting edge like that, but he was always disappointed that none of his designs made it into actual production." I took a swig of my beer. "He worked on the Nucleon."

Carl put down his beer. "Nucleon?"

"It was a concept car for a World's Fair or something like that. A nuclear-powered car, can you believe it? Atoms for peace."

Carl got a strange look on his face then. "I have something out back that I think you ought to see."

The sun was low in the sky, casting neon-orange glints off the hoods of a row of old cars all the way at the back of the yard, where we'd seldom gone before. Bees buzzed in the shrubs that grew along the fence. Near one end of the row was a bulky shape shrouded in a moss-covered olive-drab tarp. "Help me haul this off, would you?"

We pulled off the tarp and revealed one of the strangest-looking cars you've ever seen. It looked like a cross between an old Caddy with big pointed fins and a pickup truck, and where the trunk, or pickup bed, should have been there was a big square hole that went all the way down to the ground. It looked like a car with a built-in swimming pool.

It was painted in that Godawful turquoise color that was so popular in the Fifties.

On the tailgate was a name in chrome script: Nucleon.

"Sonofabitch! You've got the mockup! I didn't even know they built one!"

"Take a closer look."

I looked. It was no fiberglass mockup. It was real steel, and a little rusty. The doors were scarred with parking-lot dings. The tires were bald. The seats and the steering wheel were worn from use. The odometer showed seventy-one thousand and some miles.

There was no gas gauge.

Suddenly I got a queasy feeling in the pit of my stomach. "Carl... do you, by any chance, have... a Geiger counter?"

"You know, I think I might. Hang on a sec."

I just stood and stared slack-jawed at the thing while Carl left and came back.

"Here it is."

"Check out the back first. The reactor was really heavy; it had its own wheels. It rode in that hole, kind of like a trailer only surrounded by the car." Carl waved the Geiger counter's wand around inside the hole. There was a slight increase in the chattering noise it made, but only a little. "Any idea how much radiation is too much?"

"Not a clue."

"Still, it doesn't seem too bad."

"No."

"But it's not zero. That means this car once had a nuclear

25

reactor. It was a fucking *nuclear car!*"

"Jesus."

We sat in the grass, leaning our backs against a nearby Camaro, and watched the air shimmer over the Nucleon's sun-warmed roof. Crickets chirped. Carl plucked a long stalk of grass and chewed on it thoughtfully.

"Where did you get this thing, anyway?" I asked.

He stared off at the setting sun for a while, then shook his head. "Sorry, I don't remember. I know it wasn't here when I bought the place back in '48."

"How can you forget buying an atomic car? You remember everything else about this place."

"It's a funny thing." He looked down into his cupped hands. "Usually it's pretty simple. Like, suppose you wanted a carburetor for a '52 Mercury. I'd know where to look, and I might find one or I might not. But sometimes, like with the Nucleon here" — he gestured at it with the stalk — "I remember exactly where it is, but I don't remember remembering it before, if you catch the distinction." He looked right at me then, his eyes hard. "I'm only telling you this because you're an artist. If I told my buddies at the VFW they'd have me locked up."

"My lips are sealed."

"I knew you'd understand."

The sun was setting behind the Nucleon, and the breeze was cooling. "What are we going to do with this thing?" I asked. "I sure don't have any place to park it."

"Cover it over with the tarp again, I guess. Maybe it'll be here tomorrow, maybe not. There's no telling."

We hauled the tarp back over that impossible car and walked back to the gate in silence. Then I turned to him and said, simply, "Thank you."

"You're welcome," he replied. He closed the gate behind me, and as I drove off I saw him sitting on the porch, staring off into the darkening sky.

After another year or so the blush was off the apple and I was no longer the hot new thing. Just as well, really; I was tired of junklets, tired of juggling assignments, tired of airports. I settled back into a career that was a lot like it had been before, only now I had a cushion of investments that meant I didn't have to hustle so hard between assignments. I was happy enough, I suppose, though sometimes I missed those crazy junklet days.

I was doing a lot of stuff based on natural forms and landscapes then, getting my reference photos on nature hikes, and I didn't see Carl very often. We always exchanged Christmas cards, though. Then one day I got a phone message from him: would I please come out to the yard, as soon as possible?

"Glad you could make it," he said as I walked up his porch steps the next day. He was sitting on a battered wire milk crate, looking like a broken gray umbrella. His health had been poor for months, though he rarely complained.

"No problem," I said. "How did you get my number?" He'd never called before.

"It was on your checks. Listen, I know this is going to seem strange, but I found this at the bottom of a coffee can full of bolts and somehow I just knew it belongs to you." He held out a small metallic object.

It was a key, a scarred brass thing, one of those ones that's the same on both sides. Smaller than a car key, bigger than a suitcase key. "I don't recognize it."

"You're sure? I don't get these feelings often, and when I do they're usually right."

"I'm pretty sure. Sorry."

"Well, keep it anyway. Memento of an old man's folly. Sorry I dragged you out here for nothing."

"That's OK, I was thinking of coming out for a visit anyway." We spent a pleasant hour on the porch, watching the leaves fall and talking about contact lenses, fast food, and the weather. Then I bought some flowerpots and went home.

Two weeks later I got a call from Laurel Hernandez, Carl's lawyer. Carl had died in his sleep, at the age of 78, and I was mentioned in his will. The funeral was Tuesday; the will would be read the next week.

I met dozens of people at the funeral, all of whom Carl had touched in some significant way. A woman for whom Carl had found a vibrating chair that was the only thing that made her bad back tolerable. A man who had kept a fleet of delivery trucks going with spare parts from Carl's yard. A family that had rebuilt a shoddy old house into a showplace, using materials and fixtures provided by Carl, and helped to revitalize their whole neighborhood. We spent the afternoon swapping Carl stories; it was a sad occasion, but not somber.

The will reading was a lot less crowded. There was me, and Ms. Hernandez, and a clerk, and a couple of cousins. The cousins got the investments, which were not trivial. I got the junkyard.

I told Ms. Hernandez I needed a couple of days to think about my options. But I was only halfway down the stairs from her office when I realized I already knew exactly what to do. I sat down right there on the steps and cried, overwhelmed by the generosity of Carl's final gift.

Ms. Hernandez drove me out to the yard after the transfer of title, a complicated ceremony involving the signing of more papers than I'd ever seen in my life. "Are you sure you don't want me to find a management company to run the business for you?" she asked as we got out of the car.

"I'm sure. I plan to keep on as a contract artist part-time, at least for a while, but this is what I want to do. Where I want to be. However, I'd appreciate the services of an experienced business lawyer."

"I would be happy to help."

The gate was padlocked. I'd never seen it padlocked before.

I stood there for a moment, not knowing what to do, and then I put my hands in my jacket pockets and felt something hard. It was the key Carl had given me the last time I saw him, which was also the last time I'd worn that jacket.

On impulse, I tried it in the padlock.

It worked.

We got inside and wandered around the yard. Ms. Hernandez didn't seem to think it was odd that I had a key to the gate, and I decided not to mention the circumstances under which I'd acquired it.

We paused before a rank of vacuum cleaners, a faded rainbow of aqua and pink and beige plastic. "Mr. Tatyrczinski was one of my favorite clients," Ms. Hernandez said. "He gave me a bust of Kennedy for my birthday one year. Kennedy was my hero, but I don't think I ever mentioned that to him. Somehow he always knew just the right thing to do."

"Maybe he didn't know. Maybe the junkyard knew."

"What?"

"Never mind. Wait a minute, I just remembered something." I walked down to the end of the row of appliances, paused a moment, turned left. There, on a battered chrome dinette table, was a jar of buttons. I opened it, dug around for a moment. "Here. I think Carl would have liked you to have this."

It was a campaign pin in red, white, and blue. It was a little faded, but still plainly readable: RE-ELECT JFK IN '64.

"This must have been some kind of joke," Ms. Hernandez said.

"Maybe. Or maybe it's a little memento from a time that never was. A time that was better than this one."

"What a... a lovely thought. In any case, if I were your business lawyer I would caution you against giving away merchandise to friends and relatives. It's a common problem for new business owners."

"OK, I'll take three bucks for it. Naah, make it two fifty."

"It's a deal."

We stood side by side and watched the sun set over the junkyard.

I Hold My Father's Paws

THE RECEPTIONIST HAD FEATHERS where her eyebrows should have been. They were blue, green, and black, iridescent as a peacock's, and they trembled gently in the silent breath of the air conditioner. "Did you have a question, sir?"

"No," Jason replied, and raised his magazine, but after reading the same paragraph three times without remembering a word he set it down again. "Actually, yes. Um, I wanted to ask you... ah... are you... transitioning?" The word landed on the soft tailored-grass carpet of the waiting room, and Jason wished he could pick it up again, stuff it into his pocket, and leave. Just leave, and never come back.

"Oh, you mean the eyebrows? No, sir, that's just fashion. I enjoy being human." She smiled gently at him. "You haven't been in San Francisco very long, have you?"

"No, I just got in this morning."

"Feathers are very popular here. In fact, we're having a special this month. Would you like a brochure?"

"No! Uh, I mean, no thank you." He looked down and saw that the magazine had crumpled in his hands. Awkwardly he tried to smooth it out, then gave up and slipped it back in the pile on the coffee table. They were all recent issues, and the coffee table looked like real wood. He tested it with a dirty thumbnail; real wood, all right. Then, appalled at his own action, he shifted the pile of magazines to cover the tiny scratch.

"Sir?"

Jason started at the receptionist's voice, sending magazines skidding across the table. "What?"

"Would you mind if I gave you a little friendly advice?"

"Uh, I... no. Please." She was probably going to tell him that his fly was open, or that ties were required in this office. Her own tie matched the wall covering, a luxurious print of maroon and gold. Jason doubted the collar of his faded work shirt would even button around his thick neck.

"You might not want to ask any of our patients if they are transitioning."

"Is it impolite?" He wanted to crawl under the table and die.

"No, sir." She smiled again, with genuine humor this time. "It's just that some of them will talk your ear off, given the slightest show of interest."

"I, uh... thank you."

A chime sounded—a rich little sound that blended unobtrusively with the waiting room's classical music—and the receptionist stared into space for a moment. "I'll let him know," she said to the air, then turned her attention to Jason. "Mr. Carmelke is out of surgery."

"Thank you." It was so strange to hear that uncommon name applied to someone else. He hadn't met another Carmelke in over twenty years.

CS

Half an hour later the waiting room door opened onto a corridor with a smooth, shiny floor and meticulous off-white walls. Despite the art—original, no doubt—and the continuing classical music, a slight smell of disinfectant reminded Jason where he was.

A young man in a nurse's uniform led Jason to a door marked with the name Dr. Lawrence Steig.

"Hello, Mr. Carmelke," said the man behind the desk. "I'm Dr. Steig." The doctor was lean, shorter than Jason, with brown eyes and a trim salt-and-pepper beard. His hand, like his voice, was firm and a little rough; his tie was knotted with surgical precision. "Please do sit down."

Jason perched on the edge of the chair, not wanting to surrender to its lushness. Not wanting to be comfortable. "How is my father?"

"The operation went well, and he'll be conscious soon. But I'd like to talk with you first. I believe there are some... family issues."

"What makes you say that?"

The doctor stared at his personal organizer as he repeatedly snapped it open and shut. It was gold. "I've been working with your father for almost two years, Mr. Carmelke. The doctor-patient relationship in this type of work is, necessarily, quite intimate. I feel I've gotten to know him quite well." He raised his eyes to Jason's. "He's never mentioned you."

"I'm not surprised." Jason heard the edge of bitterness in his own voice.

"It's not unusual for patients of mine to be disowned by their families."

Jason's hard, brief laugh startled both of them. "This has nothing to do with his... transition, Dr. Steig. My father left my mother and me when I was nine. I haven't spoken to him since. Not once."

"I'm sorry, Mr. Carmelke." He seemed sincere; Jason wondered if it were just professional bedside manner. The doctor opened his mouth to speak, then closed it and stared off into a corner for a moment. "This might not be the best time for a family reunion," he said finally. "His condition may be a little... startling."

"I didn't come all the way from Cleveland just to turn around and go home. I want to talk with my father. While I still can. And this is my last chance, right?"

"The final operation is scheduled for five weeks from now. It can be postponed, of course. But all the papers have been signed." The doctor placed his hands flat on the desk. "You're not going to be able to talk him out of it."

"Just let me see him."

"I will... if he wants to see you."

Jason didn't have anything to say to that.

03

Jason's father was lying on his side, facing away from the door, as Jason entered. The smell of disinfectant was stronger here, and a battery of instruments bleeped quietly.

He was bald, with just a fringe of gray hair around the back of his head. The scalp was smooth and pink and shiny, and very round — matching Jason's own round head, too big for the standard hardhats at his work site. "Big Jase" was what it said on his own personal helmet, black marker on safety yellow plastic.

But though his father's head was large and round, the shoulders that moved with his breathing were too narrow, and his chest dropped rapidly away to hips that were narrower still. The legs were invisible, drawn up in front of his body. Jason swallowed as he moved around to the other side of the bed.

His father's round face was tan, looking more "rugged" than "wrinkled." Deep lines ran from his nose to the corners of his mouth, and the eyebrows above his closed eyes were gray and very bushy. It was both an older and a younger face than what he had imagined, trying to add twenty years to a memory twenty years old.

Jason's gaze traveled down, past his father's freshly-shaved chin, to the thick ruff of gray-white fur on his neck. Then further, to the gray-furred legs that lay on the bed in front of him and the paws that crossed, relaxed, at the ankles, with neatly trimmed nails and clean, unscuffed pads.

His father's body resembled a wolf's, or a mastiff's, broad and strong and laced with muscle and sinew. But it was wrong, somehow. His chest, narrow though it was, was still wider than any normal dog's, and the fur looked fake—too clean, too fine, too regular. Jason knew from his reading on the plane that it was engineered from his father's own body hair, and was only an approximation of a dog's natural coat with its layers of different types of hair.

He was a magnificent animal. He was a pathetic freak. He was a marvel of biotechnology. He was an arrogant icon of self-indulgence.

He was a dog.

He was Jason's father.

"Dad? It's Jason." Some part of him wanted to pet the furry shoulder, but he kept his hands to himself.

His father's eyes flickered open, then drifted closed again. "Yeah. Doctor told me." His voice was a little slurred. "What the hell'r you doing here?"

"I ran into Aunt Brittany at O'Hare. I didn't recognize her, but she knew me right away. She told me all about... you. I came straight here." *It's my father*, he'd told his boss on the phone. *He's in the hospital. I have to see him before it's too late.* Letting him draw the wrong conclusion, but not too far from the truth.

His father's nose wrinkled in distaste. "Never could trust her."

"Dad... *why?*"

He opened his eyes again. They were the same hard blue as Jason's, and they were beginning to focus properly. "Because I can. Because the Consti... *tu*tion gives me the right to do whatever the hell I want with my body and my money. Because I want to be pampered for the rest of my life." He closed his eyes and crossed his paws on the bridge of his nose. "Because I don't want to make any more damn decisions. Now get out."

Jason's mouth flapped open and closed like a fish. "But Dad..."

"Mr. Carmelke?" Jason looked up, and his father rolled his head around, to see where Dr. Steig stood by the door. Jason had no idea how long he had been there. "Excuse me, I meant Jason." Jason's father put his paws over his face again. "Mr. Carmelke, I think you should leave your father alone for a while. He's still feeling the effects of the anesthetic. He may be more... open to discussion, in the morning."

"Doubt it," came the voice from under the crossed paws.

Jason's hand reached out—to stroke the forehead, to ruffle the fur, he wasn't sure which—but then it pulled back. "See you tomorrow, Dad."

There was no response.

As soon as the door closed behind him, Jason leaned heavily against the wall, then slid down to a sitting position. His eyes stung and he rubbed at them.

"I'm sorry." Jason opened his eyes at the voice. Dr. Steig was squatting in front of him, holding a clipboard in his hands. "He's not usually like this."

"I've never understood him," Jason said, shaking his head. "Not since he left. We had a good life. He wasn't drinking or anything. There weren't any money problems—not then, anyway. Mom loved him. I loved him. But he said 'there's nothing here for me,' and he walked out of our lives."

"You mentioned money. Is that what this is about? You know he's given most of it to charity already. What remains is just enough to pay for the craniofacial procedure, and a trust fund that will cover his few needs after that."

"It's not the money. It was never the money. He even offered to pay alimony and child support, but Mom turned it down. It wasn't the most practical decision, but she really didn't want anything to do with him. I think it was one of those things where a broken love turns into a terrible hate."

"Does your mother know you're here?"

"She died eight years ago. Leukemia. He didn't even come to the funeral."

"I'm sorry," the doctor said again. He sat down, let his clipboard clatter to the shiny floor next to him. They sat together in silence for a time. "Let me talk with him tonight, Mr. Carmelke, and we'll see how things go in the morning. All right?"

Jason thought for a moment, then bobbed his head. "All right."

They helped each other up.

ᛣ

Jason's father jogged into the doctor's office the next morning, his lithe new body bobbing with a smooth four-legged gait, and hopped easily up onto a carpeted platform that brought his head to the same level as Jason and the doctor. But he refused to meet Jason's eyes. Jason himself sat in the doctor's leather guest chair, fully seated this time, but still not fully comfortable.

"Noah," Dr. Steig said to Jason's father, "I know this is hard for you. But I want you to understand that it is even harder for your son."

"He shouldn't have come here," he said, still not looking at Jason.

"Dad... how could I not? You're the only family I have left in the world, I didn't even know if you were dead or alive, and now... this! I had to come. Even if I can't change your mind, I... I just want to talk."

"Talk, then!" His face turned to Jason at last, but his blue eyes were hard, his mouth set. "I might even listen." He lowered his head to his paws, which rested on the carpeted surface in front of him.

Jason felt the little muscles in his legs tensing to rise. He could stand up, walk out... be free of this awkwardness and pain. Go back to his lonely little house and try to forget all about his father.

But he knew how well that had worked the last time.

"I told them you were dead," he said. "My friends at school. The new school, after we moved to Cleveland. I don't know why. Lots of their parents were divorced. They would have understood. But somehow pretending you were dead made it easier."

His dad closed his eyes hard; deep furrows appeared in the corners of his eyes and between his brows. "Can't say I blame you," he said at last.

"No matter how many people I lied to, I still knew you were out there somewhere. I wondered what you were doing. Whether you missed me. Where did you go?"

"Buffalo."

Jason waited until he was sure no more details were forthcoming. "Is that where you've been all this time?"

"No, I was only there for a few months. Then Syracuse. Miami for a while. I didn't settle down for a long time. But I've been in the Bay Area for the last eleven years." He raised his head. "Selling configuration management software for Romatek. It's really exciting stuff."

Jason didn't care about his father's job, but he sensed an opening. "Tell me about it."

They talked for half an hour about configuration management and source control and stock options—things that Jason didn't understand and didn't want to understand. But they were talking. His dad even managed to make the topic seem interesting. A wry smirk came to Jason's lips when he realized he was getting a sales presentation from a dog. A dog with his father's head.

 CB

Jason and his father sat in the courtyard behind the clinic, under a red Japanese maple that sighed in the wind. The skyscrapers of San Francisco were visible above the fence, which was painted with a colorful abstract mural. A few birds chirped, and the slight mineral sting of sea salt flavored the air, reminding Jason how far he was from home.

A phone with two large buttons was strapped to his father's left foreleg. He could push the buttons with his chin to summon urgent or less-urgent assistance. He sat on the bench next to Jason with his legs drawn up beneath him, his head held high so as to look Jason as much in the eye as possible.

"I would have had to have something done with the knees one way or the other," he said. "They were just about shot, before. Arthritis. Now they're like new. I was taking laps this morning, before you showed up. Haven't been able to run like that in years. And being so close to the ground, it feels like a hundred miles an hour."

Jason translated that into kilometers and realized his dad wasn't speaking literally. "But what about... I dunno, restaurants? Museums? Movies?"

"After they do the head work I'll have different tastes, and I'll get nothing but the best. Museums—hell, I never went to museums before. And as far as movies, I'll just wait for them to come out on chip. Then I'll curl up with my handler and go to sleep in front of them."

"Of course, the movie will be in black and white to you."

"Heh."

Jason didn't mention—didn't want to think about—the other changes that the "head work" would make in his father's senses, and his brain. After the craniofacial procedure, his mind would be as much like a dog's as modern medicine could make it. He'd be happy, no question of that, but he wouldn't be Noah Carmelke any more.

Jason's dad seemed to recognize that his thoughts were drifting in an uncomfortable direction. "Tell me about your job," he said.

"I work for Bionergy," Jason replied. "I'm a civil engineer. We're refitting Cleveland's old natural gas system for biogas... that means a lot of tearing up streets and putting them back."

"Funny. I was a civil engineer for a while, before I hired on at Romatek."

"No shit?"

"No shit."

"I was following in your footsteps, and I didn't even know it."

"We thought you were going to be an artist. Your mom was so proud of those drawings of the barn, and the goats."

"Wow. I haven't done any sketching in years."

They stared at the mural, both remembering a refrigerator covered with drawings.

"You want me to draw you?"

Jason's father nodded slowly. "Yeah. Yeah, I'd like that."

Someone from the clinic managed to scare up a pad and some charcoal, and they settled down under the maple tree. Jason leaned against the fence and began to sketch, starting with the hindquarters. His father sat with his hind legs drawn up beneath him and his forelegs stretched straight out in front. "You look like the Sphinx," Jason said.

"Hmm."

"You can talk if you like, I'm not working on your mouth."

"I don't have anything to say."

Jason's charcoal paused on the page, then resumed its scratching. "Last night I read a paper I found in the restaurant. The *Howl*. You know it?" The full title was *HOWL: The Journal of the Bay Area Transpecies Community*. It was full of angry articles about local politicians he'd never heard of, and ads for services he couldn't understand or didn't want to think about.

"I've read it, yeah. Buncha flakes."

"I found out there are a lot of different reasons for people to change their species. Some of them feel they were born into the wrong body. Some are making a statement about humanity's impact on the planet. Some see it as a kind of performance art. I don't see any of those in you."

"I told you, I just want to be taken care of. It's a form of retirement."

The marks on the page were getting heavy and black. "I don't think that's it. Not really. I look at you and I see a man with ambition and drive. You wouldn't have gotten all those stock options if you were the type to retire at 58." The charcoal stick snapped between Jason's fingers, and he threw the pieces aside. "Damnit, Dad, how can you give up your *humanity*?"

Jason's dad jumped to his four feet. His stance was wide, defensive. "The O'Hartigan decision said I have the right to reshape my body and my mind in any way I wish. I think that includes the right to not answer questions about it." He stared for a moment, as though he were about to say something else, then pursed his lips and trotted off.

Jason was left with a half-finished sketch of a sphinx with his father's face.

છ

He sat in the clinic's waiting room for three hours the next day. Finally Dr. Steig came out and told him that he was sorry, but his father simply could not be convinced to see him.

Jason wandered the lunchtime crowds of San Francisco. The spring air was clear and crisp, and the people walked briskly. Here and there he saw feathers, fur, scales. The waiter who brought his sandwich was half snake, with slitted eyes and a forked tongue that flickered. Jason was so distracted he forgot to tip.

After lunch he came to the clinic's door and stopped. He stood in the hall for a long time, dithering, but when the elevator's ping announced the arrival of two women with identical Siamese cat faces he bolted—shoving between them, ignoring their insulted yowls, hammering the Door Close button. As the elevator descended he gripped the handrails, pushed himself into the corner, tried to calm his breathing.

He landed in Cleveland at 12:30 that night.

ଔ

The other hard-hats at his work site gave him a nice card they had all signed. He accepted their sympathies but did not offer any details. One woman took him aside and asked how long his father had. "The doctor says five weeks."

Days passed. Sometimes he found himself sitting in the cab of a backhoe, staring at his hands, wondering how long he had been there.

He confided in nobody. He imagined the jokes: "Good thing it isn't your mother... then you'd be a son-of-a-bitch!" Antacids became his favorite snack.

The little house he'd bought with Maria, back when they thought they might be able to make it work, became oppressive. He ate all his meals in restaurants, in parts of town where he didn't know anyone. Once he found a copy of the local transpecies paper. It was a skinny little thing, bimonthly, with angry articles about local politicians and ads for services he wished he didn't know anything about.

Four weeks later, on a Monday evening, he got a call from San Francisco.

"Jason, it's me. Your dad. Don't hang up."

42

The handset was already halfway to the cradle as the last three words came out, but Jason paused and returned it to his ear. "Why not?"

"I want to talk."

"You could have done that while I was there."

"OK, I admit I was a little short with you. I'm sorry."

The plastic of the handset creaked in Jason's hand. He tried to consciously relax his grip. "I'm sorry too."

There was a long silence, the two of them breathing at each other across three thousand kilometers. It was Jason's father who broke it. "The operation is scheduled for Thursday at 8 am. I... I'd like to see you one more time before then."

Jason covered his eyes with one hand, the fingers pressing hard against the bones of his brow. Finally he sighed and said "I don't think so. There's no point to it. We just make each other too crazy."

"Please. I know I haven't been the best father to you..."

"You haven't been any kind of father at all!"

Another silence. "You've got me there. But I'd really like to..."

"To what? To say goodbye? Again? No thanks!" And he slammed down the phone.

He sat there for a long while, feeling the knots crawl across his stomach, waiting for the phone to ring again.

It didn't.

ଓ

That night he went out and got good and drunk. "My dad's turning into a dog," he slurred to the bartender, but all that got him was a cab home.

Tuesday morning he called in sick. He spent the day in bed, sometimes sleeping. He watched a soap opera; the characters' ludicrous problems seemed so small and manageable.

Tuesday night he did not sleep. He brought out a box of letters from his mother, read through them looking for clues. At the bottom of the box he found a picture himself at age eight, standing between his parents. It had been torn in half, the jagged line cutting between him and his father like a lightning bolt, and crudely taped together. He remembered rescuing the torn photo from his mother's wastebasket, taping it together, hiding it in a box of old CD-ROMs. Staring at it late at night. Wondering why.

Wednesday morning he drove to the airport.

CR

There was a strike at O'Hare and he was rerouted to Atlanta, where he ate a bad hamburger and floated on a tide of angry, frustrated people, thrashing to stay on top. Finally one gate agent found him a seat to LAX. From there he caught a red-eye to San Francisco.

He arrived at the clinic at 5 am. The door was locked, but there was a telephone number for after-hours service. It was answered by a machine. He stomped through menus until he reached a bored human being, who knew nothing, but promised to get a message to Dr. Steig.

He paced the hall outside the clinic. He had nowhere else to go.

Fifteen minutes later an astonished Dr. Steig called back. "Your father is already in prep for surgery, but I'll tell the hospital to let you see him." He gave Jason the address. "I'm glad you came," he said before hanging up.

The taxi took Jason through dark, empty streets, puddles gleaming with reflected streetlight. Raindrops ran down the windows like sweat, like tears. Jason blinked as he stepped into the hard blue-white light of the hospital's foyer. "I'm here to see Noah Carmelke," he said. "I'm expected."

CR

The nurse gave him a paper mask to tie over his nose and mouth, and goggles for his eyes. "The prep area is sterile," she said as she helped him step into a paper coverall. Jason felt like he was going to a costume party.

And then the double doors slid open and he met the guest of honor.

His father lay on his side, shallow breaths raising and lowering his furry flanks. An oxygen mask was fastened to his face, like a muzzle. His eyes were at half-mast, unfocused. "Jason," he breathed. "They said you were coming, but I didn't believe it." The sound of his voice echoed hollowly behind the clear plastic.

"Hello, Dad." His own voice was muffled by the paper mask.

"I'm glad you're here."

"Dad... I had to come. I need to understand you. If I don't understand you, I'll never understand myself." He hugged himself. His face felt swollen; his whole head was ready to implode from sadness and fatigue. "*Why*, Dad? Why did you leave us? Why didn't you come to Mom's funeral? And why are you throwing away your life now?"

The bald head on the furry neck moved gently, side to side, on the pillow. "Did you ever have a dog, Jason?"

"You know the answer, Dad. Mom was allergic."

"What about after you grew up?"

"I've been alone most of the time since then. I didn't think I could take proper care of a dog if I had to go to work every day."

"But a dog would have loved you."

Jason's eyes burned behind the goggles.

"I had a dog when I was a kid," his father continued. "Juno. A German Shepherd. She was a good dog... smart, and strong, and obedient. And every day when I came home from school she came bounding into the yard... so happy to see me. She would jump up and lick my face." He twisted his head around, forced his eyes open to look into Jason's. "I left your mother because I couldn't love her like that. I knew she loved me, but I thought she deserved better than me. And I didn't come to the funeral because I knew she wouldn't want me there. Not after I'd hurt her so much."

"What about *me*, Dad?"

"You're a man. A man like me. I figured you'd understand."

"I *don't* understand. I never did."

His father sighed heavily, a long doggy sigh. "I'm sorry."

"You're turning yourself into a dog so someone will love you?"

"No. I'm turning myself into a dog so I can love someone. I want to be free of my human mind, free of decisions."

"How can you love anyone if you aren't *you* any more?"

"I'll still be me. But I'll be able to *be* me, instead of thinking all the time about being me."

"Dad..."

The nurse came back. "I'm sorry, Mr. Carmelke, but I have to ask you to leave now."

"Dad, you can't just leave me like that!"

"Jason," his father said. "There's a clause in the contract that lets me specify a family member as my primary handler."

"I don't think I could..."

"Please, Jason. Son. It would mean so much to me. Let me come home with you."

Jason turned away. "And see you every day, and know what you used to be?"

"I'd sleep by your feet while you watch movies. I'd be so happy to see you when you came home. All you have to do is give the word, and I'll put my voiceprint on the contract right now."

Jason's throat was so tight that he couldn't speak. But he nodded.

℞

The operation took eighteen hours. The recovery period lasted weeks. When the bandages came off, Jason's father's face was long and furry and had a wet nose. But his head was still very round, and his eyes were still blue.

Two deep wells of sincere, doggy love.

ༀ

Zauberschrift

A CRUEL WIND TUGGED AT Ulrich's cloak and threw rain in his face as he topped a small rise. The weather had worsened steadily as they neared the village, and the mood of his traveling companions Agnes and Nikolaus had soured along with it. But now, as they emerged from the trees, Ulrich's spirits rose as he recognized the ragged cluster of buildings that had been his home nearly twenty years ago.

"Welcome to Lannesdorf," said Agnes, her expression grim.

At first it seemed that little had changed. There was the mill, its wheel turning rapidly in the swollen creek; there the tiny church, there the cottages of Konrad and Georg. But as they approached, Ulrich saw how badly the village had been battered by months of constant rain and wind. Several houses had collapsed completely. From those that remained, thin ribbons of smoke rose only a short distance before being shredded by the relentless downpour. A few dispirited goats stood in the street, their ears drooping and their wool hanging soddenly. No people were visible.

The feeling that lodged in Ulrich's throat was a strange compound of nostalgia, hope, and despair. He prayed he would be able to find some way to help.

ଔ

Ulrich had barely recognized Agnes when she had first appeared at his shop in Auerberg. The ample, jolly woman he had called "foster mother" during the three years of his apprenticeship had become thin and stooped, her face lined and most of her teeth gone. Behind her, the young man she had introduced as Nikolaus the pastor clutched his hat to his chest; he was as thin as she, and his shaven cheeks were sunken. Ulrich was keenly aware of their worn and smelly clothes, and hoped they would leave before any of his more prosperous customers saw them.

"Why have you come all this way to ask *my* help? I am no wizard—I never even finished my apprenticeship. I am just a dyer."

"I know," said Agnes, "but Johannes always said you showed great promise."

A twinge went through Ulrich at those words—the pain of lost opportunity. He had been making excellent progress in his apprenticeship when his father and three older brothers had been taken by the bilious fever. Suddenly, unexpectedly, he had found himself in charge of his father's business. It brought him a tidy income, to be sure, but also a thousand spirit-sapping tasks that left him exhausted at the end of each day.

"Tell Johannes I thank him for his generous words."

"Alas, we cannot," said Nikolaus, "for he passed away twelve years ago."

"May God keep his soul," Ulrich said. "But what of his partner Heinrich?"

Agnes' face was bitter. "He and Johannes had a great argument, and he left Lannesdorf not long after you did. In any case, he too has passed on."

"Have you asked your lord for assistance?"

"Graf Erhart sent soldiers, but they could do nothing against the weather. This is wizards' business."

Ulrich began to appreciate their predicament. "And no wizard will help you?"

"We lack the money for a master wizard, and no ordinary wizard will touch another's spell. But you were Johannes' own apprentice; surely that gives you some special connection with his work?"

"Perhaps... I don't know. It's been twenty years."

"Please, sir," said Nikolaus. "Our crops are drowned. Men and beasts alike are sick with hunger. Please. You must help us."

Ulrich turned away and pretended to busy himself with a length of dyed cloth, so as not to meet Nikolaus' miserable eyes. "I'm sorry," he said. "I have my business to tend to." Three journeyman dyers, constantly in need of instruction and correction. A roof that needed mending. Taxes to be paid. He sighed.

"There is one more thing," said Agnes. "Bechte daughter of Wolfgang lies grievously ill."

Ulrich's head snapped around at that name. "Bechte?" She had been too young to marry when he was forced to leave.

"Bechte. She has the lung fever." Agnes' expression was knowing, but sympathetic. "She asked specially for you."

They left for Lannesdorf that very day.

೦೩

Agnes the widow of Friedrich lived with her family in a typical two-room peasant cottage, with wattle and daub walls, a dirt floor, and a roof of thatched straw. By comparison with Ulrich's three-story house in Auerberg, it was little more than a box made of sticks held together with mud. It lacked windows, chairs, and chimney; smoke from the hearth-fire exited through a simple hole in the roof. "Mind the wall, there," she said as they entered. "You could put your elbow right through it if you're not careful. We keep trying to patch it up, but in this weather nothing ever dries."

Ulrich dropped his traveling bag on the table. "Take me to Bechte," he said. "I must see her at once."

Agnes' son Michel looked up at that, his eyes wide. "Oh, sir... you may see her, but I fear she cannot see you."

"What do you mean?" Ulrich asked, though he already knew the answer.

"She died this morning, sir."

ℭ℘

Bechte lay in state on the table at her cottage, her weeping husband and children by her side. She was as beautiful as he remembered, though her death-pale skin was blotchy from the fever that had killed her. Weakened by hunger, she had not been able to put up much of a fight against it.

Ulrich felt a pang of envy for Bechte's husband... but then he realized they shared a common pain. Both of them had loved Bechte, then lost her through no fault of their own. He embraced the man and offered his sympathies.

Finally he leaned down and delicately kissed Bechte's brow. It was cold and waxy. "Rest in peace, my wife that never was," he whispered. "I swear to you I will find some way to help your village." He straightened and looked around at the thin and haggard faces of Bechte's family, Agnes, and Nikolaus. They looked back at him with expressions of hope.

But what could he do to help them? He had never even finished his studies, and had forgotten most of what he had learned.

"I will visit the wizards' house in the morning," he said at last. "Perhaps I will find something there."

They all joined hands and Nikolaus led them in a prayer for salvation.

ℭ℘

Ulrich bedded down on a pestilential straw mattress with Agnes, her sister, her sister's husband, and seven or eight children. The smell, the constant fidgeting and sniffling, and the moist oppressive heat kept him awake at first. He was used to cool linen sheets, wooden floors, and breezy windows.

And yet... and yet he found the presence of those others strangely comforting. It reminded him of his apprentice days, when he had slept with the wizards and their families. His duties had been small and well-defined, then, though they had seemed enormous at the time. He not known how happy he was.

Ulrich snuggled against the warm breathing bodies and passed into sleep.

ൠ

The wizards' cottage was well away from the rest of the village, off by itself in a stand of beech. It was abandoned and weather-beaten, but showed no signs of vandalism. "People avoid this place," Agnes explained. "It's known to be haunted."

"Indeed," Ulrich replied. "Wizards rarely leave their homes or possessions unprotected. I should go in by myself first."

He pushed the crumbling door aside and ducked beneath the collapsed lintel. Inside he found dripping water, weak daylight streaming through holes in the thatched roof, and a swampy smell of mud and decay. The back half of the roof had collapsed; a heavy beam lay across the cracked hearthstone, and rotting straw lay everywhere.

For a moment he just stood, taking it in, trying to reconcile this ruin with his happy memories. Johannes' writing-desk had been there, Heinrich's chest of herbs and compounds there. Now there was nothing but disorder and decay. Johannes' favorite chair lay overturned in a corner; when he tried to pick it up, it fell to pieces in his hands. He flung the rotten boards away.

Enough delay. There were problems to be solved here.

All morning he had strained his mind, trying to piece together bits of memory. He had remembered three of Johannes' *tessera* — words of command over daemons — and hoped that would be enough. He cupped his hands to his mouth and called them out, one after another. There was no reaction to the first or second, but at the third he felt a movement in the mud and rotten straw under his feet.

Gingerly at first, careful of his fine clothing, then more and more enthusiastically he swept the mud away with hands and feet. Finally he grinned as the iron-bound lid of Johannes' coffer appeared. It appeared to be intact, and the third *tesserae* had released the ward on its lock. "Nikolaus! Agnes!" he called. "Come in! I think it's safe, and I need your help!"

The three of them dragged the heavy coffer out of the sucking mud and onto the hearthstone. Ulrich cleaned the grime away from the hinges and hasps as well as he could, then rinsed his hands in a puddle before raising the lid.

The large bound volume of spells was inside, as he'd hoped. But it was covered with mold and mildew. Black and green tendrils engulfed the book in a wild profusion of corruption.

"God in Heaven," Ulrich breathed. "With the shape this thing is in, we're lucky the weather is no worse than it is."

Ⳡ

"Demons?" Konrad the reeve cried, touching the saint's medal pinned to his doublet. They had hauled the coffer with its precious, damaged contents to Agnes' cottage for a more careful inspection, and Konrad, Graf Erhart's representative in Lannesdorf, had joined them there. His long face was very lined and hard for a man so young, and he carried himself with an authoritative swagger.

"Not demons, *daemons*," Ulrich explained, remembering his

own panicked reaction when Johannes had used the word for the first time. "The word is Latin; it is closer in meaning to *Geist*, spirit, than *Dämon*, demon. Philosophers disagree over where daemons come from, even whether or not they exist before they are bound to a task, but they are *not* devils or angels. Only God may command those, but daemons are subject to human will."

"Demons or spirits, they are still evil," said Konrad.

"Not evil. Just mindless and powerful." Johannes had been fond of comparing them to an imbecile child with the strength of a bull. "When properly controlled, they are beneficial. The daemons bound by these spells gave you twenty years of exceptionally good weather."

"It's true, Konrad," Agnes said. "Up until this year we hadn't had a crop failure since before Ulrich was an apprentice. You're too young to remember, but we used to have a bad harvest at least one year in four."

"But now they have turned against us," said Konrad.

"Not really," said Ulrich. "Look." He gestured at the book open on the table before them.

Spell-books were never beautiful like illuminated Scriptures; they consisted of nothing but line upon line of the convoluted legalistic Latin called *Zauberschrift*. But this spell-book was truly ugly. The center of each page was still legible, but the edges were discolored and many of the letters were unreadable.

"You see how badly damaged the words are," said Ulrich. "The daemons are still doing their best to obey these commands, but they are so garbled the results are disastrous."

Agnes looked puzzled. "But if the book was damaged by the rain, and the rain came from the damage to the book... which came first?"

Ulrich had to think about that. "The mold must have come first," he said after a time. "It probably started years ago, while the weather was still good. The damage to the book caused the rain, not the other way around." But something nagged at the back of his mind.

Konrad's angry voice interrupted Ulrich's thoughts. "Surely to control the weather is a violation of God's will!"

"God sends the rain," Nikolaus said, "but it is no violation of His will to wear a hat. Perhaps these daemons have been something like a hat for the whole village."

"But now they are destroying it!" Konrad replied. "And we must destroy them. Burn the book!"

"It's not so simple," said Ulrich. "The daemons will try to follow their commands even as the book burns." Ulrich recalled a demonstration Heinrich had given him. He had bound a very simple protective daemon to a yew tree, then had set fire to the spell. The tree had become a twisted heap of splinters in an instant. "These weather daemons are very powerful. I would not want to be here if you did anything to damage this volume any further!"

"There must be some way to dispel the daemons," Nikolaus asked.

"Yes, but breaking a spell is an exceedingly complex spell in itself. Only a master wizard would even attempt it."

"So what do you propose to do?" said Agnes.

"Clean away the mold, repair the vellum and binding, re-ink the damaged places. That should put things back the way they were. And then you can store the book someplace dry."

"I thought you said you were not a wizard," said Konrad.

"Only a wizard can write a new spell, but even an apprentice should be able to repair one. All I have to do is make up some ink, cut some quills, and read and write a few words of Latin. I did those things every day." *And I pray I can still remember how after twenty years,* he added silently.

There was one other thing he did not mention. The sealing of the spell with blood, and the risk of death that went with it. But he had an idea to avoid that.

"Very well," said Konrad. "But if the weather does not improve soon, I will take matters into my own hands."

os

Ulrich sat at Agnes' trestle table, grinding charcoal into a fine powder with a mortar and pestle he had found in the ruins of the wizards' cottage. Nearby, Agnes dipped goose feathers into a cauldron of boiling water to soften them for cutting. Ulrich's goose-bitten finger throbbed, a reminder of the eternal enmity between geese and the scribes who steal their eggs for ink and their feathers for quills.

"You said these weather daemons are very powerful," said Agnes. "Why work such great magic in such a tiny village?"

"Many villages have a weather daemon or two. But Johannes and Heinrich together were able to bind stronger daemons than either of them could alone." He paused in his grinding, lost in memory for a moment. "It's a pity they didn't stay together. Do you know why Heinrich left?"

"It was his ambition. Johannes was content to stay where he was born, and work more and better spells for the benefit of the village. Heinrich was always pushing, always reaching for more and more power. He ached to be a king's wizard. Finally it came to a huge screaming fight, and he left the village in a foul temper. But without Johannes he was nothing. He eventually became wizard of Mehlen, and died there."

"I do not know Mehlen."

"I'm not surprised—it is an even smaller town than Lannesdorf."

"I remember how Heinrich treated his horse—whipped the poor beast so hard I feared for her life. I wondered sometimes why Johannes put up with him."

"He told me once that he had tolerated Heinrich for the sake of

57

the magic they could do together. But in the end it was Heinrich who left, and good riddance."

CB

Ulrich set down his quill and rubbed his eyes. After two weeks of scrubbing, stitching, and inking, the letters seemed to swim upon the page like a thousand tiny black fish. But this was the last of it.

The sound of Agnes' family snoring in the outer room mingled with the drum of rain on the thatched roof, the hiss of wind through the cracks in the walls, the rhythmic splats from the mud puddle under the leak in the corner. The smoky flame of the tallow candle wavered in the draft. He wondered what hour of the night it might be.

He turned back over the pages, looking for any remaining spots of mold or illegible words. Here and there he touched up a letter, but he knew he was only delaying the inevitable. Finally he brought from his belt-bag the fragments of the wax seal that had closed the spell-book — wax mingled with wizards' blood. He melted the fragments together in the candle's flame, let the melted wax fall onto the cord that held shut the book. Then, fingers trembling, he pressed his father's signet ring into the wax.

Nothing happened. The spell was sealed, and he still lived.

He let out a breath he had not even known he was holding, and knelt to thank God for his success. Then he dragged his weary body off to bed. He did not even bother to undress.

CB

A short time later he was jerked from sleep by an enormous clap of thunder.

He sat up, trying to shake the sleep out of his head. A long flash of lightning showed the wide eyes of Agnes and her family, huddled together in fear — the thunder followed just a moment later, seeming to smash a lid of darkness down over the scene. Between peals of thunder Ulrich heard a tremendous rattling roar — hail pelting the roof and walls.

The youngest child wailed. Another bolt of lightning showed Ulrich her terrified face, and one tiny hand reaching out to grasp at Agnes' sleeve. Thunder rolled across the roof.

Ulrich struggled out of the bed, groped for a candle. Then the roar of hail doubled in volume as the front door was flung open. A flash of lightning revealed Konrad and a dozen other villagers, their dripping faces contorted with rage and fear.

"Enough of wizardry!" Konrad yelled. "Agnes, stoke the fire. We will burn the cursed book this very night!"

"There is no telling what might happen then!" Ulrich shouted.

"Silence!" Konrad replied. "It could scarcely be worse than this. Nikolaus, bring the book."

"No!" Ulrich yelled, and dashed into the inner room. He snatched up the spell-book.

Lightning flared again, a long stroke that cast a net of blue-white fire across the scene. Nikolaus and Agnes blocked the door, their eyes hard; Konrad stood behind them. Water trickled down the windowless walls. No escape.

Ulrich clutched the book to his chest. Then, with a growl, he lowered his head and charged — straight at the wall.

The rain-sodden clay gave way and he crashed through, feeling the sticks within the wall claw at his face and arms. He tried desperately to protect his eyes and the book at the same time. He got his head and upper body through, but then his legs met resistance and he tumbled face-first into the cold mud outside.

Hail battered his head, a sharp broken stick jabbed into his thigh, and his mouth and eyes were clogged with foul, clinging mud. He struggled blindly, writhing in the ruins of the broken wall. Hard clods of clay fell onto his back and head.

Then he felt hands grabbing at his feet. Panicked, he surged forward, finally winning free—all save one shoe, pulled off by someone inside the house. Freezing mud squelched between the toes of the bare foot.

Ulrich struggled to his feet, rubbing mud from his eyes with one hand, awkwardly juggling the heavy book with the other. He heard a confusion of voices behind him as a large section of the wall collapsed, delaying pursuit. Konrad shouted something, but his words were lost in the sounds of hail and thunder.

This was clearly no natural storm. The hailstones that seemed to pound in on him from all directions were black, not white, and had the size and twisted shape of knucklebones. Lightning flared again and again, blue-white flashes mingling with greenish afterimages in his eyes. The thunder was nearly constant. And there was a weird, lightheaded sensation, as though he were falling, which he had experienced before in the presence of great magics.

"There he is!" A tremendous bolt of lightning accompanied the shouted words, revealing Konrad standing in the door of Agnes' collapsing house. His finger pointed directly at Ulrich, and two villagers began to move in his direction before the light faded.

Ulrich ran.

His head and shoulders were battered by the black hail as he ran, hunched protectively over the book, unbalanced by its weight. His bare foot slid painfully across the hailstone-littered mud and he nearly fell, but he caught himself with one hand and kept going. Shouts and the splashes of feet in puddles sounded not far behind.

Another flash of lightning revealed a fork in the path. The left fork led into the woods—the natural destination for any outlaw. He could lose himself there with ease. But unless he found shelter soon, the hail would destroy the spell-book as surely as any fire.

He took the right fork. Konrad and the others were right behind him.

Ulrich left the path and charged through the trees. Branches whipped his face; sticks and sharp rocks assailed his bare foot with every step. But it delayed his pursuers, and with his desperate haste he gained a little way on them.

Then the ground fell away from him.

Ulrich cried out in surprise as he slid down a muddy embankment and splashed into the freezing waters of the creek. He felt the book slipping from his arms as he regained his feet, and it was only with a frantic grab that he prevented it from falling into the rushing water. He heard shouts behind him. With an effort he hoisted the book over his head, then waded into the creek.

The chill water ripped at his legs, threatening to topple him over, but he pressed forward. Deeper and deeper he slogged, feeling the current tug at his leggings, then at his jacket. He had no idea how deep the water might be after months of rain, but he forced himself to keep going. Water splashed to his waist, his chest, his armpits, sucking all warmth from his body. He could feel nothing from his feet. His arms burned from the effort of holding the heavy book above his head. He kept going.

Finally the creek bed began to slope upward. He struggled on, feeling his body grow heavier and heavier as he rose step by step from the roaring water. At last he reached the bank and collapsed onto a log, letting the book fall into his lap. His muscles twitched from exhaustion and he trembled all over from fatigue and fear.

Another bolt of lightning illuminated the scene. Three villagers stood, pointing, on the opposite bank. Konrad was half-way across, his face set in an expression of determination and hatred.

Ulrich hauled himself to his feet and stumbled up the bank, seeking higher ground. Hoping to lose himself in the trees.

He staggered through a black world, freezing cold and lit only by irregular flashes of lightning. Again and again he ran headlong into a tree or fell into the mud. Thunder roared like God's mocking laughter. Blood pounded in his ears, even louder than the thunder;

breath rasped in his throat.

Then, just as he entered a clearing at the top of a small hill, his bare foot snagged on a protruding root and he sprawled full length, the book flying from his hands. Desperately he scrambled forward on hands and knees, found the book caught in the branches of a thorny bush. The cover was still closed; he prayed none of the pages had been damaged. He levered himself to a standing position, clutching the book to his chest.

A flash of lightning revealed Konrad's lined face not three feet from his own.

Ulrich backed away from the apparition, his free arm flailing as he toppled backward into the bush. Thorns clawed at his hands and face, caught his clothing. His own weight and that of the book pinned him to the bush, whose branches hampered his arms so that he could not rise.

Trapped.

Konrad smiled as he stepped forward. "You look tired, sir," he said. "Let me take that heavy book for you."

Ulrich struggled against the entrapping bush.

Konrad reached for the book.

And then a blue-white sheet of fire stretched across the sky, accompanied by an immediate smashing pressure of sound. It was all too huge for Ulrich's eyes, his ears, his brain to comprehend, and he lost consciousness.

Some time later—he had no way of knowing how long—he was able to see and hear again, to move his limbs, to wrench himself free of the bush. The night was still dark; the lightning and hail still raged.

Konrad lay unmoving on the ground, already covered with a layer of the black hailstones. His hat and shoes were missing; much of his clothing looked burnt.

Wearily Ulrich picked up the book and began walking.

After an eternity, he came to the mill. Its wheel groaned loud enough to be heard even over the ringing in his ears.

He splashed through the creek and into the darkness under the mill-wheel's axle. Here was a small space where he had spent many a pleasant hour with Bechte. As he ducked inside there was a sudden movement, and a fox dashed out between his legs. The space was foul and muddy, but at last he was shielded from the pounding hail.

Shivering, he wrapped himself into a ball around the book. He would wait here until daybreak, then find a better hiding place.

ଏ

He awoke with a start to the sight of Agnes' dripping face. Her mouth was set in a scowl, and he scrambled back away from her, cracking his head on a projecting timber.

"Agnes!" he gasped, stupidly. "How did you find me?" His own voice sounded peculiar to him; his ears felt stuffed with straw.

"I grew up by this mill. You are not the only one who knows of this trysting-place."

A little wan daylight seeped through chinks in the wall, and outside the hail had been replaced by a driving rain. Thunder still rolled.

"I'm sorry I broke your wall."

"You should be!" she snapped. "Half the house collapsed behind you."

"I'm sorry," he said again, and meant it. "I should never have come here."

"Be quiet and move over. My bottom's getting soaked."

He moved away from the entrance, letting Agnes pull herself fully inside. There was just room for the two of them. Agnes' eyes were white in her mud-smeared face, and Ulrich knew he must look far worse.

They sat in silence for a time. Finally he said "Are you going to tell them where I am?"

"I don't know. Half of them want to burn the book, and God knows what would happen then. But I'm not sure what else I can do."

"You can help me. I know what I did wrong. I can fix it, I think. But I need some things."

"What kind of things?"

"A candle. And some sealing wax. And a sharp knife."

"I'll see what I can do. Are you sure this won't make it even worse?"

"I think so. I only hope I have the courage to do it."

She began to back out of the hole, then paused. "May I ask you one question?"

"Anything."

"These daemons... they control the weather. Rain, wind, sun. Why could they not keep one book dry?"

"I... I don't know."

"No matter." And she left.

ℤ

But it did matter. It tugged and tugged at Ulrich's mind while he waited for Agnes to return. She was right; keeping the spell itself safe from harm was a simple and standard part of any spell. How could a wizard of Johannes' abilities have forgotten it?

Ulrich cast his mind back over the last two weeks of work. He had not read every page—much of the *Zauberschrift* was beyond him in any case—but he did remember seeing a clause for protecting the spell-book.

He broke the seal. A twinge went through him at that, but the weather did not seem to worsen, and he leafed through the book in search of the passage he recalled. The light was terrible, there was barely room to turn the pages, and his vision was blurred from exhaustion, but eventually he found it.

It was indeed, as near as he could puzzle out, a clause for protecting the spell-book. But there was an addition in Heinrich's crabbed hand: *you and all your brothers shall in this, and in all things, be obedient to Heinrich the wizard above all others.*

Tired though he was, Ulrich seethed. That power-besotted bastard Heinrich had given himself personal command of all the daemons, hiding it here in this obscure clause. And worse, he had done it badly. He had inserted his text in the phrase that invoked the protective daemon, and the insertion had mangled the language of the invocation. This error had left the spell-book completely unprotected. It was a wonder the book had lasted as long as it did.

Just then Agnes returned. "I brought your materials, and something to eat. But I think they may search the mill soon. You must hurry."

Ulrich wolfed Agnes' bread and cheese, spitting crumbs as he explained to her what he had found. Taking the knife, he scraped away Heinrich's words, replacing black treason with a pure expanse of creamy vellum. He read and re-read the remaining words, trying to reassure himself that this change would have the desired effect and no other. He thought that it would, but there was much here he did not understand, would not have understood even if his ears were not still ringing.

And now came the part he had been dreading. "A spell is a compact between wizard and daemon," he explained to Agnes as he lit the candle with flint and tinder, "It must be sealed with blood. There are errors, in the spell or in the sealing, that can cause injury. Or death. So when the time came to seal the spell, before, I took the coward's way. I re-sealed it with the old wax. With the two original wizards' blood. I hoped that would seal the spell without involving me. But it didn't work. The false seal inverted the meaning of the spells. Brought disastrous weather instead of good." He dripped fresh wax onto the cord, picked up the knife.

"This time I use my own blood. This time I take the risk upon my own head. And may God forgive me if I have made any mistake." He pricked the ball of his left thumb with the knife, squeezed a few drops of blood onto the hot wax. Then he dripped more wax onto the cord and took up his father's signet ring.

The moment he pressed the ring into the wax, a blue light burst from the book, illuminating the dank hole like the legendary lighthouse at Pharos. With the light came a great whispering roar like the wings of ten thousand butterflies, and the flavor of cinnamon and salt.

"How will we know if you have succeeded?" asked Agnes.

Ulrich sat gape-mouthed for a moment. "Did you not see the light?"

"What light? The day does seem a bit brighter, if that is what you mean." Indeed, the light outside was stronger, and the rain seemed to be slackening.

"Yes, it does," he said. Though the light and sound had lasted only a moment, the taste of cinnamon and salt remained on his tongue and a peculiar tingling suffused his limbs. "I think that means I have succeeded."

ༀ

Mud-caked and aching, Ulrich leaned heavily on Agnes as they slogged wearily back to her half-ruined cottage. The spell-book lay in the crook of Ulrich's arm, miraculously clean. Clearly the protective daemon was hard at work.

The sun raised wisps of steam from the sodden ground and glinted from the puddles that lay everywhere. A hungry winter lay ahead, but there might be time for one small harvest before the snows and there was the promise of an early, daemon-driven spring.

As they approached the village square they saw that a celebration was already in progress. People danced in circles, joyous at the sun's warmth on their upturned faces.

"Ulrich," Agnes said, "it has been twelve years since Lannesdorf had a wizard of its own. Will you consider staying here with us?"

Ulrich stopped walking. He stared at the shiny red seal on the spell-book. At last he spoke. "I will consider it. If I can find a wizard to complete my instruction. If my journeymen have not destroyed the shop in my absence. And if the village will build a proper house for me. One with wood floors."

"I do not know if these things can be arranged," she said. "But we will see. Come, now, let us enjoy the fine weather."

Agnes took Ulrich's arm, and together they joined the celebration in the village square.

಄

Rewind

A FLASH OUTSIDE THE VENETIAN blinds sent a crazy striped parallelogram of flickering orange light splashing across the wall of Clark Thatcher's room. The plastic IV bag hanging at the head of his bed caught some of the light and reflected it onto his legs, a bright orange amoeba that danced and jiggled for a moment until the crash of the explosion frightened it away. Then he heard sirens, and shouting.

Thatcher craned his neck, straining against the straps that held him to the bed, but all he could see outside was a pale yellow flicker and moving shadows. Through the small window in his door, nothing but the same hospital-sterile light he'd seen since he'd been here.

How long was that? Hours. Maybe a day. Ironic, for a Knight not to know the time. But something soft filled his mouth, and no matter how hard he bit down his system would not activate.

He heard gunshots. More shouting. Was it getting closer? Hard to concentrate. The cold fluid seeping into his arm turned his muscles to putty and his brain to jelly. He pulled again against the straps. If he could get loose, maybe he could escape in the chaos of — whatever was happening out there.

If he couldn't get loose, this was the end of the line. They would cut him open, take out the central stabilizer and a few other

69

expensive and delicate parts, and let him die on the table. They probably wouldn't even bother sewing him up again.

Knowing Duke—knowing what he knew now about Duke—they might not even put him under first.

Duke, you bastard, he thought, *you used to be my hero.*

Movement outside the door. Voices. Thatcher held his breath, listened with his whole body.

"Halt!" A pause, then: "This area's restricted, ma'am."

"Thank God I found someone!" A woman's voice, torn with panic. "They came through the window! They're in the staff lounge on the third floor!"

"Shit! Preston, stay here with the nurse."

Thudding of boots down the hallway.

"Preston, was it?"

"Yes, ma'am."

"Mister Preston, I... oh my God! Behind you!" Then a gunshot—astonishingly loud in the enclosed space, though it sounded like something small-caliber.

The doorknob rattled. A face in the window, briefly. Voices again: the woman, and others. Talking too softly for Thatcher to make out over the rapid thudding of his heart. Another shot, even louder, and the door shattered open. The hard fluorescent light cut solid slices in the dusty air. Sharp sting of gunpowder in Thatcher's nose.

Three people entered the room: a nurse, and two men in fatigues, with blackened faces. The nurse and one of the men dragged a body in with them—one of the door guards. "Is that Thatcher?" said the other man, low and hard. He had a beard.

"Yeah," said the first man. "Thatcher, we're from the CLU. We're getting you out of here." A pang ran through Thatcher's chest and stomach at the words—a feeling of being pulled in two. No going back now.

The first man pulled a scuba knife from his boot and began cutting Thatcher's straps, while the bearded one braced his shoulder against the door and peered out the window. The woman ducked down below the foot of the bed. "You can call me Bravo," the man with the knife said while he cut. "The other man is Judah, and the woman's Angel."

As soon as one arm was free, Thatcher pulled the tape off his mouth. It hurt. "Can you walk?" asked Bravo.

Thatcher spit out a plastic horseshoe, but before speaking he bit down three times, then twice more. Green digits appeared in his peripheral vision: it was 2:35 AM. "I'm a little woozy," he said. Other readouts glowed, green and yellow, as his system came on-line. System status was OK but energy levels were very low. He helped the man free his legs and sat up on the edge of the bed. He saw that the woman, Angel, had pulled on camouflage over her white dress and was smearing black paint on her face. "You're not a nurse," he said stupidly.

At that, the man at the door, Judah, looked at her. "What are you doing?" he said. "We might need the nurse outfit for a bluff!"

"Too late," she said. "I've already put on the paint." She pulled on a black knit cap and shoved most of her hair under it.

"Save it for later," said Bravo. To Thatcher: "Do we need to find you a wheelchair?"

Thatcher got to his feet. "No." Then he had to sit down again on the edge of the bed. "Maybe."

The two men supported him while Angel took point, moving down the hall. Thatcher felt hideously exposed in his inadequate hospital gown. At the first corner, Angel started to peer around it, but Judah pulled her back. "Keep your head down," he whispered. She glared at him, but crouched low and stuck her head out at knee level. Then, with another glare, she waved them forward.

Two more corners. They didn't meet anyone—they must all be dealing with the explosion and fire. "The front door guard has a gun under the desk," Thatcher said. He knew this hospital well; he'd spent seven months here having the system put in.

"Thanks," said Judah, "but we've already taken care of that." They rounded a final corner to find the door guard—his name was Dave and he had a girl, five, and a boy, three -- on the floor, eyes open and unseeing. Beyond him were glass doors, black mirrors reflecting the bullet-shattered desk.

"You didn't have to do that," Thatcher said.

"Just another victim in the government's war on the people," said the woman. "Come on."

They crouched low and scuttled to the doors, acutely conscious that the brightly lighted lobby was plainly visible to anyone outside in the blackness. The doors slid open—Thatcher's heart jumped at the sudden motion—and they ran through to the shelter of a concrete traffic barrier.

The west wing of the hospital was on fire, flames roaring and clawing the sky. Fire trucks and medic vans twitched in the shifting orange light; silhouettes of firemen sprayed water on the burning building. Someone was cursing, over and over.

"We came through the fence over there," the bearded man said to Thatcher, pointing into the darkness on the far side of the parking lot. "Doesn't look like they've noticed it yet."

"OK, let's go," said the other man. They kept low and moved quickly from car to car. The pavement was rough under Thatcher's bare feet, and they splashed in cold water—runoff from the fire hoses. Bitter smoke mingled with the gasoline and asphalt smells of the parking lot.

Bravo was in the lead as they reached the edge of the parking lot—just a few yards of scrubby grass between them and the fence. As he stepped over the curb, yellow flashes of gunfire burst out of the night to his left and he fell with an "Agh!"

Angel raised her rifle and returned fire, while Judah pulled Thatcher back into the cover of a black Ford Bronco. "Get *down!*"

Judah said to Angel, but she fired again and again while bullets buzzed past.

Finally she ducked back behind the Bronco. "I think I got one of them."

"And how many more are there?" The bearded man kept his voice down, but it was taut with rage.

"Just one, I think," she replied in a matching tone, "and if *someone* doesn't take him out pronto we're dead." She checked her rifle, then jumped out from behind the car and began firing into the darkness. Answering fire cracked back at her and the van's windshield shattered.

"Crazy bitch," muttered the bearded man. "Come on, maybe we can find another way out." He pulled Thatcher in the opposite direction.

"Wait." Thatcher bit down twice, then once—code 21. Green digits read fifteen percent. "I think I can get us out of this."

Angel came back behind the Bronco, breathing hard. "Sonofabitch clipped me." Blood, black in the sodium light, stained her ear.

"Give me a rifle," said Thatcher. "I guarantee I can take down that shooter. But after that I won't be good for much of anything. You might have to carry me. Understand?"

Judah stared in incomprehension. "Got it," said Angel. "Here. Three rounds left."

"Thanks." Thatcher bit down again, code 323. He looked over the rifle, then stepped out from behind the car and fired three times—waiting and watching carefully after each shot, making no attempt to conceal himself.

There was a flash and a bullet slammed into his side. He felt the crunch of ribs shattering and a cold numbness spreading from the entry wound. As he stumbled from the impact, he bit down once.

Rewind.

Uninjured, Thatcher stepped out from behind the car. He turned to his left and loosed one precise shot into the darkness. He heard a grunt and a thud as the shooter fell. Then he collapsed, his face slamming into the dirt.

He drifted in and out of consciousness. The bearded man and the woman carrying him between them. Streetlights going by, seen from below through a car's rear window. Gunshots. Screaming. The car rocking crazily back and forth. Sirens.

Blackness.

ᘓ

Thatcher awoke to too-bright sunlight and a cracked, cobwebbed ceiling. He groaned and covered his eyes. It was 10:53 AM. Goblins were tightening a metal band around his head, and his side throbbed with pain—remembered pain, pain from shots that had never been fired, but real pain nonetheless.

"Welcome back," said a woman's voice. Angel. "How do you feel?"

"Uhh. I hurt all over. And I'm starving."

"All I can offer is aspirin, and some cold fried chicken. If it's still good."

"I'll take it. And where's the bathroom?"

"Just out the door, to your left."

He pulled the hospital gown closed as best he could while he limped to the door. She stared, but didn't say anything about the scars that webbed his entire body. He hoped she wouldn't.

She sat at the foot of the bed while he polished off two thighs and a wing, a little styrofoam tub of cold mashed potatoes, and a half-gallon bottle of coke. Black paint stained the furrows of her brow, the crows' feet of her eyes. She had a bandage on one ear.

"Where are we?" he asked between bites. The room was tiny, barely bigger than the bed. A grimy rectangle on one wall showed where a picture had once hung.

"My apartment. Belltown."

"Is it safe here?"

"I don't know. I don't know if anywhere is safe. We got ambushed at the rendezvous point. They shot Judah when he got out of the car." She sniffed, and wiped her nose on an already-black sleeve. "I never even knew his real name." She began to sob, tears making black streaks on her face.

Not knowing what else to do, Thatcher patted her on the arm. She leaned into him and cried on his shoulder. She was all bones, her skin soft and loose, her hair colorless and wiry. She smelled of gunpowder. Thatcher held her awkwardly, wanting to give comfort but disquieted by her touch. He kept thinking about how his instructor Dr. Collins had been killed in a CLU attack.

This was crazy. He was a soldier in the most elite unit in the Army; she was a member of the terrorist "Committee for the Liberation of the USA." They should be trying to kill each other, not huddling together in a squalid little bedroom in Belltown. *Damn you, Duke,* he thought. *You've turned everything upside down.*

After a while the sobs subsided and she sat up, wiping her eyes.

"I'm sorry about your friend," Thatcher said, "but how on Earth did a nice little old lady get involved with a bunch of terrorists in the first place?"

"I'm 48, and we aren't terrorists!" she shot back. "It's the government that's waging an undeclared war on the people. We're just fighting back."

"Tell that to Dave's wife. He was the door guard at the hospital."

Her look was icy. "If that's the way you feel about it, I'll give you bus fare back there."

"Oh jeez, I'm sorry. It's just—I didn't think I was getting involved with the CLU! I just wanted out of the Army."

"Who else did you think could break into a military hospital and rescue your sorry ass?"

"I wasn't supposed to need a rescue! All I wanted was fake papers. The next thing I know I'm strapped to a bed and waiting to die. I didn't know Duke was tapping my phone. I didn't know my friend-of-a-friend would call in the CLU."

"Who's Duke?"

"Major T. K. Duke. My commanding officer. Used to be my friend."

"Used to be?"

"We had a... disagreement. About a girl."

A harsh pounding rattled through the room. "Police!" came a voice. "Open up!"

"Oh Jesus," said Angel. Her face suddenly looked like dirty white plastic.

"Keep calm." Thatcher looked out the window. It was five stories down. No fire escape. "Do you have a gun?"

"A rifle. But it's hidden on the roof. Couldn't risk getting caught with it."

The cop would be armed. No way he could take him on without a weapon, not as shaky as he felt. "Have you ever been arrested?" He looked in the closet.

"No."

The closet overflowed with clothes, shoes, and junk, but there might be enough room. "They might not have your picture, then. I'll hide in here. You answer the door. If there's trouble I'll come out and help, but with any luck he'll just ask a few questions and leave. Whatever happens, keep calm!"

"Calm. Right." She took a deep breath, then left.

He checked and armed his system as he closed the door of the tiny closet, hearing the cop's rough voice asking Angel "have you seen this man" and demanding to search the apartment. Thatcher tried to visualize the place from the brief glimpse he'd had earlier, hearing heavy footsteps moving from the front door to the kitchen, to the bathroom... the cop seemed to be making a pretty cursory search of it. This just might work.

Booted feet came to the bedroom door. It squeaked open. Creak of the cop's leather jacket and gunbelt as he looked from side to side. A pause. Two more steps.

The closet door jerked open. Thatcher saw his own terrified face in the cop's black visor as he bit down.

Rewind.

Desperate, exhausted, Thatcher slipped under the bed as the cop's footsteps moved from the kitchen to the bathroom. Sipping air he wanted desperately to gulp, he tried to ignore the smell of the worn and filthy carpet and make as little noise as possible. More footsteps; the door squeaked open. Dusty black boots trod inches from his face, while he held his breath. The closet door opened, then closed.

The boots paused, looking around. Drops of sweat slithered down Thatcher's sides.

The boots departed.

Thatcher clutched the carpet, trembling with fear and fatigue, as the cop admonished Angel to report immediately if she saw this man, then tromped off. He blacked out for a moment, then saw Angel's face, creased with worry. "I thought you were in the closet!"

"I was."

She helped him out from under the bed, but even with her help he couldn't stand up. "Angel. Please. Help me."

"How?"

"Food." He passed out again. When he came to, the apartment was silent.

Thatcher spent a long dead time staring stupefied at the scuffed and rusty leg of the bed before Angel reappeared with a warm and fragrant white paper sack. The burgers inside were leathery and greasy. The most delicious things he'd ever eaten.

ℭ

After he'd eaten the last tiny fragment of french fry, he felt human enough to sit at the kitchen table. "All right, Thatcher," Angel said, "If I'm going to risk my neck for you and keep feeding you like some mama bird, I want some answers."

"I'll tell you what I can."

"First and foremost: what makes you so special? I've never seen the Committee risk so many people in an operation. Why?"

"You don't know who I am?"

"Bravo never told me anything he didn't think I had to know."

"I'm from the Knights. K Division."

"Jesus." She sat back and crossed her arms on her chest. "That explains a few things. And opens up a lot more questions. Like, why should we trust you?"

"You saw how they had me tied down and drugged. They were going to kill me. I'm not going back."

"Could be a set-up."

"Um." How could he prove...? "Wait. I shot that guard. By the fence. That wasn't a set-up. They couldn't know where we were going. He was really shooting at me. I really shot him." *Oh my God,* he thought, *I probably know him – knew him. I wonder who it was?*

"That's another thing. How did you do that? You just stepped out there and whipped one shot into pitch darkness. Got him in one. Can you see in the dark? X-ray vision? Telekenesis? What is the big secret that makes you K Division troops so damn unstoppable?"

"Sorry. Classified."

She stood up, leaning over the table, heedless of the chair clattering to the floor behind her. "Fuck that, soldier-boy. You're in bed with us now, like it or not, and you're going to have to put out."

"No."

Without warning she slapped him across the face. "Two people died to get you out of there, maybe a lot more. You *owe* us. So talk!"

He stared silent negation at her, but her gray eyes burned back unblinking and he had to drop his gaze. He found his hands were clenched together on the table before him. Silver scars laced his fingers like meridian lines.

He thought about all the different kinds of pain those scars had caused him.

Finally he spoke. "We call it 'rewind.'"

"Go on."

"It's a kind of time travel. We can go back in time, just a few seconds. Do things over."

"I don't get it." But she pulled the chair back up onto its feet and sat down in it. Willing to listen.

"Let me give you an example. I got shot at the fence last night."

"Not that I saw."

"No. You didn't. I rewound, back to a point before the shot. I saw where the shot had come from — was going to come from — and fired at that spot before he could shoot. You have to have a good memory and better aim to make it into the Knights."

"So it never happened."

"It never happened. But I remember it. And it still hurts." The ache was sharp. It would take another couple of days for the pain to fade. There were some wounds he'd taken years ago that still twinged, even though he had no scars to show. Not from those wounds, anyway.

"How does it work?"

"I don't understand the principles. God knows I tried, but I barely passed the exams and I've forgotten what I knew then. It's bioelectrical, I know that. My body is an integral part of the system. Circuitry along the spine. Wires around every bone." Seven months in the hospital to put the system in. Hoarse from screaming, sometimes.

"So you have... what, an atomic reactor inside?"

"It runs off ATP, the chemical that powers your muscles. When I'm rested and well-fed I can do six, maybe seven jumps. Right now if I tried I'd probably just pass out." Eleven percent, said the green digits.

"OK," she said, standing up. "It sounds plausible enough. I'd like to take you to my superiors. If what you say is true, we can use someone with your talents. Your knowledge."

Again he felt as though he was being torn in half. He hated Duke, didn't care about the government—but he couldn't betray his unit. They were all he had. Job, friends, and family all rolled into one.

He bit his lip and nodded, not meeting Angel's eyes. Maybe if he played along and paid attention, an opportunity to escape would present itself.

"Wait here," Angel said. "I'm going to make some phone calls. And buy you some clothes."

೫

Wind whistled through a leaky passenger-side window, patched with duct tape, as they headed towards a rendezvous somewhere in Eastern Washington. Angel was at the wheel; Thatcher leaned against the door, eating trail mix and scratching. He didn't know where she'd found the clothes he was wearing, but the shirt was too small and it itched.

The radio was talking again about the terrorist attack on a hospital in Seattle. It had been talking all day, yet somehow had avoided the detail that the hospital was a top-secret military facility. Thatcher switched it off.

"Time travel," Angel said into the silence. "Sonofabitch. We thought it was a force field, or telekenisis. This explains everything." She was looking at him like he was a bug under glass.

80

He wished she would watch the road, and not just because he was afraid of an accident. "Did you ever use it for... personal reasons? Like, go back and undo something stupid you did when you were a kid?"

"I wish. My personal best is eleven seconds. Duke says he can do twenty-eight." He watched wheat fields passing for a moment. There was nothing else to see, no other traffic. "Anyway, I've never regretted anything that much. Until recently."

"Lucky. I can think of a hundred things I'd change if I could."

"Like what?"

"My parents died in a car accident when I was sixteen. I wished every day for years that I could go back and keep them from going out that night. It was like I could feel another world, right nearby, where they were still alive. It just kept getting farther and farther away."

"I'm sorry."

She snorted. "Don't be sorry. You weren't even born yet. Save your sorries for stuff you've got something to do with." She looked at him again. "Like the coup."

"What? I was eight years old."

"Yeah, but it was K Division that made it possible. There's no way Haig and his little bunch of hotheads could have taken the White House without you. And you've kept them in power ever since."

"I'm not going to apologize for that," he said, sitting up. "I wanted out, yeah, but that was just a personal problem between me and Duke. I'm proud of the Knights and everything we've done. *Everything.* Before the coup we had stagflation and the misery index, and we were getting our butts kicked in the Mideast. Now we have a roaring economy and every country in the world respects the USA."

"The world *fears* the USA. Most of the citizens fear it too. Look, you're too young to remember what it was like before. Back in the last millennium," she said with hard irony, "there was no barbed wire at the borders. No Citizen Checkpoints, no curfews, no National Identity Cards. And no fucking forced labor!"

"The new millennium doesn't start until next year, we wouldn't need those national security measures if it wasn't for terrorists like the CLU, and don't give me that 'forced labor' crap. Workfare keeps the country strong. Honest work instead of handouts, and a strong national defense to boot."

Thatcher saw her knuckles whiten on the wheel. "Oh, we've still got handouts! It's just that now the government hands out workers to the defense industry. Workfare laborers get paid minimum, and the average—the *average!*—lifespan on the job is under five years." Her eyes glistened with tears. "I watched my little sister Cherry die of beryllicosis."

"What's... gorillacosis?"

"Beryllicosis. Sort of like black lung disease, only not so pretty. Comes from inhaling beryllium dust. It's what happens to people who run machine tools at aerospace plants where there are no Goddamn workplace safety rules!" Her face was set in a rigid mask of hatred and grief, tears running down like rain. "It took her eighteen months to die, and they didn't even cover the hospital bills. I joined the CLU the week after the funeral."

"Uh, maybe you'd better pull over."

"I am not going to fucking pull over!" she screamed, her face bunching up like a fist. "I am going to keep driving this Goddamn car until we get to the rendezvous and I can hand you over, so I never have to think about you or the fucking K Division ever again!"

"You're weaving all over the road! You could get us both killed!"

"What the hell," she said. "One less soldier, one less freedom fighter, it all evens out..." And then she jerked the wheel savagely to the right and slammed on the brakes. The car skidded to a halt on the shoulder, crunching through gravel, the left rear wheel still on the pavement. Angel crossed her arms on her chest and leaned her head on the wheel, crying uncontrollably, her voice making a discordant chord with the sound of the horn.

Thatcher fumbled with his seat belt, ran around to the driver's side. He opened the door, leaned in, and held Angel in his arms. She hugged him fiercely back. The gravel was hard under his knees.

"I'm sorry," he said. "I'm really, really sorry." There were tears in his eyes too.

"I'm sorry too," she sobbed. "I've been stupid." She pushed him away, wiped her eyes on her sleeve. "We need to get out of here before the cops show up."

"Maybe I should drive."

"Maybe you should."

They got back on the road, and after a nervous half-hour Thatcher was ready to believe that no flashing blue lights were about to appear in his rear-view mirror. He kept rigidly to the speed limit.

Angel sat with one hand on her forehead, staring off at the point where the road met the horizon. Her eyes were still wet but her breathing had returned to normal. "I shouldn't have said some of those things," she said at last. "You seem to be a good kid. You've just been part of something bad."

He started to protest. But then he thought about what she'd said about her sister—about Workfare. About the radio, and how it never told the whole story. About Duke.

He'd told Angel that he'd had a disagreement with Duke about a girl. That was true, as far as it went.

She must have been beautiful, before. Now that perfect, sweet face was frozen in an expression of pain and fear and despair, spattered with flecks of dried blood. The same blood that stained Duke's hands. *I'm sorry you had to see this,* he'd said, *but I'm sure you'll understand.*

He understood, all right. As he helped Duke dispose of the body, he finally understood that Duke was running K Division as his own private hunting club. It was while he was washing the blood off his hands that he decided to get out of the Army.

But it was only now, with Angel's story fresh in his ears, that he thought about how Duke fit into the system. How his superiors must have known what he was doing, and had left him alone. It must go all the way to the top.

"What does this 'rewind' feel like?" she asked.

He blew out his cheeks. "Like having your bones pulled out of your body, all at once. Some guys can't take it. Go through all the surgery, all the training, and after the first time they just can't pull that trigger again."

"What happens to them?"

"They get transferred out." Like Duncan Mackenzie. He remembered clearing out Mackenzie's quarters, packing up his stuff for shipment to Fort Benning, laughing and joking with the other guys about the "washout."

Mackenzie had never answered his letters. Thatcher had assumed he was too ashamed to write back. But now he thought about Duke, leaning over him in the hospital bed. *Do you know how much the central stabilizer on your spine costs?* he'd said. *Ten and a half million dollars. They have to build twenty thousand of them to get one that works. You didn't really think we were just going to let you walk away with that, did you?* Suddenly he wondered where those boxes of Mackenzie's stuff had really wound up.

"They get transferred out," he repeated, more thoughtfully. "At least, that's what they say."

"You can never trust them. They said they'd keep Cherry and me together, but when space got tight in the orphanage they transferred me to another facility. I had to kick and scream to get us together again. As soon as I turned eighteen I got us both out of there."

"That must have been hard. Supporting two people at eighteen."

"It was. But somehow we survived. I gave up a lot to keep her safe." She closed her eyes. "I'd give up anything to bring her back. But I know that's not going to happen, so I work to bring down the system that killed her. I'd give my life for that."

"You came damn close back there. And at the hospital. If you don't take a little more care, you'll wind up an angel for real."

"Yeah, I know." She slumped in her seat. "But ever since Cherry died, I don't really care a lot about me."

"You should," he said. "You're worth caring about."

"Thanks."

But she didn't seem convinced.

og

They reached the rendezvous point—an abandoned gas station near Ellensburg—just after sunset. There they found a couple of men who identified themselves as Dusty and Wolf.

Dusty was a round man with a gray beard and a black leather cap and jacket. "We've done some checking on Thatcher's story," he said to Angel, "and it seems to check out, but we need to interrogate him."

"I don't like the sound of that," said Thatcher.

"Sorry, but we have to take precautions," said Wolf, a large muscular man in jeans and a flannel shirt. "With the ambush day before yesterday, we think there may be a mole in the Committee. We're not going to torture you or anything, just ask you some questions."

Wolf had a key to the empty gas station, and they went inside and sat around a table in what had been the repair area. The windows in the garage doors were covered with newspaper; the space was illuminated by a hissing gas lantern. Angel, Wolf, and Dusty became faces floating in the darkness.

They asked him a *lot* of questions, some of them over and over. Thatcher explained about the Knights, about Duke, about why he'd left. When he told them about the girl he'd seen Duke kill, Angel's eyes went wide and she put her hand on his.

"Couldn't you just transfer out?" asked Dusty.

"With what I'd learned about Duke, I didn't want to be anywhere in the same Army with him. Anyway, I don't think he would have let me go in one piece." Poor Mackenzie.

Some of the questions they asked about the Knights' technology were very perceptive. They seemed to know a lot about the system already, seemed to be probing to see how much he was willing to reveal.

He told them everything. Classified, Top Secret, Maximum Secret—he let them all go.

The other Knights seemed to be standing in the darkness behind Wolf, staring at him with disapproval. He knew them all—their names, their faces, their voices, their habits—and their scorn burned him. But behind Angel stood her sister Cherry, the girl Duke had killed, and Duncan Mackenzie, their eyes pleading for mercy. The girl had no name, and Cherry no face—but somehow those three were more important to him than all the Knights put together.

There was one other presence in the darkness. Duke. He seemed to stand behind Thatcher. His stare made the hairs rise on the back of Thatcher's neck.

"One last question," said Dusty. "How can you kill a Knight in combat?"

Even after all the secrets he'd betrayed, this was the hardest. It took him a long time to form the words. "You have to shoot him in the head, and it has to be a surprise. If you can kill him before he can bite down, his system can't save him." In the darkness, the

Knights shook their heads, turned, and walked away.

Wolf and Dusty looked at each other. Dusty nodded. Wolf said "All right. We're going to take you to a safe house a few miles from here. We have another defector there. I hope that you and he together can give us a weapon we can use to overthrow the government. Any questions?"

"Can we get something to eat first? I'm starving."

They hid Angel's car under a tarp behind the gas station and all got into a van. They drove to a little mom-and-pop diner, where Wolf called the safe house from a pay phone. Thatcher ate a huge meal of meatloaf, mashed potatoes, green beans, biscuits, and two slices of apple pie a la mode. The conversation was pleasant and trivial.

It was 11:03 when they came to a farm: a house and a barn and a couple of outbuildings surrounding a dirt courtyard. Moths fluttered in the cone of mercury light coming from a fixture near the peak of the barn.

Dusty was driving, and Thatcher could see his brow furrow in the cold blue light. "What's wrong?"

"Where's Booter?"

"Probably in the barn," said Wolf.

"Who's Booter?" said Angel.

"The dog," said Dusty. "He's kind of our chief of security. Whenever a car comes by, he's out here barking his head off."

"He's probably just asleep somewhere."

"I don't know." Dusty stopped the van. "I'm inclined to be a little paranoid right now. I think I'd like to back off and reconnoiter." He put the van into reverse.

Machine gun fire rang out of the darkness; Thatcher couldn't see from where. Steam spurted from under the van's hood, and the engine coughed and died.

"Shit!" said Wolf.

"I think we're in trouble," said Dusty.

87

Thatcher's system was at eighty percent. "Give me the gun," he said, meaning the rifle they'd brought with them from Angel's car. "I can hold them down while you make a run for it. We'll go out the back door."

"Why should we trust you?" said Wolf.

"We can trust him," said Angel. Dusty nodded. "Good luck," said Angel, handing him the rifle and a spare clip of ammunition.

"I'll go off to the left. Give me half a minute, then go right. Good luck."

Thatcher checked the rifle over — safety off, seven rounds in the clip plus one in the chamber — then clambered over boxes and tarps to the back door. He eased the latch open, then quickly threw the door open and jumped out.

The van sat in a rutted driveway between fields of winter wheat, a sketch in silver and black in the mercury light from the farm and the beams of a full moon. Thatcher kept low, hurried into rustling wheat. He dropped to one knee and examined the barnyard through the rifle's telescopic sight. Nothing moved. Finally he sighted on the light that illuminated the scene, shattered it with one shot.

There was an immediate response, shots flashing from the darkness in the vicinity of the barn. He ducked and ran, moving to the left, forcing his way through the rough rattling stalks.

Thatcher poked his head up above the wheat, eyes beginning to adapt to the moonlit dark. He saw a heavy figure — Dusty — emerge from the van and run into the wheat to his right. Then two more figures. But instead of running away, they headed toward the farm!

Wolf was nearly carrying Angel, who struggled to no effect. Thatcher cursed and raised his rifle, but their jerky movements and the darkness prevented a clear shot at the traitor Wolf. He hurried after them, but the van was closer to the barn than to him and they reached the barnyard before he did. They vanished into the black square of the open barn door. A moment later, gunfire flashed out of that square at him, and he ducked back into the field.

Thatcher considered his options. He could run, hide out in the fields, try to make his way to safety on foot. It was what he'd advised the others to do. But now the situation was different.

He scurried back to the shelter of the van. At least it would block some of the bullets. A few shots rang out as he emerged from the field, but as he reached the van he heard a voice on a bullhorn. "Hold your fire!" It was Duke! "Sergeant Thatcher, listen to me. We have your co-conspirators. We have your girlfriend. Surrender, and they will live."

Faintly, he heard Angel protest: "I'm not his fucking girlfrien..." The sentence ended with the smack of hard plastic against flesh.

Thatcher panted against the van door for a moment, then poked his rifle out from behind the bumper. He put five shots into the barn doorway, was rewarded with screams and an answering hail of flashes. He ducked back, hearing a bullet slam into the van's tire.

He leaned out again and fired two more shots, then pulled back and inserted the second clip. Deep breath, then he charged out from behind the van. He would take as many of them down as he could. Then he stopped short.

Duke was standing in the middle of the courtyard, plain as anything. His face was cool and pale in the cold moonlight, features sharp and unperturbed, though he held the struggling Angel to his chest with a pistol to her head. Even his fatigues were crisp.

"Let's not drag this out," he said, not shouting—speaking just loud enough to be heard. "It's quite simple. Deactivate your system, throw down your weapon, and the woman lives. Otherwise, she dies."

In response Thatcher raised his rifle, sighted between Duke's eyes, and fired. But even as he squeezed the trigger Duke ducked out of the way. He tried again; same result. Even a head shot was no good in this situation, when Duke was ready for him and looking right at him.

Duke ducked down behind Angel, putting her head between him and Thatcher. "Nice try, Sergeant," he said, panting a little. "But I'm losing patience." His finger tightened on the trigger. "You have five seconds to surrender. Four. Three."

"Don't let him use me against you!" Angel shouted, and threw back her head into his nose. He ate the pain—did not rewind—but he was distracted for a moment.

Angel's face filled the gunsight. Her eyes were hard, looking right at him. She knew that the head shot was the only way to kill a Knight. I'd give up my life to bring down the government, she'd said. "Do it!" she said through clenched teeth.

He couldn't do it. He dropped the gun, held up his hands. "You win."

"Excellent choice. Deactivate your system."

He bit down on his tongue. "Done," he lied.

"Come forward. Private Keene, bring the syringe."

"No!" said Angel, and elbowed Duke hard in the ribs. His grip relaxed and she twisted, caught him in the groin with a heel.

"You little bitch." Duke's finger tightened on the trigger and Angel's head exploded.

Thatcher growled, a fierce animal sound, as he bit down hard. *Rewind.*

"You have five seconds to surrender. Four. Three."

"Don't let him use me against you!" Angel shouted, and threw back her head into his nose. Her face filled the gunsight. "Do it!"

Thatcher pulled the trigger. Watched as the bullet slammed into Angel's face, and through it. Into Duke's face behind hers. Into the brain behind that face.

Stopping that brain before it could rewind.

Thatcher ran as hard as he could toward the courtyard even as the two bodies buckled. There was a stunned pause, then bullets flashed from the barn toward him. One caught him in the shoulder -

- he ignored the pain and kept running. He reached Angel, scooped her up, held her tight against his chest, and bit down hard.

Rewind.

"You have five seconds to surrender. Four. Three."

It hadn't worked. Angel was still in Duke's arms.

He had to kill her again.

"Do it!"

He did it. Again. Then he stayed where he was, turned and fired shot after shot into the barn door before those inside could react. Blinking away tears.

In the end, he killed enough of them that the CLU members in the barn could overpower the rest. He took two bullets doing it, but neither of them hurt him as much as the ones he'd fired into Angel's head.

ଔ

"You don't have to do this, you know," Dusty said.

"I do have to," Thatcher replied. "I owe it to Angel."

He lay on a couch in the farmhouse's living room. An ATP/glucose mixture dripped cold into his left arm, and a power cord was alligator-clipped to wires that emerged from a bandaged incision at the base of his neck. His blood seemed to be fizzing.

"We could really use you right here and now."

"If this works, you won't need me here and now. It'll be a whole new world." He turned to the defector, Dr. Collins. He was a former K Division scientist; Thatcher had been told that he'd been killed in a terrorist attack. Somehow he was not surprised to find him here. "How many seconds again?"

"Seven hundred million. That'll put you in early April of 1978, give you six months to find Fessler and stop him."

"Someone else might discover the same thing," said Dusty, "and it'd be all the same."

"Maybe," said Collins. "But I've been all over the theory. Fessler's discovery was a complete fluke."

Dusty held out his hands, supplicating. "We don't even know if a six-year-old brain can handle a twenty-eight-year-old mind! And even if it works, what can a kid do?"

"I was a tough kid." Thatcher bit down, and the green digits appeared—digits only he could see. Seven hundred million seconds. Jesus. One more bite would activate the sequence. "Let's do it."

"Good luck." Collins flipped a switch, and Thatcher's blood felt like it was boiling.

He bit down, and it all vanished.

ଓ

Fear of Widths

WHEN THEY GOT OFF THE PLANE at Mitchell Field, there was nobody there to meet them. That's when it really sank in.

He had to sit down in the waiting area until the sobs stopped coming. His wife held him, awkward in the hard airport chairs; passing strangers looked concerned but did not stop, intent on their own business. After only a little while of this he blew his nose and joined the crowd. He was already pretty much cried out. But his heart sat in the hollow of his chest like a lonely farmhouse on the vast prairie.

So many times I've flown to this airport, he thought as they walked to the baggage carousel, and now I barely recognize it. Every time before, his parents had met him at the gate. Smaller and smaller, grayer and grayer. After the heart attack Dad lost weight (finally, after years of nagging) but it didn't make him look healthy; instead he looked shriveled, like all the juice had been squeezed out of him. Mom just got smaller and rounder every year, and moved more and more slowly.

And now they were gone. Run down in a crosswalk by a drunk who ran a red light. The funeral was tomorrow.

The rent-a-car place wanted to give him some American tuna boat instead of the Japanese compact he'd reserved. When he received the news, he felt for a brief unreal moment that he stood on a vast whistling plain, cold and alone -- but the feeling passed as his wife began to protest. He touched her arm to quiet her and said to the agent "We'll take it."

He didn't realize until later that the car was a Plymouth, like the one his folks had when he was in sixth grade.

The airport interchange was under construction. The Billy Mitchell bomber that had once stood triumphantly at the entrance to the airport was now stuck on a pedestal like some drab and awkward butterfly, tiny and barely visible to the speeding traffic. Nothing was familiar. But when the car pulled onto the freeway, he saw the hotel where he'd attended a high school job fair. The gas station where he'd tanked up on the way out of town, returning to college after Christmas break. Billboards for a bank whose logo had changed, but whose name brought a thirty-year-old jingle ringing into his head.

And the horizon.

How could he have forgotten the horizon?

In Portland there was no horizon. Not like this. In Portland there was always something between you and the edge of the planet: trees, or mountains, or clouds. Even in those places where there was a bit of horizon, there was something to draw the eye away from it. Something important and grandiose, like Mount Hood.

Here there was nothing bigger than the horizon itself. Oh, there were stands of trees here and there, but they were funny little round things, just beginning to bud—a bare wisp of greenery like a teenager's underfunded beard. They didn't have a chance against the line that went all the way around.

The horizon was a lariat whirling around his head at eye level. A shimmering, dangerous line. But who was twirling it?

The blare of a horn and his wife's gasp brought his attention back to the road, and he braked hard. The red lights ahead got much too close much too fast, but the squeal of tires did not end in a crunch, and a few minutes later he was back up to highway speed.

He gripped the steering wheel harder to still the trembling in his hands, to maintain his focus.

It was difficult to watch the road when the infinite horizon sucked at his attention. It was so very flat here. Even the tiny rise of a freeway overpass was enough to give a view for miles. A panorama of factories and churches, standing out from a background of boxy little houses: tiny square things, brick and clapboard, with pointed roofs against the snows. So simple, like a child's drawing of a house. Each with a little concrete stoop, just two or three steps high, and a simple, flat lawn of green grass. Perhaps a bush or two. Not like the overhanging roofs, deep porches, and sprawling rhododendrons of his neighborhood in Portland.

How could a cartoon of a house keep you safe from the vast open spaces? Portland houses had solidity; those overhanging Craftsman roofs enclosed, protected, defended. Just in case Mount Hood decided to blow off its lid like Mount St. Helens, revealing the horizon beyond, they were ready. Milwaukee houses were naive, defenseless. They clung to the flat landscape like lumps of chewed gum; their only strategy was to be too inoffensive to bother with.

The houses were tidy here, but the cars were in bad shape. The one passing him right now was nothing but a lace of rust, its bumpers held on by bungee cords. Back home — back in Portland — a car that age might have five more years in it if you kept the oil changed. But here they salted the roads.

Or was it the salt, really? That was what his father had told him. But how he felt it was the great widths of this flat landscape that sucked the life out of cars. Storms swept hard across the prairies, with no mountains to block their effect; maybe the North Pole, its effects also undamped by terrain, pulled molecules of metal out of cars, leaving them riddled and weakened. Then the weather finished them off.

They got off the freeway and headed west on Capitol. Parks and fast-food places that might have been anywhere; suburbs whose names he'd forgotten. Seen from street level, the houses weren't really so tidy: paint was peeling, shingles loose. Midwestern winters were hard on houses. Or maybe it was the neighborhood; he had not lived here in so long, he didn't know if this was one of the bad ones. Probably that was it. There were too many boarded-up storefronts here for a "good" neighborhood.

But something in him believed those stores were not closed, just boarded up against the pull of the prairie — the infinite widths of horizon that kept drawing his eyes from the road ahead of him. Like a hurricane, he thought. He imagined cautious Milwaukee shopkeepers boarding their windows against the horizon: grim Germanic faces, starched white aprons, pencils tucked behind ears... and ten-penny nails clamped between white lips, eyes glancing over shoulders as the shopkeepers nailed up another sheet of plywood.

Unlike a hurricane, though, the horizon never went away.

He turned right on Brookfield. Though closer to home, this area was less familiar. It had been farm country while he was growing up; now it was all strip malls and condominiums. Square boxes bolted to the land, with parking lots like scabs.

He gripped the wheel so hard his knuckles whitened, but his hands still trembled. He was sure his wife could feel the car shimmy. She touched the back of his hand, an offer of comfort. He held her hand briefly, then clutched the wheel again. Not speaking.

His father had always gone very quiet at times of high emotion. His silences burned like pure hydrogen, a hot invisible flame.

Left on Bluebird. Lots of new houses, but there was the Johanssens' place. Someone had stuck a cedar deck onto it and given it a hideous sky-blue paint job.

And now his house. This tiny, cartoon thing, with its faded yellow paint, had been his home for sixteen years? That gable, that black window, had been his bedroom? He had often wished for a tree outside his window, like the trees down which boys in adventure stories climbed, but he had had nothing but a sheer drop to the concrete patio. That drop didn't look like so much from here.

It wasn't his bedroom now. It was his mother's sewing room. Had been. Empty now. Empty of people; full of possessions, of memories. All had to be sorted, cleared, sold off. His wife had told him about clearing out her grandmother's trailer after the funeral. But there had been sisters and cousins to help there; it had been a family event. He was an only child.

"Are you sure you don't want to stay in a hotel?" He realized he'd been sitting in the driveway with the ignition off for some time. Still gripping the wheel. Staring up at the bedroom window.

"No. Waste of good money, when there's a whole house sitting here empty." It was exactly what his mother would have said.

"Well, we should go inside then." She opened her door, and a polite repeated chime sounded from under the dashboard. A cold March wind tugged at her hair. "Are you OK?"

"I'm... good enough. Just leave me here for a moment." He pulled the keys from the ignition, silencing the chime, and handed them to his wife. "The key with the yellow thing on it opens the front door. I'll be along in a minute." She kissed him on the cheek and closed the door behind herself. He heard the trunk open and close.

The horizon was tremendous. Terrifying. Three hundred and sixty degrees across. He was glad of the car's roof pillars, glad of the tiny house and the garage, glad of anything that could hide a little of it.

The sun was beginning to set, that enormous sky shading orange to purple, brushed with trails of cloud like finger paints. Lights came on in the house.

Finally he could delay no longer. He unbuckled his seat belt. He opened the door.

He clung to the armrest as he climbed unsteadily out of the car. Gravel crunched under his shoes.

He stood next to the car, holding onto the door with both hands.

Then, knowing what awaited him, he swallowed and let go of the door.

Slowly at first, he fell away from the car. Gravel sliding under his shoes, then under his knees. When he hit the black plastic edging at the edge of the driveway he began to tumble, rolling over and over across the flat, green lawn. It was like all the times he'd rolled down grassy hillsides as a child, the dirt and grass thudding against his shoulders and elbows. But as he tumbled faster and faster he began to panic. Clawed at the grass, pulling up clumps of sod and earth with his fingernails. No use. The tidy little house with the glowing windows, clinging like a limpet to the flat, flat prairie, dwindled each time it came into view. Then he was no longer tumbling, but falling.

Falling free.

He fell all the way to the horizon.

ೞ

Brotherhood

GUS COLLINA DIED ON A SUMMER day, when the light slanted down through Kensington Steel's tall soot-streaked windows and cut hard-edged columns through the filthy air. Outside those windows the Monongahela River oozed past the town of Monessen, water cooked brown and thick as pudding by the July heat; inside the plant it was hotter still, the year-round heat of the furnaces made even more intolerable by the blazing sun outside. It was one of those days where the sweat pools at the base of your spine, crawls across the palms of your hands under the thick leather gloves, and drips from your forehead onto the lenses of your safety glasses.

Gus was working the coil line that day, where red-hot iron ingots were rolled out into long sheets. He was just coming to the end of another double shift, pushing hard to meet the impossible quotas management demanded. After sixteen hours on the job he was bone-tired, but it was 1937 and he knew he was lucky to have a job at all, and so he kept on working. Until he stumbled, just a little, and one foot caught on the other. He put out a hand to steady himself—and touched the four-foot-wide band of steel, four hundred degrees hot and moving forty-five miles an hour.

Tony Collina saw him die. Tony was Gus's brother, two years younger, and he watched from a catwalk fifty feet away as Gus was pulled into the works without even time to scream. Tony prayed to

Saint Sebastian, the patron of steelworkers, as his steel-toed boots rang down the steps and pounded across the gritty concrete floor, but even as he rushed he knew it was already too late.

They found nothing but blood. Every solid particle of Gus's body had been crushed out of existence between the turns of hot steel on the ten-ton roll at the end of the line.

&#x0cg;

Tony moved through the crowd of friends and relations at Gus's wake, accepting condolences as he passed the hat for Gus's wife — widow, now. Anna had two daughters, and a baby on the way, and no insurance or savings.

Gino Mattioli came through the front door still in his work clothes, his face filthy and bearing the red marks of his safety glasses. Not even death could slow the production lines at Kensington Steel. "Tony, I'm so sorry I missed the funeral. I came as quick as I could."

"'S'okay, Gino." Tony held up his hat, which rattled with silver and paper. "For Anna."

Gino's handsome face pinched into a scowl as he dug in his pants pocket. "Jesus, what a situation. How's she taking it?"

"Not well. My wife's with her now."

Gino pulled his hand from his pocket, stared down into it for a moment, then with an expression of resignation dumped the whole pathetic handful of change into Tony's hat. "Sorry, that's all I've got."

"Thanks anyway."

The two men embraced, the hatful of money jingling in Tony's ear. Before letting go, Gino asked "How about you?"

"Me?"

Gino pulled back, held both of Tony's shoulders. "Yeah, you. How are *you* taking it?"

100

Fireworks of emotion exploded in Tony's chest like the sparks from a Bessemer converter. Tony had always been the shortstop to Gus's pitcher. They'd played together, fought together, got in trouble together, worked together. Gus had handled everything when Pop died of tuberculosis in '34, shielding Tony from the diagnosis as long as he could. Gus had been the best man at Tony's wedding, less than a year ago. And now... all of a sudden, at 27, Tony was the papa of the entire family.

"I'm all right," he said. He turned away so Gino couldn't see his face. "I'm all right."

Gino squeezed Tony's shoulder. "I'd better go in and pay my respects."

"Yeah. You do that." He wiped his eyes quickly and turned back. "Thanks."

Gino walked into the living room, where Gus and Anna's wedding photo sat atop a plain pine coffin and a huge cross of flowers perfumed the air. Tony tried not to remember that the coffin was empty except for a pair of bloodstained and mangled steel-toed boots, tried not to think about how much the coffin and the flowers and the priest had cost, tried not to worry about how he was going to support Anna and her kids as well as his own Sofia and little Bella... tried not to wonder how many more men would die before this job was finished.

Gino finished praying and rose to his feet. He kissed his fingers and touched them to the coffin. "It's a damn shame," he said, looking over his shoulder. "That's — what, six already this year?"

"Seven."

"Jesus." He shook his head. "They're killing us. Honest to God, Tony, they're killing us with this schedule."

"I know. But if we don't make this deadline you know they'll give the damn bridge contract to Inland and then every single one of us will be on the W.P.A."

"Now you're talking like management."

Tony pursed his lips, drew in a breath through his nose. "I have to go and give this money to Anna." But as he turned to go, Gino caught his shoulder.

"We don't have to take this. We can fight them. We can unionize."

Tony slapped Gino's hand away. "And we can lose our jobs. Or worse. Remember Republic Steel?"

Everyone knew how the Republic Steel strike had ended. On Memorial Day 1937, a crowd of picketers were met by armed policemen as they approached the plant. Ten men died in the resulting melee, hundreds were injured, and the strike was broken. The newsreels called the strikers a bloodthirsty mob, but the steelworkers' grapevine said they were just a Memorial Day picnic crowd, including women and children, armed with nothing but placards. Either way, the strike had been a disaster for the union.

Gino's dark brows drew together as he stared hard into Tony's eyes. Then he turned away and waved dismissively at Tony. "Go on, then. Tell Anna, if there's anything I can do..."

"I'll tell her."

On the way to the back bedroom where Sofia comforted the grieving Anna, Tony passed through the kitchen. Warm smells of the lasagna and porcetta and ravioli brought by the aunts and neighbor women enticed his nose, but the stove was cold. Cold as death.

ଔ

Tony sat up in bed. "Who's there?"

At first there was no sign of what had woken him. Sofia snored gently beside him, and little Bella breathed peacefully in her crib beside the bed. Similar sounds came through the door, where Anna and her two children slept in the living room. Six people made a tight crowd in the four-room company house, but Tony could not shirk his family obligations.

Just as Tony was about to settle back down and close his eyes, he saw something move. It might have been the curtains stirring in the fitful breeze, but no—it was at the foot of the bed. Something rippled in the stripes of yellow light cast by the street light through the Venetian blinds.

Tony's eyes snapped open and his heart pounded. "Anna? Is that you?"

"Don't you know me, you moron?" The voice was familiar, but it sounded like a long-distance telephone call from the bottom of a freezer, and the hair rose on the back of Tony's neck.

"Gus?"

"Who else?"

Tony squinted into the darkness. Was that a human figure perched on the footboard? Or was it just a shadow? Tony could see right through it to the Blessed Virgin on the wall behind it.

"You're not Gus," he hissed. He gripped the sheet so tightly he felt it start to tear.

The figure leaned forward, the stripes of light shifting across its face, and Tony thought he saw Gus's big ears and prominent Adam's apple. Just like his. "Who else would know about the deal you and I made with Walter Ailes?"

Goosebumps pricked Tony's forearms. "I never should have let you talk me into it in the first place."

The shadow seemed to shake its head. "I'm sorry about that, now."

Tony closed his eyes, pinched the bridge of his nose hard. "This is a dream, right?"

"Maybe. But even if it is, there's one thing I want you to remember when you wake up."

Tony let go of his nose, stared at the shadowy figure.

"You're going to have to decide who your real friends are, little brother. Ailes gives you money, but..."

"I have Anna and *your* kids to support! There's no way I can back out now."

"Don't make the same mistake I did." And then, without transition, Gus was gone.

Tony gazed on the face of the Blessed Virgin. Her cheap printed smile was not very comforting. *It was just a dream*, he told himself. But then he put out a hand to the footboard where his brother's ghost had sat. The wood was cold under his fingertips, though the July night was sweltering.

Tony put the pillow over his head, just like when he was a kid, and shivered until he fell asleep.

∞

Molten steel glowed orange-red as it seethed from the giant ladle into the ingot molds laid out at Tony's station. He pulled a bandana from his pocket and wiped the back of his neck as he watched the pour, then stuffed it quickly away before guiding the ladle to the next mold. Hot air and sparks roared out of the mold as the steel poured in, burning the scowl on Tony's face.

Bruno the foreman slapped him on the shoulder. "You're wanted at the office," he shouted over the clang and rush of the plant.

The oak and glass office door closed with a thud, blocking out most of the sound from the plant floor beyond. "I'm Antonio Collina," he said to the suspicious-looking clerk behind the counter.

Walter Ailes, the plant's director of personnel, emerged from a back room a few minutes later. His hair and skin were very pale, and wire-rimmed glasses perched atop his hatchet-thin nose. Tony was ashamed of his own swarthy, grimy complexion.

"Thank you for coming, Mister Collina," said Ailes. "Won't you please come this way?" His skinny hand was cool and surprisingly strong, easily matching the pressure of Tony's callused fingers.

Together they moved from the concrete of the plant floor onto hardwood. Tony became increasingly uncomfortable as they walked, acutely aware of the gray grit imbedded in his coveralls, his face, his hair. He was afraid to touch the clean cream-colored walls; he knew he stank of sweat and hot metal. "What's this all about, Mister Ailes?" Tony whispered. "You said never to come into the office."

"Yes. But Mister Kensington wanted to have a word with you." Ailes opened a heavy door on which OFFICE OF THE PRESIDENT was written in gold leaf.

The office behind the door was bigger than Tony's entire house, with high ceilings and oak bookcases full of ledgers. The desk, also of oak, was the size of the altar at St. Cajetan's. Behind the desk hung a portrait of OUR FOUNDER, Joseph G. Kensington. And below the portrait sat Joseph G. Kensington II, President of Kensington Steel. He stood and held out his hand.

Tony had never met a Kensington before. He was nearly as pale as Ailes, but his nose was round and pink and his jowls seemed to bulge from his high starched collar like a big bubble-gum bubble. "Mister Collina, I was so sorry to hear about your brother Giuseppe."

"Thank you, sir." Kensington's hand felt like a bunch of uncooked sausages. Tony didn't want to grip it too firmly, for fear it would burst.

"I like to think of everyone here at Kensington Steel as family. And families stick together in time of hardship, do they not?"

"Uh, yes, sir."

Kensington wiped his hand with a white silk handkerchief, then dropped it in the wastepaper basket. "I am aware," he said, "that some members of the Kensington Steel family do not have the family's best interests at heart. Mister Ailes tells me that the weekly reports that you and your brother have written on these agitators' activities have been most informative."

"Thank you, sir." Tony gritted his teeth at the memory of the men who had lost their jobs as a result of those reports. But the extra six dollars a week in his pay envelope, which had been a luxury for a family of three, were a necessity for six. It would be even worse when Anna's baby came.

"I want to make sure that these reports continue. Despite the unfortunate circumstances."

"Of course, sir." *You cold-hearted bastard,* he thought.

"We believe," said Ailes, "that there may be an increase in... antisocial activity, in the wake of your brother's death."

"I don't understand, sir." But Tony knew what he meant, and he felt sweat trickling down his sides.

"We are talking about *unionization*, Mister Collina!" Kensington thundered. "Communists and anarchists. Bloodthirsty men who desire nothing less than the destruction of the American way of life!" His pink cheeks grew pinker.

"All we ask," said Ailes in a soothing voice. "is that you appear to cooperate with any attempt to unionize the men, and keep us informed of the organizers' actions."

"I, uh..." The room was suddenly hotter than the August sun and the proximity of the blast furnaces could explain. "Yes, sir." He would have to avoid Gino. If nobody asked him to join, he wouldn't have anything to report on.

"However, Mister Collina," said Ailes, and his words were suddenly as thin and strong as his fingers, "please do keep in mind that you are not our only such... reporter. If your reports are not complete and accurate, we *will* know it."

Six dollars a week. "You can depend on me, sir."

૯౩

As Ailes was escorting Tony back to the plant floor, a Serbian laborer came up to him with a large, heavy box. "Where you want this, Mister Ailes?"

Ailes's face betrayed a sting of annoyance. "Put it with the others."

"Yessir."

As the Serb turned away, Tony noticed the words stenciled on the end of the wooden box: AXE HANDLES, TWO DOZ. Aghast, Tony watched as the Serb opened a store-room door. Behind that door were more boxes of axe handles, and other things: tear gas grenades, rifles, and riot guns with barrels the size of beer bottles.

Ailes's eyes narrowed with anger. "You should not have seen that, Mister Collina. I trust you will keep this information... confidential?"

"Uh, yes sir."

"Good. And I hope you will understand that we are prepared to defend Kensington Steel from the forces of anarchy." He lowered his voice and leaned in close. "By *any* means necessary. Do you understand, Mister Collina?"

"Yes, sir."

CB

Later, back in the noise and stench of the plant floor, Tony recalled what Gus had said about deciding who his real friends were. But that had just been a dream. The six dollars a week was real, and it would keep his brother's children from going hungry.

Even so, and even in the heat of the blast furnaces, Tony shivered.

CB

Weeks went by. Tony filed his reports, usually nothing more

than repeating his co-workers' grumbles and anti-management jokes, and the money came in every week. He kept his conversations with Gino focused on baseball and their wives' cooking. After a while he started to relax.

Then, one night, he dreamed of Gus. They were playing stickball in the street by the house where they'd grown up, though they were both adults and wearing their steel-mill coveralls.

"Heads up!" shouted Gus, and hit a long high ball to Tony.

"Got it!" He reached for the ball, but it sailed past his outstretched fingers and into the bramble bushes behind Uncle Ottavio's house.

"It wasn't my fault!" Tony cried.

"I may have hit it," Gus said, "but you blew your chance to catch it. Now you have to go into those brambles and fetch it out."

The bramble bush was very dark and tall, and seemed to grow as Tony watched. "I'm scared," he said, and turned back to Gus.

Gus was covered with blood, and sharp points of broken bones emerged from his cheeks and forehead. The eyes were white and staring in his ruined face. "You should be."

Tony woke screaming. The sheets were soaked with sweat, and Bella began to cry. Sofia got up to comfort her, but as she patted and rocked the baby she asked Tony "Is everything all right?"

"Yeah," Tony said. "Just a bad dream."

Six dollars a week. He hoped he hadn't sold himself too cheaply.

ः

The next day Tony sat heavily on a bench in the break area. He took off his hard hat and rested his head in his hands.

"You heard we lost another one?" said Gino as he sat down next to him.

"Aw, Jesus. No, I just didn't sleep well last night. Who?"

"Negro boy down in the coke yards. Pietro Dani—you know him?—he fell asleep running a crane and dropped a whole load of coke right on top of the guy."

"Jesus."

"We're not going to take this any more. We're going to take action."

Tony's heart felt as though it had just stopped. "Don't tell me this, Gino."

"I know you don't want to hear it. But we've got to do something. We're meeting down at Polish Hall tomorrow night at eight. We've got a man from the C.I.O. to help us organize."

Tony swallowed. "No thanks."

"Please. It's important. We've been talking about doing something for a long time, but Gus's death was what finally got us moving. It would mean a lot if you could show your support."

"Yeah," said Arturo Cavenini as he sat down on the other side of Tony. "You should come."

You are not our only reporter, Ailes had said. Could Arturo be one of the others? Now Tony would have no choice but to write Gino up. "I really wish you hadn't asked me."

"C'mon," said Arturo. "What can it hurt?"

Tony thought about axe handles, and gas grenades, and riot guns. "It can hurt a lot." He stood up to leave.

Then he felt a cold touch at the back of his neck, and heard a voice like a long-distance phone call in his head. *Go to the meeting,* it said. *Do it for me.*

"What's wrong?" said Gino. "You look like hell all of a sudden."

"It's nothing. Just gas."

Go, said the voice.

"OK, I'll go."

A broad smile broke out on Gino's face. "Thanks, Tony. I mean it."

Tony shook his head to clear it, but the voice and the cold were already gone.

CB

There were about seventy-five men at Polish Hall, shifting and muttering uncomfortably on the long wooden benches. Tony twisted his cap in his hands. *It's not too late to leave*, he thought. If he left before the meeting started it would look funny, but then he could tell Ailes he didn't know who the ringleaders were. He felt like Judas Iscariot.

Tony's decision was made for him then, as the doors closed and Gino took the stage. "Thanks for coming," he said. "I'm proud to see so many members of our Kensington family here tonight." An ironic chuckle ran through the crowd. Tony felt sick. "This is a great night for the workers of Kensington Steel, because tonight we begin to reclaim our lives. For the last sixteen months we have struggled with double shifts, impossible production quotas, and tragic losses." He gestured at Tony, and a few men muttered "yeah." Tony managed a wave and a weak smile.

Gino began to pace back and forth, the stage floor creaking under his boots. "We've been cooperative. We've been polite. We've tried to work with management. But the situation just keeps getting worse. As you may already know, they aren't even going to give us Labor Day off." Tony found himself growling right along with the rest of the crowd. The news was a surprise to him. "Are we going to take that?"

About a dozen men yelled "No!"

"Are we going to keep working double shifts for twenty-four dollars a week?"

"No!" This time it was most of the crowd.

"Are we going to watch our brothers die, one after another, until no one is left?"

"*No!*" Tony yelled it too.

"That's right!" Gino said. "Because tonight, we organize!" He raised his fist, and the crowd responded with applause and shouts of encouragement.

When the noise died down, Gino introduced Mike Kelley of the Congress of Industrial Organization, a beefy, florid man with a brusque manner and a thick working-class Irish accent. He spent the rest of the evening outlining a strategy for organizing a union, passing out packets of leaflets and buttons, and getting men to volunteer as shift captains and other key organizers. The mood of the crowd was upbeat as it dispersed into the night.

As Tony walked home, though, a weight settled onto his shoulders. For one thing, he knew he had to write up a report on the meeting. If he named names, men would lose their jobs; if he didn't, Ailes would cut off his money for shirking. For another thing, he knew that any serious attempt at rebellion would be met with well-informed, well-armed resistance. He wanted to run from the whole situation, but both Gino and Ailes—for their own reasons—would expect him to continue attending meetings.

In the dark between streetlights, Tony spotted a beer bottle in the gutter. He kicked it savagely and it flew through the air to smash against the curb on the other side of the street.

The shower of glass fragments seemed to hang in the air for a moment.

Tony swallowed.

The glittering cloud of glass splinters did not fall to the pavement. Instead, it swirled into a manlike form. Gyrating like a swarm of bees, it churned across the street to where Tony stood paralyzed in the dark.

"What's wrong, little brother?" Gus's voice came as a scraping and grinding of broken glass. Tiny particles escaped from the swarm, pattering on the sidewalk and stinging Tony's face.

"G-g-g-..." Tony stammered, then clamped his jaws together.

"Gus, I d-don't know what to do." He shivered in the hot August night.

"Remember who you are. Stick with your own kind."

"But if I stick with the union, I'll have to tell Ailes everything!"

"Yes..." The final *s* sounded like a bucket of sand being poured out.

"If they march on the plant and Ailes knows they're coming, people will be killed! Is that what you want?"

A tinkling chuckle came from the figure's midsection. "I'm not the only one who wants to see a few deaths in the Kensington family." Then the swarm of fragments clattered to the sidewalk, peppering Tony's shoes and pants. He slapped at a sudden pain in his cheek, and drew out a sliver of glass. His own blood on his fingers was black in the light from the distant streetlight.

"Gus, you bastard," he said. But there was no one there.

Gus had gotten him into this mess in the first place. Could his ghost be trusted?

 og

The phone booth at the back of Johnson's Restaurant smelled of cigarette smoke and fried fish. Tony had to try three times before he got the nickel into the slot, and his fingers trembled as he dialed the number.

"Ailes here."

"Mister Ailes, this is Tony Collina."

"Ah yes, Mister Collina. What can I do for you?"

"Mister Ailes, I want out. I don't want to write reports for you any more."

Ailes chuckled. "You don't want me to know about the meeting at Polish Hall, do you?"

Tony drew in a shuddering breath. "If you already know about it, what do you need me for?"

"God gave us two eyes and two ears for a reason, Mister Collina. I always like to keep several men on the hook... I mean, as reporters. Each provides a check on the others."

"I'm sorry, sir, but I still want out."

"I'm afraid that would be... inconvenient. To you."

"To me?"

"Yes. If certain reports, in your handwriting, were to be made available to the other members of your nascent union, the results might be... unfortunate."

Tony gaped into the phone.

"Do we understand each other, Mister Collina?"

Tony gulped. "Yes."

"Very well then. I expect to see your complete and accurate report on my desk this Thursday as usual. Good evening, Mister Collina."

"Good evening, sir." But the line had already gone dead.

∞

Two weeks later the crowd at Polish Hall was up to a hundred and fifty men. They planned a big Labor Day rally at Monessen City Park with all the wives and children, then they'd move to the plant entrance for the three o'clock shift change, to distribute leaflets urging men to join the union. The anger and resentment of men forced to work sixteen hours on a holiday would be sure to pay off in a big groundswell of support. They were excited and confident, and they chattered among themselves in Italian and English as they left the hall.

Tony accosted Gino as he locked the doors. "Gino, this isn't going to work."

"Sure it will! Management is playing right into our hands. Anything they try to do to stop us will just add to our support."

Tony could not meet Gino's eyes. He turned away and watched

moths circling the streetlight nearby. "They know what we're doing."

"What do you mean?"

"They have spies. In the plant. In the union. And they're ready to hit us back. *Hard*."

Gino put a hand on Tony's shoulder. "Spies? Who? How do you know?" He tried to turn Tony around, but he resisted.

"I can't tell you. I just don't want to see anyone else get killed."

Gino's hand tightened on Tony's shoulder, then he pushed him away with a disgusted sound. "You're just chicken. If we *don't* organize, more men *will* get killed. Like Gus. Remember Gus?"

Tony still did not meet Gino's eyes. "Yeah. I remember Gus."

"*He* wouldn't be afraid to do the right thing."

"Don't be so sure."

Gino stood silent for a moment, then turned and walked away. Tony listened to his footsteps fading away into the dark.

ॐ

Labor Day dawned hot and clear, with a big blue sky relieved by a few puffy clouds. The carpenters and the plumbers and the printers were up early, preparing their floats for the afternoon parade. The steelworkers of Kensington who weren't on shift were up early too, but they didn't have a float—instead they were cranking out mimeographed leaflets and painting placards.

By lunchtime City Park thronged with people. Women in their Sunday outfits carried picnic baskets; children laughed and ran across the grass. The smells of fried chicken and porcetta were everywhere.

Tony observed the festivities as though from inside a Mason jar. *Labor Day's going to be just like Memorial Day*, he thought. At best, the union organizers would lose their jobs; at worst, they'd lose their lives, and the lives of the women and children as well.

Tony had tried to convince Gino and Mike Kelley not to go through with it, but they refused to listen. He'd made clear in his reports that the workers intended no violence, but knowing Ailes he expected deadly force in reaction to any action at all. He'd even thought about leaving town, but where else could he find work?

So here he was, at City Park on Labor Day, feeling like the ghost at the feast. He would keep his own family away from the plant, and take any action he could to prevent violence. But he didn't feel very confident he could make much of a difference.

A great cheer erupted from the bandstand at the center of the park. "Come on," said Sofia. "We're missing everything!" She settled Bella more firmly on her hip and ran ahead with Anna's two girls, leaving Tony with the picnic basket and Anna with her very pregnant tummy to struggle along behind.

They laid out their picnic blanket in the shade of an oak, ate their roasted-pork sandwiches, and listened to politicians make speeches and brass bands play. For a while Tony could almost forget the coming confrontation. But at one o'clock Gino called through a bullhorn for all the off-shift Kensington workers and their families to gather to the left of the stage.

"Sofia," Tony said, "I want you to take Anna and the kids home."

"Why?"

"Just do it, okay?"

"But I wanna go with you, Uncle Tony!" said Lizzie, Anna's oldest. "All the other kids are going."

"Sorry, kiddo," he said, and swung her around by her arms. She laughed and laughed as she flew through the air, then he set her down and bent down to her level. "You be good for your mama and Aunt Sophie, okay?"

"Okay."

"I love you." He hugged her, and over her little shoulder he saw Sofia give him a look of deep concern. He straightened quickly and marched away, not wanting her to see the expression on his face.

The crowd around Gino was festive, men and women in their best clothes laughing and singing as they distributed placards and packets of flyers among themselves. Gino and Mike Kelley made inspirational speeches, they all cheered, and then they set off across the grass toward the Kensington Steel plant. Tony found himself carrying a sign that said WIN WITH THE C.I.O.

As the crowd walked down Fourth Street toward the plant, a shadow crossed the sun and the laughter dimmed a bit. It was only the smoke pouring from the plant's smokestacks, but to Tony it seemed like a bad omen.

They got closer to the plant. Even from a mile away the plant dominated the horizon, but now they were only a few blocks from the main gate and it seemed bigger than the world—a looming gray wall that, even from here, smelled of hot iron and sulfur.

The crowd walked on in silence.

One block from the main gate they could read the sign above it: KENSINGTON STEEL BUILDS AMERICA. And below the sign they could see a line of men.

"Finks," muttered a man next to Tony. Professional strikebreakers. Muscular, leering men armed with axe handles and riot guns. There were policemen in the line as well, carrying truncheons and rifles.

The leading members of the crowd of workers paused at the sight. The ones behind them came on, unknowing. Between the two groups a press of confusion developed.

One of the policemen stepped up and raised a bullhorn to his lips. "All right, you anarchists. This is as far as you go today. You are ordered to disperse."

The man next to Tony slowly bent down and set down his picket sign, then picked up a large piece of brick from the street. Others around him did the same.

A cop cocked his riot gun with a metallic *ch-chunk* that cut through the sounds of the plant.

Tony grabbed the wrist of the man with the brick. "Don't do anything stupid!" he hissed. But the man just shook him off in annoyance.

"You are ordered to disperse," the bullhorn repeated.

Tony began to back up, pushing his way through the crowd.

Then the tense silence was cut in two by the three o'clock whistle that marked the end of the first shift.

Despite the heat and humidity, Tony felt a sudden chill at the sound—but he did not shiver. Instead, insanely, he was comforted. For some reason it made him think of snowmen, and snowball fights, and snow forts. A protective cocoon of cold.

Tony and Gus stood together within a swirl of snow. They were wearing their winter coats.

"Don't run," said Gus. "I need you to stay here."

"And get killed?"

"You have to trust me."

"Trust you? Damn it, Gus, you talked me into this deal with Ailes, and then you *left* me!" Hot tears cooled quickly as they ran down his cheeks.

"I know. I'm sorry. I screwed up, okay? But from... where I am, I can see things I couldn't before. I can fix it. I *gotta* fix it. But I need your help."

Tony's breath huffed out of his mouth in big white clouds. At last he said "What do you want me to do?"

"Just relax, and let me do all the talking."

Tony gazed on his dead brother's face for a moment more, then closed his eyes.

The shift-change whistle was just dying away as he opened his eyes again. He felt funny, like he was under water. Cold water. But it was still a comforting kind of cold.

Tony's legs began to move, and he found himself pushing through the crowd until he stood between the two groups. His arms raised themselves in the air and he waved for attention.

"Put down your weapons," he said to the workers. Though the words came from his own mouth, they were a surprise to him, and his voice sounded as though he were talking over a long-distance line. "Too many have died here already." Amazingly, many of those who had picked up rocks and bricks did put them down. And even though Tony had not raised his voice, he saw men way at the back of the crowd reacting to his words.

Tony turned to the line of men at the factory gate. "Put down your guns and clubs. These people are not your enemies." Some of the finks lowered their axe handles, but the cops were more disciplined and retained their weapons.

Seeing this, the men in the crowd who had not put down their bricks gripped them tightly, and a few men bent down to pick up new ones. Despite the cocooning cold, Tony began to sweat.

Just then the first-shift workers began to pour from the plant's doors. But this was not the usual tired shift-change procession. These men were still wearing their work clothes and safety gear, running hard. One man screamed in horror.

Tony had no idea what was happening. Neither did anyone else. Cops, finks, and workers looked around, uncertain of what to do.

The policeman raised his bullhorn. "You strikers are still under an order to disperse!" But no one moved.

The first men to emerge from the plant passed through the main gate. They ran wide-eyed and staring, intent on putting as much space between themselves and the plant as possible.

The bullhorn spoke again. "Pinkerton men, see to the disturbance inside the plant! Officers, disperse these strikers!" The finks turned and ran toward the steel mill; the cops moved forward, raising their weapons. Several men in the crowd of workers raised bricks over their heads, prepared to throw them.

"*No!*" Tony cried, raising his hands, and a wave of cold seemed to burst from him, rings of stillness spreading like ripples in a pond.

He faced the crowd of workers—his friends, his co-workers, their wives and children—and said "*Go home!*" As one they backed away from him. He turned to the policemen, and to them he did not even speak—he only stared at them, and they shrank back.

Without a word, the workers turned and walked away, back toward the park. They moved as though in a dream. The cops stood where they were, equally entranced.

Only Gino seemed to remember himself. "Mother of God," he whispered. "Tony, what's happened to you?"

"I'm not Tony," came the words from his mouth, and he strode purposefully toward the plant. Gino followed him.

When they reached the plant, the last few first-shift workers were just emerging from the doors, and most of the finks were already inside. The sounds of the working steel mill had never paused, but now they were joined by screams and gunshots.

"What the hell is going on in there?" asked Gino, but Tony just kept walking.

Soon they passed through the door of the plant. "By the Blessed Virgin," said Gino.

The steel mill was running at full capacity—ladles pouring molten steel, huge stamping mills pounding ingots into plates, rolling mills pressing out continuous sheets. But the men running the mill...

Some of them were gray and transparent, like half-developed photographs of themselves. Others were horribly burned, leaving flakes of charred flesh behind them as they moved. One man had a steel pry-bar thrust through his chest, oozing blood from both sides. Everywhere were torn and mangled limbs, flayed skin, cracked skulls.

Those whose faces were still intact seemed to be having a wonderful time. Tony even recognized one of them — it was Marco Costanza, who'd bled to death after his arm was crushed by a falling girder. He was moving fine, hauling heavy bundles of steel rebar one-handed, though the other arm dangled uselessly at his side.

The dead men paid no attention to Tony and Gino, or to the strikebreakers. One of the finks stood stock-still, petrified by fear, and was crushed by a forklift driven by a headless machinist. Another fink fired his pistol at the gray shadow of a crane operator; the bullet ricocheted off the crane cab and grazed his skull, knocking him over.

"What the blue blazes is going on here?"

Tony turned to the sound of the voice, to see Kensington and Ailes emerging from the office. Kensington was puffing like a locomotive, his pink face glowing like a blast furnace.

The dead steelworkers all turned to the voice as well. All action in the plant stopped. They began to move toward Kensington.

Kensington was clearly terrified, but to his credit he pressed on regardless. "You men will stop this... Halloween prank, or whatever it is, and get back to work this instant!" But the dead men closed steadily in around him. "Get back to work!" he gasped again, with no effect. "Get... back..."

A ring of burnt, shredded, and broken flesh closed around Kensington, and from the center of it came a strangled scream and a sound like broomsticks breaking.

Tony turned his attention to Ailes, who was pressed against the office wall, arms and legs trembling. He was even paler than before.

"Mister Ailes," Tony said. "Nice to see you again. You have records. Files. Reports."

"Y-yes..."

"Take me to them."

Ailes turned and half-ran, half-stumbled through the office. Tony followed at a steady pace. Gino came behind him.

They entered Ailes's private office. "Here they are," he said, and pointed to a file cabinet.

"All of them?"

"All of them."

Tony pointed at the file cabinet, and all four drawers flew open. The papers within burst into the air like a thousand fat snowflakes. Tony waved his hands and the flying papers aged, browning and curling, two hundred years in a moment. Then they all crumbled to dust, leaving nothing but a smell like dead leaves.

Tears ran down Ailes's cheeks. Gino muttered one prayer after another.

"Now I can go," Tony said, and the world went black.

 os

When he came to, he was outside the plant and Gino was leaning over him. "Are you awake?"

"I think so..."

"Do you remember what happened in there?"

"There were dead men. I saw Marco. Lots of others."

"Yeah. Hundreds. I think it was every man who's ever died in a Pennsylvania steel mill."

"Kensington."

Gino snorted. "Yeah, but he doesn't count."

"Are they still in there?"

"No. I think they all vanished when you passed out. There's nobody in there right now but a half-dozen dead finks."

"Ailes?"

"He's talking with Mike Kelley. I think they're coming to an agreement."

"That's good." He closed his eyes.

CB

Gus Collina was born on an autumn day, when the cool light streamed in through the windows of the new house his mother shared with his Uncle Tony and Aunt Sofia. The first face he saw in this life was Tony's.

He met Tony's eye and winked. And then he had a good long cry.

CB

Circle of Compassion

GLISTENING IN THE FIRELIGHT, a drop of sweat gathered at the tip of Su Yuen's nose. It was a distraction, a thing of the world, and she strove to ignore it, to empty her mind of all thought as she knelt in prayer. *Namu kuan shih yin pu sa*, she prayed over and over: I bow to you, being of wisdom, who hears the cries of the world. The drop swelled until it fell from her nose, landing with a small explosion of dust on the pounded-earth floor of the mud hut in which she knelt. It was followed by another, and another. But though the little hut was sweltering hot, when she finished her prayers she found herself hesitant to leave — unwilling to return to her master, General Chang, and the noise and smoke and stink of death that surrounded him.

Su slipped the bracelet from her wrist. The air of Xian would calm her.

The bracelet was of bronze, and depicted the Dragon of the West with its tail in its mouth. Though not elegant, it had been carefully crafted for her by Shan the metalworker, and blessed by the Mother of her order with a special charm.

Su spoke a secret word of power, and the bracelet tingled in her fingers and grew cool, a shimmer like a desert mirage filling the space inside it. She brought her nose close to the opening and smiled at the cold air that blew from it. It was breezy this night in her favorite meadow, half a day's walk from her home temple of

123

Miao Feng Shan in the country of Xian.

The breeze smelled of high mountains and cold streams. It smelled of snow. It smelled of home.

She opened the neck of her robe and allowed the air from the bracelet to flow down inside, evaporating the sweat that pooled in the hollow of her throat and the space between her breasts. But after only a short time of this she sighed. It would not do to luxuriate too long when she had so many difficult tasks awaiting her. She spoke a second word. The bracelet tingled again, and then returned to inert metal.

It was still cool to the touch, though, as she slipped it back onto her wrist. A small reminder of the snows of Xian, so many thousand leagues from the wretched little town of Guang-xi.

Su Yuen stepped from the shabby little hut into the torchlit street. Barely deserving of the name "street," it was only two paces wide and constructed of dirt, like everything else in Guang-xi. Even the walls that surrounded the town were simple bulwarks of rammed earth, not even faced with brick. They would offer little resistance to the siege engines of Yao Ming.

No townspeople were about at this hour; to defy the curfew imposed by General Chang was to embrace death. But Chang's troops recognized Su, and bowed to her as she passed.

Chang stood with his lieutenants in the great hall—such as it was—of the town's magistrate, who cowered with his family to one side. Chang had sketched a map of the town and its surroundings in the dirt floor, and indicated its various features with the pointed butt of a halberd.

Chang himself was an imposing figure, with dark intense eyes and a long gray beard that suggested his many years of successful command. He wore a long purple robe, trimmed and tasseled in red; the armored surcoat with its many square bronze plates hung on a rack nearby. "Do not depend too much on the mountains to the north," he scolded one of his lieutenants. "Yao will send at least three companies around to surprise us from behind. It may take them some days to get here, but we should be prepared. Post watchmen here, here, and here."

"But they have been riding hard for days, my lord," said a lieutenant. "For exhausted men to cross those mountains would be suicide."

"Yes," Chang acknowledged with a grim nod. "That is why he will send three companies — to be sure at least one survives."

The lieutenant gave a silent bow, conceding the truth of Chang's observation. Yao's troops were untrained conscripts, but they vastly outnumbered Chang's remaining forces and Yao was willing to spend many lives for a successful attack.

"Priestess Su Yuen," Chang said, fixing her with a dark commanding gaze, "Have you prepared yourself as you require?"

"Yes, my lord," she replied with a trembling bow.

Chang pointed to a series of parallel lines drawn on the plain below the city's south gate. "You are to scout General Yao's camp. Determine the strength of his forces, and if possible his plans."

Head still bowed, she stammered out "But, my lord, I know nothing of military matters."

Chang sighed heavily and looked heavenward. "Honored ancestors, I thank you for saving me and these remaining men at the battle of Yu-min. But why could you not have seen fit to leave me more than this one miserable priestess?" His piercing gaze returned to Su. "Can your spirit hear, as well as see?"

"Yes, my lord."

"The general's tent will be in the middle of the camp. Listen there for any numbers. How many companies, battalions, divisions, horses. Times and places. Do you understand?"

"Yes, my lord."

"Begin, then. Waste no time."

"Yes, my lord." She bowed deeply, then knelt on the dirt floor and pulled her box of incense from her sleeve.

Su made her preparations, shivering beneath her robe despite the oppressive heat. As a priestess of Kuan Shih Yin, the living expression of loving compassion, she had devoted her life to understanding and peace. Using the powers of her office for warlike purposes was abhorrent to her. But hers had been the poor fortune to be on an outreach mission to the court of Li when General Yao of the upstart state of Tung had attacked, two months ago. She had been placed under the protection and command of General Chang, who had kept her safe and never before asked for anything in return. But the last of Chang's military magicians and priests—ancestor worshippers who practiced human sacrifice, but still human beings worthy of Kuan Shih Yin's love—had been killed by Yao's forces at the recent, disastrous battle of Yu-min. Chang had no one else, and she must carry out his orders not only because he was her properly appointed commander, but because he and his men had saved her life in the initial attack and many times since.

Even so, the thought of it made her sick to her stomach.

He has not asked me to fight or kill, she reassured herself. It didn't help much.

She cleared her mind and prayed, struggling to block out the sounds and smells of an occupied town preparing for attack. After a long while, with a feeling like tearing silk, her spirit detached itself from her body.

It was always disorienting to look back on herself, yet now she found it strangely reassuring—a female Xian face, with its strong cheekbones, shaven head, and pigtail, alone among these shaggy Li men. It was almost as though one of her temple sisters were here.

Then she chided herself for delay, and sent her spirit out through the tile roof of the hall.

Su's spirit soared above the town, with its courtyards glimmering with the torches of Chang's remaining troops. Quickly she flew over the walls, and the moat beyond them, to the plain below the town where Yao had massed his army. Thousands of fires burned there, in rigid rows and columns. Su knew nothing of armies, but she could count, and even she could see that Yao's army vastly outnumbered Chang's forces.

But there, in the center of the camp, was one tent larger than the others, which swarmed with soldiers coming and going like an ants' nest. Su swooped down upon it and through its fabric roof.

She recognized Yao Ming at once—she had seen his scarred, dark-bearded face in many scrolls and woodcuts. He wore an armored surcoat, fashioned of many palm-sized squares of rhinoceros leather, over a blue robe with black trim. At the moment he and his lieutenants were bowed in concentration over a smoking brazier.

The smoke from the brazier stung her eyes as she moved closer, trying to hear their conversation. But they were not conversing— they were praying. Foul prayers to the black demons worshipped by the Tung. She would learn nothing useful from this, so she moved behind Yao, to a low table where maps were spread out.

As she peered closer, trying to make sense of the maps' rough markings, the prayers reached a feverish enthusiasm, the Tung men shrieking and swaying as they waved their hands over their heads. Finally they all shouted four words together, and Yao threw a handful of mulberry leaves into the brazier.

Su coughed in the choking smoke.

But... this was wrong. Smoke should not affect her spirit body.

This was no ordinary fire.

Panicking, she gathered her spirit self to flee. But before she reached the tent roof, a huge, taloned hand darted out of the smoke and grabbed her by the foot. "Ai!" she cried.

Helplessly she struggled as the rest of the black demon coalesced into being. It had the form of a huge, muscular man, barely able to stand erect at the center of the tent, but its face was distorted by enormous fangs and protruding eyes and its skin was charcoal-black. The hand that held her foot was hard as stone and ridged with muscle. "Release me, demon, in the name of Kuan Shih Yin!" But her words had no effect.

"What have you caught, oh my demon?" asked Yao. He had heard nothing.

"A spying spirit," the demon replied, in a voice like stones grinding together.

"Bring him here!"

"As my master wishes." The demon reached up with its other hand and grabbed Su by the neck, then pulled her down to the floor of the tent.

Her boots thumped on the dirt, and then the demon forced her to her knees.

She gasped at the pain, then gasped again at the realization of what it meant. The demon had pulled her material body into the tent!

Yao stood, as did his lieutenants. "I see that Chang is reduced to having Xian priestesses do his spying for him," he said. "An excellent sign. Release her, oh my demon."

The demon pulled her to her feet, then shoved her into the center of the circle. Yao paced around her, examining her as though she were a horse in the market. His nostrils flared. "You stink of magic," he declared.

Namu kuan shih yin pu sa, she thought over and over, willing her knees to stop their trembling. Trying to force herself to meet her end with dignity.

Yao leaned closer, stinking of sweat and blood. This was the man who had decapitated his own uncle to gain the generalship, who had slaughtered entire cities for the insult of opposing his will. So fearful was his reputation that even his most unwilling conscripts obeyed his orders instantly. He sniffed at her hair, her neck, her shoulder, then down her arm. Then he smiled, and pushed back her sleeve, revealing the bronze dragon bracelet.

"What is this pretty bauble?"

Su said nothing, clenching her teeth to prevent them from chattering.

He grabbed her queue and pulled back her head, leaning in close. "Answer me!" he roared, his foul breath hot on her face.

"It is just a souvenir!" she cried, the truth forced out of her by the press of fear. "A small magic to remind me of my home, nothing more!"

"Indeed?" He seized her forearm and pulled the bracelet off her wrist. It came easily. "I think perhaps you do not tell the whole truth." He examined the bracelet, turning it over so the firelight glinted across the dragon's scales, then squeezed it over his rough hand and onto his own wrist. "I shall hold this object for further examination." He turned away from her. "Oh my demon, you may have this spy to do with as you please."

Su turned and looked up, and up, at the demon's leering face, then shut her eyes hard.

Then a great commotion erupted from outside the tent, shouting and banging and a fierce inhuman bellow.

A soldier burst in, eyes wide. "They send fire demons against us!"

Yao's jaw clenched in anger, and he glared accusingly at Su, then turned back to the demon. "Defend the camp!" he shouted. The demon roared and plunged out through the tent flap, but the doorway was too small and the demon brought half the tent down behind itself.

Pandemonium ensued, inside and out, as the tent collapsed on Su, Yao, and his lieutenants. Su found herself struggling under the heavy fabric, blinded by smoke, while all around her men shouted and cursed. A crackling sounded, much too close. The tent had caught fire! Su dropped to the dirt and began to squirm blindly forward.

An eternity later, Su's hand reached out and found... nothing. The edge of the tent! She dug her fingers into the dirt and pulled herself free, gasping in the smoky air. Fire flickered all around, and men ran shouting in every direction. Over all sounded the roars of the demon and the bellowing of the unseen attackers. Su gathered her feet under her and ran.

She ran only a few steps before colliding with a hard surface... a broad torso covered with small square plates of rhinoceros hide.

Yao Ming.

"I won't let you go that easily, my little spy," he panted, and seized the front of her robe.

Su tried and failed to pull Yao's hand away, but her fingers recognized the dragon bracelet.

She spoke a secret word of power.

Yao screamed, and his hand released its grip... and dropped into the dirt with a sickening thud.

Su ducked away from Yao as he clutched his severed wrist, cursing, blood running down his sleeve. But as she turned to run away, she spotted a glint of bronze in the blood-stained dirt. She spoke the second word of power as she scooped up the bracelet and ran into the night.

The panicked camp was not concerned with stopping one small priestess; in addition to the general's tent, other fires burned here and there, and the fire demons bellowed and clattered all around. Su kept low and scurried. Her previous flight over the camp, in spirit form, helped her to keep her feet on the right path.

Soon she escaped into the darkness between the camp and the town. After that she met no one until she came to the moat, gasping and holding her sides. "Su Yuen!" cried the lieutenant at the drawbridge. "Thank the ancestors you are alive!"

Immediately she was conducted to Chang, where she reported what had occurred. When she described how the demon had captured her, Chang nodded grimly. "So I surmised, from what you said just before you vanished."

"But how did you summon fire demons?" she asked. "You have

no other priests or magicians."

"Fire demons?" Chang snorted. "Yao's foul habits are too well known to his conscript troops, they see demons behind every bush. No, we did nothing more than to tie burning lanterns to the tails of several bulls. But they do make an impressive noise, and do a most satisfactory amount of damage. Now go and rest. I will require your services again in the morning."

"Yes, my lord." But she did not leave. "My lord... thank you for rescuing me."

Chang gave her a curt nod in reply. "I would not abandon my only remaining priestess." Then his face softened. "I am glad you were not harmed."

She thanked him again, and bowed, then retired to her borrowed pallet. But though she was bone-weary and the hour was late, she barely slept. Whenever she closed her eyes, she saw the demon's leering eyes and fearsome teeth.

The next day, after a wholly inadequate breakfast of thin rice gruel, Su was again commanded to survey the enemy's camp. It took her half the morning to calm herself sufficiently to release her spirit from her body, and she hesitated for a long time beneath the hall's tile roof before pushing through it.

When she arrived at the camp she found Yao at the top of a small hill, with his demon beside him and all his thousands of men gathered around him. Though his missing right hand was bound up by a blood-soaked bandage, his face burned with energy and determination. Su ducked behind a rocky outcropping before the demon could spot her.

Yao stood beside a large pile of clay pots. As she peered out from behind the rock, he took a mattock from one of his lieutenants and methodically smashed them all. Then, breathing hard and holding the mattock high, he stood on the pile of shards and began to speak.

Puzzled by this display, Su shifted closer, trying to hear what Yao had to say. But as she approached, Yao's nostrils twitched and he paused, sniffing the air. Then the demon cried out and pointed straight at her. Rigid with anger, Yao ran to his war-chest and drew out a black spear that shimmered with power.

Su did not wait to find out how well the demon could throw. She flew back to the magistrate's hall with desperate haste.

"Ah!" she gasped, drawing in a breath as her spirit rejoined her physical body. Chang's lieutenants immediately bombarded her with questions, but she had to close her eyes and concentrate on her breathing for a long moment before she could even speak coherently.

Once she had made her report, Chang took a deep breath and turned away, hands gripping each other behind his back. His lieutenants were silent. "What does this mean, my lord?" she asked him.

"Yao has created a 'death ground,'" Chang replied without turning around. "Without cooking pots, his men now have only the food they have already prepared — perhaps three days' worth." He turned back then, and his face was as grim as she had ever seen it. "They know they must conquer or starve, and so they will fight without pause and without mercy."

Chang thanked Su for her report, then began discussing with his lieutenants the defense of the town. But as Su bowed and prepared to leave, he gestured for her to stay.

Chang clearly expected an attack in overwhelming force within the day. Though his words about troop emplacements, fallback positions, and supply lines were meaningless to Su, she could see the desperation of the situation in the empty faces of his lieutenants. One by one they bowed and departed, to make what preparations they could.

After the last lieutenant had left, Chang gestured Su close to him. He looked old, so old. "Su," he said, "you are a priestess of

Xian. You understand compassion, and peace. I am a man of war."
He took a deep breath. "Am I a bad man, Su Yuen?"

She considered the question carefully before replying. "It is true that many have died, on both sides of this conflict, because of your orders. But you have also saved many others who might have died. I believe you have been as good a man as you can be."

Chang sighed, and looked at his folded hands. "I have an opportunity to save many lives this day. But I fear that I will not have the courage to do so."

Su waited for the words to come.

"Yao wants me. Only me. He knows that, while I live, the people of Li will never surrender, no matter how badly defeated. But if he can parade my head on a spear to all the cities of Li, they will accept his victory and allow themselves to be quietly absorbed into the state of Tung." Chang took Su's hands. "I mean to surrender myself to Yao. If I do this thing, Yao may spare the lives of some of my men today, and thousands more will live instead of dying in a hopeless struggle against the Tung." His eyes pleaded. "Help me to be strong. Help me to carry through with this plan."

Su's heart resonated with Chang's pain, as one gong will vibrate when another nearby is struck. But she damped it down. "No," she said firmly. "I will not help you."

Chang dropped his eyes from hers. "Then all is lost."

"No!" she said again. Then, more gently: "As long as you live, not all is lost."

Chang looked up again.

"I have seen the evil of Yao, and the black demons that Tang worships. I know that any lives you save today by surrendering yourself will be lives lost in misery and despair tomorrow. Even if you die here, the people of Li will know that you died fighting, and they will do the same in your honor."

Chang shook his head with a rueful smile. "Priestess, you understand too well how to motivate an old soldier."

"I have learned from one of the best."

Chang bowed Su from his presence.

Outside the hall Chang's chief armorer, an aged craftsman with some knowledge of practical magic, awaited her with many pointed questions about the demon's exact appearance and behavior. Finally he thanked her, though his expression was grim. "From what you have said, I believe it is a taloned demon of the Fifteenth Hell. These are vulnerable to certain charms, but they must be written on silk, and we lost our scribe at Yu-min."

Su's heart leapt with hope. "I can write!"

"Thank the ancestors!"

With the armorer's help, Su wrote out the charms on dozens of strips of silk, which they tied to the shafts of arrows. She then blessed each one with a prayer to Kuan Shih Yin. "I will accept the assistance of any god who is willing to give it," the armorer said with a shrug.

After that Su set to work making bandages, blessing amulets, and praying with any soldiers and citizens who desired her assistance. As she was blessing a jade disk for a trembling young soldier, she heard horns and a distant roar like wind and surf.

The sound of an army at the charge.

Su's station was at Chang's headquarters, and she hurried to him.

"I need you to be my kite," Chang said when she arrived. "Fly high over the town and give me the strategic view."

"Yes, my lord." As she bowed, their eyes met briefly. He did not say *that will keep your spirit safe from Yao's spear*, and she did not thank him for it. But they both understood.

Exhausted and shaken as she was, it took Su a long time to send her spirit out. By the time she rose above the magistrate's hall, Yao's forces had already begun crossing the moat, the roaring demon in the lead. But as soon as it came within range, Chang's best bowmen let loose with Su's charmed arrows. At their touch the demon screamed and burst into flame, and then it was no more.

But the demon was only one part of the attack; even as it burned, massive wooden fork-carts, catapults, and scaling ladders rolled across temporary bamboo bridges. Chang's men pelted them with flaming arrows from the tops of the walls, but Yao had prepared for this: the fork-carts were protected by wooden roofs covered with fresh oxhide, which trapped the arrows and refused to catch fire.

Su reported this development to Chang, and a moment later her spirit eyes saw men with heavy crossbows charging to the defense. But they were too late. Under the protection of the hide-covered roofs, the first of the fork-carts had reached the walls. Thick braids of twisted rope sent wooden levers—each twice as long as a man and tipped with a three-tined iron fork—snapping down onto the town's earthen walls like the striking claw of a great tiger. Two or three such blows were sufficient to bring down a large chunk of wall. Though Chang's bowmen fired rapidly into the gap, killing many of the invaders, more and more of Yao's conscript soldiers were pouring over the moat. They soon began swarming over their comrades' bodies, through the gaps in the wall, and into the town.

"Fall back!" Chang ordered his lieutenants when Su told him the walls had been breached. Then he turned back to Su. "We too must retreat." She found herself leaning heavily on his arm as they hurried out of the magistrate's hall.

Chang and Su moved in the midst of a flood of screaming, panicked townspeople, heading for the garrison where the town's west wall met the mountains. The sturdy little building was not a castle, barely even a fort, but it was the most defensible structure in the town and it was large enough to hold all of Chang's troops.

But when they arrived, they found fewer than two hundred soldiers. "We have been taking very heavy casualties," reported a lieutenant whose head was bandaged up with a blood-soaked rag. "The Tung men fight like trapped rats."

"Let in five hundred civilians," said Chang, "then bar the door."

While Chang and the three lieutenants who had made it to the garrison prepared to make a last stand, Su sagged exhausted and worthless in a corner. She was too drained to send her spirit out again, and she would be no use whatsoever in a fight. All she could do was prepare her spirit for the afterlife.

But when she had finished her prayers, the final attack had still not come. "What is he waiting for?" she asked Chang.

"I do not know," he said. They pressed through crowds of terrified civilians and wounded soldiers to the outer room, where splintered furniture blocked the garrison's only door, and peered out an arrow slit.

Outside, mobs of Yao's troops crowded the street, but they had left an open space in front of the garrison. Yao himself stood in that space, his rhinoceros-hide surcoat stained with soot and blood. "Does Chang yet live?" he called out.

"I live," Chang called back, though he stood to the side of the arrow slit in case one of Yao's sharpshooters should make an attempt to change that. Su moved to another slit nearby, unable to take her eyes off of Yao.

"I would like to make you an offer," Yao replied. "You have a Xian priestess with you. Do not deny it, I can smell her. Give the bitch to me, and I will allow you and your men to live."

Chang looked at Su, his expression unreadable, but he called back "We would prefer to die, rather than live under Tung rule."

Yao gave a swift curt nod that indicated he had expected no other response. "I will give you until dawn to reconsider your decision." He raised his voice. "My offer applies to anyone in the building. Send out the Xian priestess, and all your lives will be spared."

Su's knees gave way. She slid down the wall, collapsing like a horse that has been ridden too far. But Chang stood tall, and spoke in a general's voice. "You will not be surrendered," he said to Su, and stared around at the soldiers and civilians who crowded the room. "This I promise."

The sun crept downward, and slipped below the horizon, but the garrison with its mass of people grew no cooler; Su blinked stinging sweat from her eyes as she prayed with a freshly-widowed civilian and her three small children. Then, when the prayer was done, she slipped her bracelet from her wrist. "This is a special charm," she whispered to the middle child. "It is supposed to be a secret. But now... I suppose there is little reason to hide it any longer." She spoke a word of power, and cool mountain air flowed from the bracelet.

The children gasped and cooed in pleasure, pressing their faces into the breeze, and the young widow smiled at their happiness. But then the youngest reached out for the shiny bauble, and thrust her tiny hand through the shimmering loop all the way up to the elbow. Su gasped at the memory of Yao's severed hand, but the panic lasted only a moment; she had dabbled her own fingers through the bracelet into the cool air beyond many times. It was only at the moment the charm was invoked that it was so dangerous. Still, magic was always unpredictable, and she gently grasped the child's arm and drew it back out of the bracelet.

The infant's face bunched up as though to cry, but then relaxed into an expression of curiosity and wonder as she stared at her own hand, tightly clenched in a fist. Then the tiny fingers opened.

Su too looked on in wonder.

Sparkling in the child's palm was a tiny handful of... snow.

"General Chang!" Su called as she hurried to his quarters. "General Chang! I must speak with the armorer immediately!"

Luck was with her: the armorer was among the survivors. But after he had inspected the bracelet, he shook his head and handed it back to her. "I am sorry, priestess," he said. "If it were iron, I might be able to enlarge it as you request. But bronze is not so malleable."

Su's spirits, so recently raised, fell hard.

"Still..." said the armorer, tugging on his beard, "though the bracelet cannot be hammered out, perhaps the spell can be. What do you know of its construction?"

"It partakes of the Circle of Heaven, of course, and the power of the Dragon of the West, but my own memories are the focus of the charm. It will not work unless I am touching the bracelet."

"Hmm. The Dragon can be invoked with the appropriate herbs, perhaps, but the Circle..."

Su, Chang, and the armorer talked for a long time, while the torches burned down and were replaced. Soldiers came and went, calling out watches at intervals. Finally, at the beginning of the last watch before dawn, they agreed that no better plan could be devised.

"It will be dangerous," advised the armorer. "The Dragon of the West is not easily tamed."

"I understand," said Su.

Chang's expression was serious. "Those who form the circle must remain behind. I cannot ask you to do this."

Su matched Chang's gaze with her own. "I have no choice," she said. "The charm is tied to me. All I ask is that you give me a sharp knife, so that I may choose the moment of my death."

Chang held Su's gaze for a moment, then closed his eyes and bowed his head. Without a word, he drew the sheathed knife from his own belt and handed it to her. She bowed to him as she accepted it.

"Come," said the armorer. "We have little time."

They lit incense, and burned herbs, and spilled wine upon the ground. And then Su found herself kneeling before a large stone, trembling as though from cold though the night was still sweltering. *Namu kuan shih yin pu sa,* she prayed, as she held out her bracelet in her two hands and placed it on the stone.

The armorer set his chisel on the bracelet, just where the Dragon of the West's tail entered its mouth. "When you are ready," he said quietly, and raised his mallet, awaiting her signal.

Su looked into his eyes, and took a deep breath. Then she gave a fierce nod, and as the armorer brought his mallet down she spoke a word of power.

The bracelet shimmered and tingled between her fingers for a moment before the metal parted.

"Ah!" Su cried out, as cold fire burned along her arms and across her chest. It was as though she hugged a huge, invisible tree of ice—her arms were forced into a circle by the pressure of the spell, and a cold blast of air blew upward into her face. But though the broken bracelet seared her fingers with its chill, she held on.

Then she felt warm fingers on her hands. It was Hsien, Chang's youngest surviving lieutenant. All the lieutenants had volunteered for this duty, but Chang had insisted that the skills of the other two could not be lost. Hsien held tightly to Su's trembling hands, his face impassive.

"I... I will release my left hand," Su said through chattering teeth, and Hsien shifted his grip so that his right hand held Su's left and his left grasped the bracelet.

"I am ready," said Hsien.

Su squeezed her eyes tightly shut and let go with her left hand.

Then she screamed, as a burning-cold wall of wind forced her arms apart. Hsien cried out at the same time, but he held her left hand with a firm grip.

Su opened her eyes. Her arms and Hsien's formed a nearly circular loop, the two of them grasping the broken bracelet on one side and each other's hands on the other. Looking down, though her eyes watered from the chill wind, she saw—not her own feet and Hsien's, but a pure unmarked patch of snow. "It's working!" she gasped.

Two more volunteers joined the circle. Soldiers. One cursed as the cold seared his hands; the other only clenched his jaw. The circle was now nearly a man's height across.

Hsien and the man to his right now lowered themselves to one knee and dropped their joined hands to the floor, while Su and the fourth man raised the bracelet as high as they could. The circle was now a tilted ellipse, and the fierce wind pouring out of it whipped the clothing of the men nearby.

"Go!" Chang yelled into the gale. "Civilians first, then soldiers! Officers last! Hurry!"

Women and children stepped over Hsien's hand and ducked under Su's, squinting against the wind and gasping as their bare feet touched the snow. But they pressed ahead, driven by the knowledge that Yao would soon attack. Old men followed, and more women, some carrying babies and leading children. The warmth of their bodies as they passed eased Su's chattering teeth, a little, and they stepped through the circle quickly and in good order, but as the civilians went on and on Su's trembling began to shake her entire body.

Namu kuan shih yin pu sa, she prayed, not knowing how much longer she could hold on.

Then a warm weight settled on her shoulders. It was a horse blanket, and it stank, but it helped immensely. She looked over her shoulder and saw Chang placing another blanket on the man to her left.

The parade of women, children, and men continued. Ice caked in the folds of the blanket, and Su's hands ached from the cold. *Namu kuan shih yin pu sa.*

Her prayers were interrupted by Chang's harsh, commanding voice. "This is too slow!" he said, and placed his hand on the bracelet.

"No!" Su cried out, but it was too late—Chang had inserted himself into the circle.

"Two by two!" he yelled, and the civilians complied, walking two abreast from the heat and dust of Guang-xi into the cold and snow of the Xian mountains.

"Chang, how could you?" Su called to him across the endless flow of heads and shoulders. "You cannot remain behind. The people need you!"

"The people need me now," he replied in a matter-of-fact tone. Snow was already accumulating in his beard. "And I could not allow myself to live, knowing that my brave priestess stayed behind to save me."

Su's head bowed, and her knees sagged. "Oh, Chang..." The cold bit through the heavy horse blanket, and she began to tremble anew.

And then, impossibly, Chang began to chuckle.

"What do you find funny in this situation?" she demanded of him.

"It reminds me of when I was a child," he said. "Do you know 'Little Mousey Brown'?"

Shivering, Su just looked at him.

"It is a circle dance the Li children do. You hold hands in a circle, and dance around, and sing." And then he opened his mouth, and in a frog-like bass he began to sing:

"He climbed up the candlestick,

The little mousey brown,

To steal and eat tallow,

And he couldn't get down."

To her own astonishment, Su recognized the rhyme, though she hadn't thought of it in years. She began to swing her arms gently back and forth as she joined Chang in the second verse:

"He called for his grandma,

But his grandma was in town,

So he doubled up into a wheel,

And rolled himself down."

She was nearly unable to finish the verse, she was laughing so hard. Laughing like a child in the snows of Xian. "Yes, we had this rhyme in Xian," she gasped. "And at the end, when the mousey *roooolled* himself down, we would all..."

She stopped.

"Would what?" asked Chang.

She explained how the Xian version of the dance ended. "Do you think..."

"I don't know." Chang's face grew thoughtful. "We can try."

Newly invigorated, the circle waited while the last of the civilians stepped through and the first of the soldiers followed them. Soon only a handful of soldiers and one lieutenant remained in the wind-whipped room. But then the last two scouts hurried in and barred the door behind themselves. "Yao has broken through the blockade!" said one, sweat running down his face.

"He will find a surprise," said Chang. "Go!"

The scout ducked under Su and Chang's hands, joined at the bracelet, and vanished into the snow. "Good luck," said the lieutenant as he followed, leaving the room empty save for the circle of five and the whistling wind.

Their isolation did not last long. A moment later came a heavy thud at the barred door, and the latch splintered.

"Shall we roll ourselves down?" said Chang, but though his words were light his expression was serious. None of them knew what the consequences of their action might be.

"Yes," said Su, and raised the bracelet high. "Let us roll ourselves down."

A second thud, and the door crashed into pieces.

The man opposite the bracelet took a deep breath and, without releasing his grip on either side, ran under Su and Chang's hands.

The circle turned itself inside-out.

Su felt as though she, herself, were turning inside-out.

The last thing she saw in the garrison of Guang-xi was Yao's face, livid with anger, his hair blown back by the wind from Xian.

And then she found herself standing in the snow — in a cold but gentle breeze. A natural, not supernatural, cold. The sun was just rising, causing the trampled snow to steam gently.

Su sagged to her knees, and the broken bracelet dropped to the snow beside her. It was only inert metal now.

"How far from here to the temple?" Chang said to her.

"Half a day's walk."

"Then let us begin," he said, and extended his hand.

General Chang Hua returned to Li from Xian the next spring. With the support of the priestesses of Miao Feng Shan, the advantage of surprise, and the loyalty of the people of Li, he was able to not only re-take the Li territory lost to Tung, but overcome the conscript forces of Yao and capture the Tung capital. He went on to found a great dynasty, ruling for many years with the help of his chief adviser Su Yuen.

He is known to this day as the Compassionate Emperor.

 og

Tk'Tk'Tk

WALKER'S VOICE RECORDER WAS a beautiful thing of aluminum and plastic, hard and crisp and rectangular. It sat on the waxy countertop, surrounded by the lumpy excreted-looking products of the local technology. *Unique selling proposition*, he thought, and clutched the leather handle of his grandfather's briefcase as though it were a talisman.

Shkthh pth kstphst, the shopkeeper said, and Walker's hypno-implanted vocabulary provided a translation: "What a delightful object." Chitinous fingers picked up the recorder, scrabbling against the aluminum case with a sound that Walker found deeply disturbing. "What does it do?"

It took him a moment to formulate a reply. Even with hypno, *Thfshpfth* was a formidably complex language. "It listens and repeats," he said. "You talk all day, it remembers all. Earth technology. Nothing like it for light-years." The word for "light-year" was *hkshkhthskht*, difficult to pronounce. He hoped he'd gotten it right.

"Indeed yes, most unusual." The pink frills, or gills, at the sides of the alien's head throbbed. It did not look down — its faceted eyes and neckless head made that impossible — but Walker judged its attention was on the recorder and not on himself. Still, he kept smiling and kept looking the alien in the eyes with what he hoped would be interpreted as a sincere expression.

"Such a unique object must surely be beyond the means of such a humble one as myself," the proprietor said at last. *Sthshsk*, such-a-humble-one-as-myself — Walker could die a happy man if he never heard those syllables again.

Focus on value, not price. "Think how useful," he hissed in reply. "Never forget things again." He wasn't sure you could use *htpthtk*, "things," in that way, but he hoped it got the point across.

"Perhaps the honored visitor might wish to partake of a cup of *thshsh*?"

Walker's smile became rigid. *Thshsh* was a beverage nearly indistinguishable from warm piss. But he'd learned that to turn down an offer of food or drink would bring negotiations to an abrupt close. "This-humble-one-accepts-your-most-generous-offer," he said, letting the memorized syllables flow over his tongue.

He examined the shopkeeper's stock as it prepared the drink. It all looked like the products of a sixth-grade pottery class, irregular clots of brown and gray. But the aliens' biotech was far beyond Earth's — some of these lumps would be worth thousands back home. Too bad he had no idea which ones. His expertise lay elsewhere, and he was here to sell, not buy.

The shopkeeper itself was a little smaller than most of its kind, about a hundred forty centimeters tall, mostly black, with yellow spine-tips and green eyes. Despite its insectile appearance, it was warm-blooded — under its chitin it had bones and muscle and organs not unlike Walker's own. But its mind and culture were even stranger than its disturbing mouth-parts.

"The cup of friendship," the alien said, offering a steaming cup of *thshsh*. Walker suppressed a shudder as his fingers touched the alien's — warm, covered with fine hairs, and slightly sticky — but he nodded politely and raised the cup to his lips.

He sipped as little as he felt he could politely get away with. It was still vile.

"Very good," he said.

Forty-five minutes later the conversation finally returned to the voice recorder. "Ownership of this most wondrous object is surely beyond price. Perhaps the honored guest would be willing to lend it for a short period?"

"No trial period necessary. Satisfaction is guaranteed." He was taking a risk with that, he knew, but the recorder had never failed him in all the years he'd owned it.

Tk'tk'tk, the alien said, tapping its mouthparts together. There was no translation for that in Walker's vocabulary. He wanted to throttle the thing—couldn't it even stick to its own language?—but he struggled not to show his impatience.

After a pause, the alien spread a hand—a gesture that meant nothing to Walker. "Perhaps the honored owner could be compensated for the temporary use of the property."

"Humbly requesting more details."

"A loan of this type is generally for an indefinite period. The compensation is, of course, subject to negotiation..."

"You make offer?" he interrupted. He realized that he was not being as polite as he could be. But it was already late afternoon, and he hadn't eaten since breakfast—and if he didn't conclude this deal successfully he might not have enough money for lunch.

Tk'tk'tk again. "Forty-three," it said at last.

Walker seethed at the offer. He had hoped to sell the recorder for enough to live on for at least a week, and his hotel alone—barely worthy of the name—cost twenty-seven a night. But he had already spent most of a day trying to raise some cash, and this was the only concrete offer he'd gotten.

"Seventy?"

The alien's gills, normally in constant slight motion, stopped. Walker knew he had offended it somehow, and his heart sank. But his smile never wavered.

"Seventy is a very inopportune number. To offer seventy to one of your exalted status would be a great insult."

Damn these aliens and their obscure numerology! Walker began to sputter an apology.

"Seventy-three, on the other hand," the shopkeeper continued, "is a number with an impeccable lineage. Would the honored guest accept compensation in this amount?"

He was so busy trying to apologize that he almost didn't recognize the counter-offer for what it was. But some salesman's instinct, some fragment of his father's and his grandfather's DNA, noticed it, and managed to hiss out "This-humble-one-accepts-your-most-generous-offer" before he got in any more trouble.

It took another hour before the shopkeeper actually counted the money—soft brown lumps like rabbit droppings, each looking exactly like the others—into Walker's hand. He passed his reader over them; it smelled the lumps and told him they were three seventeens, two nines, and a four, totaling seventy-three as promised. He sorted them into different pockets so he wouldn't accidentally give the luggage-carrier a week's salary as a tip again. It angered him to be dependent on the Chokasti-made reader, but he would rather use alien technology than try to read the aliens' acrid pheromonal "writing" with his own nose.

Walker pressed through the labia of the shop entrance into the heat and noise and stink of the street. Hard orange shafts of dusty late-afternoon sun glinted dully on the scuttling carapaces of the populace: little merchants and bureaucrats, big laborers and warriors, hulking mindless transporters. No cars, no autoplanes... just a rustling mass of aliens, chuttering endlessly in their harsh sibilant language, scraping their hard spiny limbs and bodies against each other and the rounded, gourd-like walls. Here and there a knot of two or three in conversation blocked traffic, which simply clambered over them. The aliens had no concept of personal space.

Once a swarm of juveniles had crawled right over *him*—a nightmare of jointed legs and chitinous bodies, and a bitter smell like rusty swamp water. They had knocked his briefcase from his hand, and he had scrambled after it under the scrabbling press of their bodies. He shuddered at the memory—not only did the briefcase contain his most important papers, it had belonged to his grandfather. His father had given it to him when he graduated from college.

He clutched his jacket tight at his throat, gripped his briefcase firmly under his arm, and shouldered through the crowd.

○3

Walker sat in the waiting room of his most promising prospect—to be blunt, his *only* prospect—a manufacturer of building supplies whose name translated as Amber Stone. Five days in transit, eight weeks in this bug-infested hellhole of a city, a fifteen-megabyte database of contacts from five different species, and all he had to show for it was one lousy stinking customer. *Potential* customer at that... it hadn't signed anything yet. But Walker had been meeting with it every couple of days for two weeks, and he was sure he was right on the edge of a very substantial sale. All he had to do was keep himself on site and on message.

The light in the palm-sized windows shaded from orange to red before Amber Stone finally appeared from its inner office. "Ah, human! So very pleased that you honor such a humble one as myself with your delightful presence." The aliens couldn't manage the name "Walker," and even "human" came out more like *hsshp'k*.

"Honor is mine, Amber Stone. You read information I give you, three days?"

"Most intriguing, yes. Surely no finer literature has ever been produced."

"You have questions?"

Questions it did have, yes indeed, no end of questions—who performed the translation, where did you have it reproduced, is it really as cold there as they say, did you come through *Pthshksthpt* or by way of *Sthktpth*... but no questions about the product. *I'm building rapport with the customer*, Walker thought grimly, and kept up his end of the conversation as best he could.

Finally Walker tried to regain control. "Your business, it goes well?"

Tk'tk'tk, the customer said, and placed its hands on its shoulders. "As the most excellent guest must surely have noticed, the days are growing longer."

Walker had no idea what that might mean. "Good business or bad, always need for greater efficiency."

"The honored visitor graces this humble one with the benefits of a unique perspective."

Though the sweat ran down behind his tie, Walker felt as though he were sliding on ice—his words refusing to gain traction. "My company's software will improve inventory management efficiency and throughput by three hundred percent or more," he said, pulling out one of his best memorized phrases.

"Alas, your most marvelous software is surely so far superior to our humble computers that no accommodation could be made."

"We offer complete solution. Hardware, software, support. Fully compatible. Satisfaction guaranteed." Walker smiled, trying to project confidence—no, not just confidence, *love*, for the product.

Tk'tk'tk. Was that an expression of interest? "Most intriguing, yes. Most unique. Alas, sun is setting." It gestured to the windows, which had faded from red to nearly black. "This most humble one must beg the honored visitor's forgiveness for consuming so much valuable time."

"Is no problem..."

"This one would not dream of insulting an honored guest in

such a way. Please take your rest now, and honor this unworthy establishment with your esteemed presence again tomorrow." The alien turned and vanished into the inner office.

Walker sat and seethed. *Dismissed by a bug*, he thought, *how much lower can you sink?* He stared into the scuffed leather surface of his briefcase as though he'd find the answer there. But it just sat on his lap, pressing down with the hard-edged weight of two generations of successful salesmen.

C&#x8;

Though the sun had set, the street was still oppressively hot and still teemed with aliens. The yellow-green bioluminescent lighting made them look even stranger, more unnatural. Walker clutched his grandfather's briefcase to his chest as the malodorous crowd bumped and jostled him, spines catching on his clothing and hair.

It didn't help his attitude that he was starving. He'd left most of his lunch on the plate, unable to stomach more than a few wriggling bites, and that had been hours ago. He hoped he'd be able to find something more palatable for dinner, but he wasn't very optimistic. It seemed so cruel of the universe to make travelers find food when they were hungry.

But then, drifting between the sour and acrid smells of the bustling street, Walker's nose detected a warm, comforting smell, something like baked potatoes. He wandered up and down the street, passing his reader over pheromone-lines on the walls advertising SUPERLATIVE CHITIN-WAX and BLUE RIVER MOLT-FEVER INSURANCE. Finally, just as he was coming to the conclusion the smell was a trick of his homesick mind, the reader's tiny screen told him he had arrived at the SPIRIT OF LIFE VEGETARIAN RESTAURANT.

He hadn't even known the *Thfshpfth* language had the concept "vegetarian." But whatever it was, it certainly smelled good. He pushed through the restaurant's labia.

The place was tiny and low-ceilinged, with a single low, curving counter and five squatting-posts. Only one of the posts was occupied, by a small brown alien with white spine-tips and red eyes. It sat quietly, hands folded on the counter, in an attitude that struck Walker as contemplative. No staff was in evidence.

Walker chose a post, placed his folded jacket on it as a cushion, and seated himself as comfortably as possible. His space at the counter had the usual indentation, into which his order would be ladled, and was equipped with a double-ended spoon, an ice-pick, a twisty implement whose use he had yet to decipher, and a small bowl of water (which, he had learned to his great embarrassment, was for washing the fingertips, not drinking). But there was no menu.

Menus were one of the most frustrating things about this planet. Most of the items listed on the pheromone-tracked planks were not in his reader's vocabulary, and for the rest the translations were inadequate—how was he supposed to know whether or not "land-crab in the northern style" was something he would find edible? Time and again he had gone hungry, offended the server, or both. Even so, menus were something he understood. He had no idea what to order, or even how, without a menu to point at.

He drummed his fingers on the countertop and fidgeted while he waiting for the server to appear. Say what you like about these creatures, they were unfailingly polite, and prompt. Usually. But not here, apparently. Finally, frustrated, he got up to leave. But as he was putting on his jacket, trying to steel himself for the crowd outside, he caught another whiff of that baked-potato smell. He turned back to the other customer, still sitting quietly. "No menu. No server. Hungry. How order?"

The alien did not turn. "Sit quietly. With peace comes fulfillment." Its voice was a low susurration, not as harsh as most of the others he'd heard.

With peace comes fulfillment? Walker opened his mouth for a sarcastic reply, but found his grammar wasn't up to the task. And he was hungry. And the food smelled good. So he took off his jacket and sat down again.

He sat with back straight and hands folded, staring at the swirled brown and cream colors of the wall in front of him. It might have come from Amber Stone's factory, produced by a huge genetically-modified life form that ate garbage and shat building supplies. He tried not to think about it too much... the aliens' biotechnology made him queasy.

Looking at the wall, he thought about what it would take to sell Amber Stone's products on Earth. They couldn't be any more incomprehensible to him than the software he had been sent here to sell, and as his father always said, "a good salesman can sell anything." Though with three failed jobs and a failed marriage behind him, he was no longer sure that description had ever really fit him. No matter, he was too old to change careers now. The most he could hope for now was to stay alive until he could afford to retire. Get off the treadmill, buy a little house in the woods, walk the dog, maybe go fishing...

Walker's reverie was interrupted when the other customer rose from its squatting-post and walked around the counter to stand in front of him. "Greetings," it said. "This one welcomes the peaceful visitor to the Spirit of Life."

Walker sputtered. "You... you server?"

"All serve the Spirit of Life, well or poorly, whether they understand it or not. This one serves food as well. The visitor is hungry?"

"Yes!" Walker's head throbbed. Was the alien laughing at him?

"Then this one will bring food. When peace is attained, satisfaction follows." It vanished through the door behind the counter.

Walker fumed, but he tried to wait peacefully. Soon the alien returned with a steaming pot, and ladled out a portion into the indentation in front of Walker. It looked like chunks of purple carrot and pale-yellow potato in a saffron-colored sauce, and it smelled wonderful. It tasted wonderful, too. A little strange, maybe—the purple carrots were bitter and left an odd aftertaste—but it had a complex flavor and was warm and filling. Walker spooned up every bit of it.

"Very good," he said to the server, which had returned to its previous station in front of the counter. "How much?"

It spread its hands and said "This establishment serves the Spirit of Life. Any donation would be appropriate." It pointed to a glass jar on the counter, which contained a small pile of money.

Walker considered. How much of his limited funds could he spare? Yesterday's lunch had cost him five and a half. This place, and the food, were much plainer. But it was the single best meal he had eaten in weeks. Finally he chose a seven from his pocket, scanned it with his reader to make sure, and dropped it in the jar.

"This one thanks the peaceful guest. Please return."

Walker gave an awkward little bow, then pushed through the restaurant's labia into the nightmare of the street.

‍

ଔ

‍

Walker waved his room key, a twisted brown stick reeking with complex pheromones, at the hotel desk clerk. "Key no work," he said. "No let me in."

The clerk took the key, ran its fingers over it to read the codes. "Ah. Yes. This most humble one must apologize. *Fthshpk* starts tomorrow."

"What is *Fthshpk*?"

"Ah. Yes. This humble one has been so unkind as to forget that the most excellent guest is not familiar with the poor customs of this humble locale. *Fthshpk* is a religious political holiday. A small and insignificant celebration by our guest's most elevated standards, to be sure."

"So why it not work, the key?"

"Humble though it may be, *Fthshpk* is very important to the poor folk of the outlying regions. They come to the city in great numbers. This humble room has long been promised to such as these. And surely the most honored guest does not wish to share it?"

"No..." The room was tiny enough for Walker alone. And he didn't want to find out how some of the equipment in the toilet-room was used.

"Indeed. So this most humble establishment, in a poor attempt to satisfy the most excellent human guest, has moved the guest's belongings to another room." It held out a new key, identical in appearance to the old one.

Walker took the key. "Where is?"

"Three levels down. Most cozy and well-protected."

The new room was larger than the old one, having two separate antechambers of unknown function. But the rounded ceiling was terribly low—though Walker could stand up straight in the middle of the room, he had to crouch everywhere else—and the lighting was dim, the heat and humidity desperately oppressive, and everything in the room stank of the aliens.

He lay awake for hours, staring into the sweltering darkness.

ɔȝ

In the morning, he discovered that his shaver and some other things had vanished in the move. When he complained at the front desk, he got nothing but effusive, meaningless praise—oh yes, the most wonderful guest must be correct, our criminal staff is surely at fault—and a bill for the previous night's stay.

"Three hundred eighty-three!"

"The usual *Fthshpk* rate for our highest-quality suite is five hundred sixty-one. This most inadequate establishment has already offered a substantial reduction, out of respect for the highly esteemed guest and the unfortunate circumstances."

"Highest-quality suite? Too hot! Too dark! Too low!"

"Ah. Yes. The most excellent guest has unique tastes. Alas, this poor room is considered the most preferential in the hotel. The heat and light are praised by our other, sadly unenlightened, customers. These most lowly ones find it comforting."

"I not have so much money. You take interstellar credit? Bank draft?"

The clerk's gills stopped pulsing and it drew back a step, going *Tk'tk'tk*. "Surely this humble one has misheard the most honored guest, for to offer credit during *Fthshpk* would be a most grave insult."

Walker licked his lips. Though the lobby was sweltering hot, suddenly he felt chilled. "Can pay after holiday?" He would have to find some other source of local currency.

Tk'tk'tk. "If the most honored visitor will please be patient..." The clerk vanished.

Walker talked with the front desk manager, the chief hotelier, and the *thkfsh*, whatever that was, but behind the miasma of extravagant politeness was a cold hard wall of fact: he would pay for the room, he would pay in cash, and he would pay now.

"This establishment extends its most sincere apologies for the honored guest's unfortunate situation," said the *thkfsh*, which was dark yellow with green spine-tips and eyes. "However, even in this most humble city, payment for services rendered is required by both custom and law."

Walker had already suffered from the best the city had to offer—he was terrified of what he might find in the local jail. "I no have enough money. What can I do?"

"Perhaps the most honored guest would consider temporarily lending some personal possessions to the hotel?"

Walker remembered how he had sold his voice recorder. "Lend? For indefinite period?"

Tk'tk'tk. "The honored guest is most direct and forthright."

Walker thought about what they might want that he could spare. Not his phone, or his reader. "Interest in clothes? Shoes?"

"The highly perceptive guest will no doubt have noticed that the benighted residents of this city have not yet learned to cover themselves in this way."

Walker sighed, and opened his briefcase. Mostly papers, worthless or confidential or both. "Paper fastening device," he said, holding up his stapler. "Earth technology. Nothing like it for sixty-five light years."

"Surely such an item is unique and irreplaceable," said the *thkfsh.* "To accept the loan of this fine device would bring shame upon this humble establishment. However, the traveling-box..."

"Not understanding."

The *thkfsh* touched the scuffed leather of Walker's briefcase. "This traveling-box. It is most finely made."

Walker's chest tightened. "This humble object... only a box. Not worth anything."

"The surface has a most unusual and sublime flavor. And the texture is unlike anything this unworthy one has touched."

Desperately, Walker dug under papers for something, anything else. He found a pocket umbrella. "This, folding rain-shield. Most useful. Same technology used in expanding solar panels."

"The honored visitor's government would surely object to the loan of such sensitive technology. But the traveling-box is, as the visitor says, only a box. Its value and interest to such a humble one as myself are far greater than its value to the exalted guest."

Walker's fingernails bit into his palms. "Box has... personal value. Egg-parent's egg-parent used it."

"How delightful! For the temporary loan of such a fine and significant object, this establishment might be willing to forgive the most worthy visitor's entire debt."

It's only a briefcase, Walker thought. It's not worth going to jail for. But his eyes stung as he emptied it out and placed its contents in a cheap extruded carry-bag.

03

Unshaven, red-eyed, Walker left the hotel carrying all his remaining possessions: a suitcase full of clothes and the carry-bag. He had less than a hundred in cash in his pockets, and no place to spend the night.

Harsh sunlight speared into his eyes from a flat blue sky. Even at this hour of the morning, the heat was already enough to make sweat spring from his skin. And the streets swarmed with aliens—more of them, in greater variety, and more excited than he had ever seen before.

A group of five red-and-black laborers, each over two and a half meters tall, waded through the crowd singing—or at least chattering rhythmically in unison. A swarm of black juveniles crawled over them in the opposite direction, flinging handfuls of glittering green rings into the air. All around, aliens large and small spun in circles, waving their hands in the air. Some pounded drums or wheedled on high-pitched flutes.

A yellow merchant with black spines grabbed Walker's elbows and began spinning the two of them around, colliding with walls and with other members of the crowd. The merchant chattered happily as they spun, but its words were lost in the maelstrom of sound that surrounded them. "Let go! Let go!" Walker shouted, clutching his suitcase and his bag as he tried to squirm away, but the merchant couldn't hear—or wasn't listening—and its chitinous hands were terribly strong.

Finally Walker managed to twist out of the merchant's grasp, only to spin away and collide with one of the hulking laborers. Its unyielding spines tore Walker's jacket.

The laborer stopped chanting and turned to face Walker. It grasped his shoulders, turned him side to side. "What are you?" it shouted. Its breath was fetid.

"Visitor from Earth," Walker shouted back, barely able to hear himself.

The laborer called to its companions, which had moved on through the crowd. They fought their way back, and the five of them stood around him, completely blocking the light.

"This one is a visitor from *h'th*," said the first laborer.

One of the others grabbed a handful of green rings from a passing juvenile, scattered them over Walker's head and shoulders. They watched him expectantly.

"Thank you?" he said. But that didn't seem to be what they wanted.

The first laborer cuffed Walker on the shoulder, sending him reeling into one of the others. "The visitor is not very polite," it said. The aliens loomed close around him.

"This-most-humble-one-begs-the-honored-one's-forgiveness," Walker chattered out, clutching the carry-bag to his chest, wishing for the lost solidity of his grandfather's briefcase. But the laborers ignored his apology and began to twirl him around, shouting in unison.

After a few dozen spins he made out the words of the chant: "Rings, dance! Rings, dance!" Desperately, not at all sure he was doing the right thing, he tried to dance in circles as he had seen some of the aliens do.

The laborers pulled the bag from Walker's hands and began to stomp their feet. "Rings, dance! Rings, dance!" Walker waved his arms in the air as he spun, chanting along with them. His breath came in short pants, destroying his pronunciation.

He twirled, gasping "rings, dance," until he felt the hot sun on his head, and twirled a while longer until he understood what that sun meant: the laborers, and their shade, had deserted him. He was spinning for no reason, in the middle of a crowd that took no notice. He stopped turning and dropped his arms, weaving with dizziness and relief. But the relief lasted only a moment—sudden panic seized him as he realized his arms were empty.

There was the carry-bag, just a meter away, lying in the dirt surrounded by chitinous alien feet. He plowed through the crowd and grabbed it before it got too badly stomped.

But though he searched for an hour, he never found the suitcase.

ଔ

Walker leaned, panting, against the outside wall of Amber Stone's factory. He had fought through the surging streets for hours, hugging the bag to his chest under his tightly-buttoned jacket, to reach this point. Again and again he had been sprinkled with green rings and had danced in circles, feeling ridiculous, but not wanting to find out what might happen if he refused. He was hot and sweaty and filthy.

The still-damp pheromone line drawn across the office's labia read CLOSED FOR *FTHSHPK*.

Walker covered his face with his hands. Sobs thick as glue clogged the back of his throat, and he stood with shoulders heaving, not allowing himself to make a sound. The holiday crowd streamed past like a river of blackberry vines.

Eventually he recovered his composure and blew his nose, patting his waist as he pocketed the sodden handkerchief. His money belt, with the two hard little rectangles of his passport and return ticket, was still in place. All he had to do was walk to the transit gate, and he could return home—with nothing to show for his appallingly expensive trip. But he still had his papers, his phone, and his reader, and his one prospective customer. It was everything he needed to succeed, as long as he didn't give up.

"I might have lost your briefcase, Grandpa," he said aloud in English, "but I'm not going to lose the sale."

A passing juvenile paused at the odd sound, then continued on with the rest of the crowd.

છ

Walker would never have believed he'd be glad to see anything on this planet, but his relief when he entered the Spirit of Life Vegetarian Restaurant was palpable. The city's tortuous streets had been made even more incomprehensible by the *Fthshpk* crowds, and he had begun to doubt he would ever find it, or that it would be open on the holiday. He had been going in entirely the wrong direction when he had found the address by chance, on the pheromone-map at a nearby intersection.

"How long *Fthshpk*?" he asked the server, once he had eaten. It was the same server as before, brown with white spine-tips; it stood behind the counter, hands folded on its thorax, in a centered and imperturbable stance.

"One day," it replied. "Though some believe the spirit of *Fthshpk* should be felt in every heart all year long."

Walker suppressed a shudder at the thought. "Businesses open tomorrow?"

"Most of them, yes. Some trades take an extended holiday."

"Building supplies?" Walker's anxiety made him sputter the word.

"They will be open." The server tilted its shoulders, a posture that seemed to convey amusement. "The most honored visitor is perhaps planning a construction project?"

"No." He laughed weakly, a sound that startled the server.

"Selling, not buying."

"The visitor is a most intriguing creature." The server's shoulders returned to the horizontal. "This humble one wishes to help, but does not know how."

"This one seeks business customers. The server knows manufacturers? Inventory controllers? Enterprise resource management specialists?"

"The guest's words are in the *Thfshpfth* language, but alas, this one does not understand them."

"To apologize. Very specialized business."

The server lowered itself smoothly, bringing its face down to Walker's level. Its gills moved like seaweed in a gentle current. "Business problems are not this one's strength. Is the honored visitor having troubles with family?"

It took Walker a moment to formulate his response. "No. Egg-parent, brood-parent deceased. This one no egglings. Brood-partner... departed." For a moment he forgot who, or what, he was talking to. "This one spent too much time away from nest. Brood-partner found another egg-partner." He fell silent, lost in memory.

The server stood quietly for a moment, leaving Walker to his thoughts. After a while it spoke: "It is good to share these stories. Undigested stories cause pain."

"Thanking you."

"This humble one is known as Shining Sky. If the visitor wishes to share further stories, please return to this establishment and request this one by name."

෪

When Walker left the Spirit of Life, the sun had already set. The *Fthshpk* crowds had thinned, with just a few revelers still dancing and twirling under the yellow-green street lights, so Walker was relatively unimpeded as he walked to hotel after hotel. Alas, they all said, this humble one apologizes most profusely, no room for the most honored visitor. Finally, exhausted, he found a dark space between buildings. Wrapping his jacket around the carry-bag, he placed it under his head—as a pillow, and for security. He would grab a few hours' sleep and meet with his customer the first thing in the morning.

He slept soundly until dawn, when the first hot light of day struck his face. He squinted and rolled over, then awoke fully at the sensation of the hard alley floor under his head.

The bag was not there.

He sat up, wide-eyed, but his worst fears were confirmed: his jacket and bag were nowhere to be seen. Panicked, he felt at his waist—his passport and return ticket were safe. But his money, his papers, his phone, and his reader were gone.

℞

"Ah, human!" said Amber Stone. "Once again the most excellent visitor graces this unworthy establishment." It was late in the morning. Robbed of street signs, addresses, and maps by the loss of his reader, Walker had wandered the streets for hours in search of the factory. Without the accustomed weight of his briefcase, he felt as though he might blow away on the next breeze.

"You requested I come yesterday," Walker hissed. "I come, factory closed. Come again today. Very important." Even without the papers from his briefcase, he could still get a verbal commitment, or at least a strong expression of interest... some tiny tidbit of achievement to prove to his company, his father, his grandfather, and himself that he wasn't a complete loss.

"Surely the superlative guest has more important appointments than to meet with this insignificant one?"

"No. Amber Stone is most important appointment. Urgent we

163

discuss purchase of software."

"This groveling one extends the most sincere apologies for occupying the exalted guest's time, and will not delay the most highly esteemed one any further." It turned to leave.

"This-most-humble-one-begs-the-honored-one's-forgiveness!"

Amber Stone spoke without turning back. "One who appears at a merchant's establishment filthy, staggering, and reeking of *Fthshpk*-rings is obviously one whose concerns are so exalted as to be beyond the physical plane. Such a one should not be distracted from its duties, which are surely incomprehensible to mere mortals."

Walker's shoulders slumped in defeat, but then it was as though he heard his father's voice in his inner ear: *Ask for the sale.* Walker swallowed, then said "Would the honored Amber Stone accept indefinite loan of inventory management system from this humble merchant?"

The alien paused at the threshold of its inner office, then turned back to Walker. "If that is what the most exalted one desires, this simple manufacturer must surely pay heed. Would fifty-three million be sufficient compensation for the loan of a complete system?"

Stunned, Walker leaned against the wall. It was warm and rounded, and throbbed slightly. "Yes," he said at last. "Yes. Sufficient."

☙

"Where the hell have you been, Walker? Your phone's been offline for days. And you look like shit." Gleason, Walker's supervisor, didn't look very good himself—his face on the public phone's oval screen was discolored and distorted by incompatibilities between the alien and human systems.

"I've been busy." He inserted Amber Stone's data-nodule into the phone's receptor.

Gleason's eyes widened as the contract came up on his display. "Yes you have! This is great!"

"Thanks." Gleason's enthusiasm could not penetrate the shell of numbness around Walker's soul. Whatever joy he might have felt at making the sale had been drowned by three days of negotiations.

"This will make you the salesman of the quarter! And the party's tomorrow night!"

The End-Of-Quarter party. He thought of the bluff and facile faces of his fellow salesmen, the loutish jokes and cheap congratulations of every other EOQ he'd ever attended. Would it really be any different if his name was the one at the top of the list? And then to return to his empty apartment, and go out the next day to start a new quarter from zero...

"Sorry," Walker said, "I can't make it."

"That's right, what am I thinking? It's gotta be at least a five day trip, with all the transfers. Look, give me a call whenever you get in. You got my home number?"

"It's in my phone." Wherever that was.

"Okay, well, I gotta go. See you soon."

He sat in the dim, stuffy little booth for a long time. The greenish oval of the phone screen looked like a pool of stagnant water, draining slowly away, reflecting the face of a man with no family, no dog, no little house in the woods. And though he might be the salesman of the quarter today, there were a lot of quarters between here and retirement, and every one of them would be just as much work.

Eventually came the rap of chitinous knuckles on the wall of the booth, and a voice. "This most humble one begs the worthy customer's forgiveness. Other customers desire to use the phone."

The booth cracked open like a seed pod. Walker stuck out his head, blinking at the light, and the public phone attendant said "Ah, most excellent customer. This most unworthy one trusts your call went well?"

"Yes. Most well."

"The price of the call is two hundred sixty-three."

Walker had about six in cash in his pants pockets. The rest had vanished with his jacket. He thought a moment, then dug in his money belt and pulled out a tiny plastic rectangle.

"What is this?"

"Ticket to Earth."

"An interstellar transit ticket? To Earth? Surely this humble one has misheard."

"Interstellar. To Earth."

"This is worth thousands!"

"Yes." Then, in English, he said "Keep the change."

He left the attendant sputtering in incomprehension behind him.

ఴ

The man was cursing the heat and the crowds as he pushed through the restaurant's labia from the street, but when he saw Walker he stopped dead and just gaped for a moment. "Jesus!" he said at last, in English. "I thought I was the only human being on this Godforsaken planet."

Walker was lean and very tan; his salt-and-pepper hair and beard were long but neatly combed, and he stood with folded hands in an attitude of centered harmony. He wore only a short white skirt. "Greetings," he said in the *Thfshpfth* language, as he always did. "This one welcomes the peaceful visitor to the Spirit of Life."

"What are you doing here?" The English words were ludicrously loud and round.

Walker tapped his teeth together, making a sound like *Tk'tk'tk*, before he replied in English: "I am... serving food." The sound of it tickled his mouth.

"On this planet, I mean."

"I live here."

"But why did you come here? And why the Hell did you stay?"

Walker paused for a moment. "I came to sell something. It was an Earth thing. The people here didn't need it. After a while I understood, and stopped trying. I've been much happier since." He gestured to one of the squatting-posts. "Please seat yourself."

"I, uh... I think I'll pass."

"You're sure? The *thksh hspthk* is very good today."

"Thanks, but no." The man turned to go, but then he paused, pulled some money from his pocket, ran a reader over it. "Here," he said, handing it to Walker. "Good luck."

As the restaurant's labia closed behind the visitor, Walker touched the money, then smelled his fingertip. Three hundred and eleven, a substantial sum.

He smiled, put the money in the donation jar, and settled in to wait for the next customer.

ଔ

Charlie the Purple Giraffe
Was Acting Strangely

JERRY THE ORANGE SQUIRREL was walking down the sidewalk one day when he saw some word balloons floating above the hedge beside him. It was the voice of his friend Charlie the purple giraffe. "A man has to have a proper garden, doesn't he?" Charlie was saying. "And what makes a proper garden? Proper plants! And what do you need for proper plants?"

After each question, Charlie seemed to be waiting for an answer. But no response was visible.

"You need proper dirt!" Charlie continued. "And what do you have to have for proper dirt?"

Intrigued, Jerry scampered to the top of the hedge and stared down. What he saw made the little lines of surprise come out of his head.

"You have to have proper worms!" Bent double, Charlie was busily tying a Windsor knot around the neck of a common garden worm. Beside him, a large tin can—its ragged-edged lid tilted at a rakish angle—squirmed with hundreds of worms in tiny top hats, spats, and bustles.

It wasn't the worms that surprised Jerry, though—Charlie did that sort of thing all the time. It was the fact that Charlie was speaking into thin air.

"Who ya talkin' to, Charlie?" said Jerry.

Charlie was so startled that his eyes momentarily jumped out of his head. But he quickly regained his composure. "The worms?"

"Worms don't have ears."

"Uh... I was talkin' to *you*, Jerry."

"You didn't even know I was here."

"Sure I did! I was just pretendin' I didn't."

"Uh huh." Jerry's words dripped frost. One linen-clad worm raised a parasol against the drips.

"As a matter of fact, I was just about to invite you in for tea. Care to join me?"

"Yeah. We can have a nice chat."

They walked from the yard into Charlie's cozy one-room bungalow. It was pink today, with cheerful curves to its walls and roof, and was surrounded by smiling purple flowers. The entire interior was wallpapered in blue and yellow stripes, which clashed with the green and black stripes of Charlie's suit.

Charlie poured tea for the two of them, holding the tiny teapot delicately between white-gloved finger and thumb. A musical note came from the pot as he set it down. He seated himself and raised his cup, pinky raised—though he did not drink, for his arms were too short to reach his head. "What brings you out on this fine morning?" he asked. His words were sprinkled with rainbows and candy canes.

Jerry sipped his tea for a moment. "Charlie... you have to admit you've been acting a little strange lately."

"Strange?" Charlie's eyes darted to one side, then returned to Jerry.

Jerry set down his cup. "You've been talking to yourself."

"Me? Talk to myself?" He slapped his knee and laughed, not very convincingly. "Why should I talk to myself, when you're so much more interesting than I am?"

"I've seen you do it. Like just now."

"I told you, I was talking to you."

"What about last week, when you were working on your car? I saw you from three blocks away. Every once in a while you'd wave your wrench and pontificate. It was like you were trying to convince someone of something, but there was nobody there."

"I was... rehearsing. I'm giving a speech to the Rotary Club next week."

Jerry hopped up on the table. "Charlie, there is no Rotary Club in this town."

"It's in... another town."

"What other town?"

Charlie passed his cup from hand to hand. He stared fixedly at a point on the wall. It was as though he were staring out a window, but there wasn't even a painting there—just the wallpaper, which was now patterned in pink and white polka-dots. His expression was grim, almost angry. Finally he brought his head down to Jerry's level, cupped his glove to his mouth, and whispered "I wasn't talking to myself."

"Oh?"

Charlie peered theatrically from side to side, then leaned in even closer. "I was talking to the readers."

Jerry crossed his arms on his chest. "There's nobody here by that name."

"It's not a name. It's... what they do. Readers. People who read."

"Who read what?"

A change came over Charlie then, like a cloud passing in front of the sun. He placed his hands flat in his lap, straightened his neck, and took a deep breath. "Us," he said at last. "They read us."

"I don't understand."

Charlie stood up and began to pace, his hands tightly clenched behind his back. His strides were long, and the house was tiny; he could only take two or three steps in each direction before having to turn around. "Jerry," he began, then paused. "Look... do you ever ask yourself, why am I here? What is the meaning of life?"

"Sure. Sometimes. Doesn't everyone?"

Charlie stopped pacing, turned suddenly and leaned down to Jerry again. "We make them laugh." His tone was deadly serious.

"Them."

"The readers. We were created to entertain them."

Jerry waved his tiny paws in a broad gesture of negation. "Whoa there, big guy. Jerry the squirrel is nobody's creation and nobody's patsy. I'm here for *me*."

"Sorry, Jerry, but it's the honest truth. We're just characters in a comic book."

Jerry fixed Charlie with a hard, beady stare. "Prove it."

Charlie's eyes closed and his shoulders slumped. He turned away from Jerry. "I can't."

"Then how do you know it's true?"

"I've always known, I think, in the back of my head somewhere. But then one day...." He turned back to Jerry, and his eyes were two black pits of fear and despair. "I had just said good-bye to Hermione the hedgehog, I turned back to go into my house, and then... suddenly everything was black. I couldn't move. I couldn't see. I was squashed flat. But somehow I knew that all around me, piled above and below me like a huge stack of pancakes, was everyone and everything I have ever cared about. They were all squashed flat too, but I was the only one who knew it. That went on for a moment that seemed like forever. And then I was right back in my house, as though nothing had happened."

A thought balloon appeared above Jerry's head: "He's bonkers!"

"I know it sounds crazy. But it was as real as anything. And ever since then... I know we're being read, and we're being laughed at."

"I get it," Jerry said with false cheer. "When you talk to yourself you are telling them jokes!"

"No!" Charlie's hands bunched into fists, and he pounded the air ineffectually. "I'm trying to *explain* myself!"

Jerry scratched his head, and a few question marks came out. "You certainly aren't doing a very good job of it now."

"Well, for instance... last week, when I was working on my car. I was just putting the engine back in for the third time, and I was explaining to the readers that this was a very delicate operation and had to be performed with the utmost care. Not funny at all."

"Charlie, you were pounding it in place with a sledge hammer. That's pretty funny. And calling it a delicate operation just makes it funnier."

Charlie stood stock-still for a moment, his lip quivering. Then he collapsed into his chair, his purple neck arching high as he dropped his head into his hands. "I know!" he sobbed, big blue teardrops running down between his fingers. "No matter what I do, no matter how hard I try to be serious, it comes out hilarious. And I'm tired of them laughing at me!"

Jerry offered his handkerchief, and Charlie blew his nose in it with an immense orange HONK.

"These 'readers'... can you hear them? Can you see them?"

"No." He didn't raise his head from his hands.

"Then how do you know they're laughing at you?"

"I just know. The same way I know they're there."

"Where are they, exactly?"

"Right now? Over there."

Jerry followed Charlie's pointing finger, but there was nothing there but the green and white flowered wallpaper. At least it was prettier than the pink and white polka-dots that had been there before. "I don't see anything."

"Neither do I. But they're there. They're always there."

"Always?"

"Well, most of the time." He lifted his head and tried to return the sodden handkerchief, but Jerry gestured to keep it. "I don't think they watch anyone else. I mean, they're watching you now, because you're with me. And they might watch you for a while after you leave here. But eventually they'll come back to me. I'm the main character in their little comic book."

Jerry's tail bristled. "Why you? Why not me?"

"I don't know. I wish I did. That's just the way it is, I guess."

Jerry paced back and forth on the table for a time, thinking. Finally he spoke. "I think you ought to talk with Dr. Nocerous about this."

Charlie shook his head, a slow rueful motion. "Okay... but I don't think it will do any good."

ʚɞ

Doctor Nocerous's office walls were completely covered in diplomas, from such institutions as THE SCHOOL OF AARD VARKS and WAZUPWIT U. The doctor himself was a stout gray rhino, nearly as wide as he was tall, whose wire-rimmed glasses perched incongruously at the top of his horn. He wore a white lab coat, and a small round mirror was strapped to his forehead. He never used the mirror in any way. "Hmm," he said as he held his stethoscope to the side of Charlie's neck, and "Hmm" again as he stood on a stepladder to peer down Charlie's throat, and "Hmm" one more time as he held Charlie's lapel between two fingers and looked at his watch.

"Well, doctor," said Jerry when the exam was finished, "what's wrong with him?"

"My examination has discovered no physical infirmities whatsoever. Superficially, he is salubrious as an equine."

"What?" said Charlie.

"Healthy as a horse," explained the doctor.

"I told you."

"But he's *seeing* things!" said Jerry.

"Indeed. These phantasmagorical manifestations are most worrisome," the doctor muttered, puffing on his pipe. A few small pink bubbles emerged as he pondered. "I recommend that we keep your friend under observation."

"How ironic," Charlie said to the wall, then returned his gaze to the doctor. "I am not seeing things, or hearing things! I just *know* things. Is that so bad?"

Jerry jumped up on the doctor's desk. "Charlie, listen to me. I'm your friend, right? I've never steered you wrong?"

"Of course not."

"Then get this through your thick purple skull: *there are no 'readers.'* You are not the 'main character' in anyone's 'comical book.' You're just a person like anyone else, and you're here to muddle through your life the same as the rest of us. Nothing more."

"The veracity of your diminutive companion's statement is incontrovertible," said the doctor, waving his pipe. "These megalomaniacal misapprehensions must be immediately terminated. They jeopardize your physical integrity and the overall stability of the community."

"What?"

"You're a danger to yourself and others."

Charlie jumped out of his seat. "I'm no danger to anyone! So what if I talk to myself? That doesn't mean I'm going to pick up a big mallet and start flattening people!"

"Solipsistic delusions are frequently merely the initial manifestation of a general insensitivity to the legitimacy, even the existence, of external personalities. If allowed to go unchecked, these tendencies could escalate into antisocial or even injurious behavior!"

"What?"

"He thinks you might pick up a big mallet and start flattening people," said Jerry.

Charlie stood with his feet planted wide and his fists clenched.

The white fabric of his gloves was bunched and strained. He stared at the wall. "You think this is funny, don't you?"

"Nobody's making any jokes here, Charlie," said Jerry. "We're serious."

"I wasn't talking to you." He turned around, pointed at a different spot on the wall. "This has all been arranged for *your* amusement! Are you happy?"

Jerry and Dr. Nocerous looked at each other.

Charlie pulled a big mallet from his pocket and began pounding on the wall. "Are you laughing now? Huh? Are you?" The WHAM of the mallet on the wall was huge and black. "Just let me get out there and I'll show you what comedy is all about!"

"This situation necessitates immediate incarceration!" said the doctor as he ran behind his desk.

"Ditto!" said Jerry as he dived under a chair.

The doctor pressed a button under the desk; no sound came out, but a few small lightning bolts appeared. Moments later two enormous gorillas, their white coats stretched taut over bulging muscles, burst through the door. There was a swirl of motion, and when it cleared Charlie was on the floor, trussed in a straitjacket.

"Don't let them put me away!" Charlie cried.

"It's for your own good," said Jerry, and waved encouragingly as the gorillas hustled Charlie away. But as soon as they were gone, Jerry's shoulders slumped. "What are you going to do, Doctor?"

"His prognosis is not encouraging. However, he will be the recipient of the most advanced experimental treatments modern medical technology has to offer." From his pocket, the doctor drew one end of a set of heavy jumper cables. Sparks flew from the sharp copper teeth as he touched them together, and a small strange grin appeared on his face.

ॐ

Charlie's sad, desperate eyes peered through the slot in the metal door. "You've got to get me out of here, Jerry." His word balloons squeezed through the slot like bubbles from a sinking ship.

"Hang in there, buddy. Dr. Nocerous tells me you're coming along nicely."

"He's been saying that for weeks." Charlie shook his head, bringing his blackened horns briefly into view. "But I know the score. I'm not going to get out of here until I show some improvement, but since there's nothing wrong with me I'm never going to get any better than I am now."

"Charlie, you must accept that you have a problem. It's the first step on the road to recovery."

Charlie chuckled ruefully. "I have a problem, all right. I've learned that there are worse things than being laughed at."

"Nobody's laughing at you, Charlie. You need to understand that these 'readers' are nothing more than a projection of your own feelings of self-doubt and inconsequentiality."

"That's just what the rhino told you to say. But you're right— nobody's laughing at me. The *readers* aren't laughing at me. And that's the problem."

"I thought you didn't want them to laugh at you."

"I didn't. But since I've been here in this padded cell, tied up in this straitjacket all day long with nothing to do... they're *bored*."

"Well, that's an improvement, isn't it? Maybe now they'll watch someone else instead."

"They've tried. But—no insult intended—none of you guys are as funny as I am." Jerry's tail bristled. "So they're leaving. They're going away completely. And that scares me."

"You should be glad to be rid of them!" Jerry fumed.

Charlie's eyes closed for a moment. When they opened again, Jerry saw a bit of the old manic fervor. "Listen... do you ever think about the nature of time?"

"What?"

"Time. How it passes, from moment to moment. Haven't you ever noticed how some things change when you aren't looking at them?"

"Like the wallpaper?"

"Exactly. I believe that time is... divided. Into moments, or segments. Within each segment we are alive and awake, but in between... there are gaps. That's when things change."

"What does this have to do with anything?"

"I think the readers live their lives in the gaps between our time segments. They live in our time too, somehow — I know because they can see us. But in the gaps... they have the universe to themselves."

"Charlie, you're not making any sense."

"I know it sounds crazy. But I'm dead serious. And here's the important part: when the readers aren't watching us... *we don't exist!*"

Jerry shook his head and turned away, but after a moment's thought he turned back. "OK. Suppose I accept this theory of yours. Suppose there *are* gaps between moments. But time still *feels* continuous to us. See?" He waved a paw rapidly back and forth. "So it doesn't really matter!"

"It doesn't matter as long as they keep coming back. But if too many of them get bored... if they all go away and don't come back... then the gap will just go on and on, and we'll never exist again. It'll be the end of the world, Jerry. Squashed flat in the dark, forever." Charlie's eyes were desperate, sincere, pleading. "You've got to get me out of here. I'll joke, I'll pratfall, I'll do anything to keep the readers coming back. To keep us all alive. Please."

Jerry closed his eyes, unable to bear his friend's gaze. "There are no readers, Charlie."

In the end, he was right.

ⒸⓈ

Falling Off the Unicorn
by David D. Levine
and Sara A. Mueller

SAILING IN SLOW MOTION ABOVE the sand of the arena floor, Misty thought "This is going to hurt."

Just a moment ago she'd been in the saddle, nudging Vulcan through a shoulder-in, concentrating on moving the unicorn's right back hoof toward his left shoulder, getting him used to working in this building. It was new, still smelled of paint, and was making all the animals edgy.

And then some moron in the stands had lit up a goddamn cigarette.

Misty's spur caught on the saddle as Vulcan whirled out from under her, alabaster coat and flaxen mane blurring past her eyes. She couldn't get her hip under her and hit the ground on her left knee. It did hurt—it hurt like a sumbitch. She gasped from the pain, pulling in a breath full of shavings and manure dust as she rolled away from Vulcan's sharp cloven hooves. The last thing she needed was an enraged four-hundred-pound unicorn stepping on her head.

Somewhere on the stands, she could hear her groom Caroline shouting. There was shouting all around, and the metal voice from the announcer's booth called out "Loose unicorn, Harry, close the gate!" No one wanted a Persian stud running loose on the fairgrounds.

Misty kept one arm wrapped around her throbbing knee and the other over her head, but she could still see Vulcan rearing and pounding the rail with his iridescent hooves, making the hollow steel ring and tipping his head sideways to lunge through the rails with the double-edged spiral of his horn. His scream of rage echoed in the high hollow ceiling as he struggled to reach the offending smoker. Caroline pushed the stupid addict toward the exit, bellowing "Whoa, Vulcan! God-dammit, *whoa!*"

And the stupid beast whoa'd. He dropped right to his feet and gave a self-satisfied snort, pleased and proud that he'd defended his rider from the vicious cigarette. Misty rocked, holding her knee. Damn idiot animal. Caroline vaulted over the rail, dropped the six feet to the arena floor, and caught Vulcan's reins. Crisis controlled.

Misty tried to sit up as the announcer cleared the arena. Brighter pain stabbed in her knee; it felt full of white-hot glass shards. She pushed herself up on her arms, spitting and snorting out sand and the ground-up shreds of old sneaker soles. Caroline walked Vulcan over, the animal placidly lipping her dark buzz-cut as if to say "did I do good, boss?"

Caroline crouched down and cradled Misty's knee in her hands, sliding her thumbs across the top of the kneecap. Only six weeks older than Misty, Caroline had always looked after her like a beloved little sister. She whispered under her breath, and a brief tingle of investigative magic slipped through the crackle of pain. "Can't tell how bad it is, but it's not broken. Think you can get up, blondie?" Though she kept her words light, concern tightened the skin around her eyes.

"I'd rather not."

Caroline gave a little smirk and hauled Misty to her good foot.

"Ow!" Misty leaned hard on Caroline and hopped to keep her balance. That was a mistake—the injured knee screamed with pain at the jolt. "Sonofa—" But she bit off the curse, sucking air through her teeth and blinking hard. There were a lot of things that unicorn riders weren't supposed to do, and one of them was swear out loud, especially not in front of an entire arena full of riders who'd love to see her disqualified.

Double especially not in front of Mary Frances Schwartz, the only other girl here with a real shot at the Nationals. Mary Frances was a barracuda in a double-A bra, five years younger than Misty's seventeen and almost as tall. She'd be too tall to ride Persians next year, unless she turned out to be a "teeny little freak" like Misty. She sidled her own unicorn Angel over, threateningly close to Vulcan, who laid his ears back and arched up at the other stud. "Are you all right?" she asked with nearly authentic sympathy.

"It's so sweet of you to ask," Misty ground out through clenched teeth. At least two reporters were taking notes, so she couldn't say what she was really thinking. She put one arm over Caroline's shoulder and the other over Vulcan's saddle, clutching the saddle horn as the three of them hobbled slowly out of the arena to the stable.

It took them almost ten minutes to cover the hundred yards to their stalls, Misty leaning into the lithe strength of Caroline's body. Vulcan was limping too; maybe he'd hurt himself attacking the rail. The dusty fairground was painfully bright after the mercury-lit dimness of the arena.

Once they reached the shade of the stall, Caroline eased Misty onto a shrink-wrapped sawdust bale. Misty sighed and rested her head in the soft hollow of Caroline's neck, smelling clean sweat and the cotton of her shirt collar. "Thank you," she said, and squeezed her hand.

Caroline squeezed back for a moment, then pulled away and turned back to Vulcan. Misty felt a childish urge to pout—Vulcan had to be secured in his stall, but the knee didn't hurt as much when she held Caroline's hand.

Caroline unbuckled Vulcan's bridle, replacing it with a halter cross-tied to each side of the open stall door. You never let that horn loose around people if you could help it. Once the unicorn was secured, Caroline brought Misty an ice pack from the trailer. "I told your mother those damn spurs were going to be trouble."

"Since when does she listen to either of us?" Misty sucked in a breath as Caroline laid the ice pack over the ruined knee of her pink Wranglers. She didn't want to let on just how much it hurt. "Anyway, it wasn't the spurs, it was me. You'd never have lost your seat." Caroline had grown too tall to show unicorns, but on a horse she was a study in long-limbed grace.

"I'm just the groom, shorty."

Misty gave Caroline a mock glare. "I'm gonna hit five feet this year, you wait and see."

"Dream on." Caroline crouched by Vulcan's front leg, inspecting the suspect hoof. "Looks like you've got a bruised hoof there, son."

"Seriously, Caro, it should be you out there on Vulcan, not me. You trained him, after all. I just sit on him. He's the proverbial push-button pony."

"I'm too tall, and you know it. I can ride 'em, I just don't look good on 'em." She picked up Vulcan's bruised foot and cupped it between her hands for a moment, muttering a healing charm like a prayer whispered in a lover's ear. Vulcan let his head hang in the cross-ties, eyes half closed as the magic flowed through his injured hoof.

"Even if you can't ride professionally, you could be a real trainer, in a real stable! Jack Thornton would hire you in a minute if he could. Why do you hang around this one-unicorn outfit?"

Caroline rose and busied herself with Vulcan's girth, not looking at Misty. "I like it here."

"Where's *here*? Caro, we're *nowhere*. Mom treats you like a servant, I know as well as you do that you haven't had a raise in three years, and we've been to the nationals, what, five times?"

"But you still haven't won."

As if I cared. But she didn't say it... it would hurt Caroline so much. She'd worked so hard, put up with so much, all for Misty's sake; the least Misty could do in return was to make sure she got the accolades that would come from training a national champion unicorn.

Then Vulcan growled and tossed his head in the cross-ties. That meant some other stud was nearby, or...

Misty's mother announced her presence with a sandpaper screech of "I leave for *ten minutes* and what the hell happens!" She was already decked out in her Professional Show Mother outfit of white leather blazer, white leather skirt, and white Tony Lama boots—everyone on the circuit called her The Great White when she wasn't in earshot—but a chic silk turban concealed her bleached hair.

"I'm fine, Mother. Thanks for asking." Misty wondered if her mother's voice hurt her own ears, after all the vodka Bloody Marys she'd consumed when Misty had qualified for the finals last night.

"Let me see that knee." She grabbed Misty's calf, making big bright spots dance across Misty's vision, and yanked off the ice pack. The knee had swollen out to the limits of Misty's jeans. "These'll have to be cut off, I suppose. At least you had the sense not to practice in your competition outfit."

Caroline's eyes widened and she dropped the saddle unceremoniously onto its rack. "Misty! You didn't tell me it was that bad!" She knelt down in front of Misty and peered at the taut cloth. "We need to call the doctor."

Mother whirled on her. "No doctors! If some milksop gives her pain-killers, she'll blow the blood test." She turned back to Misty, pointing with one pearl-manicured finger. "This is probably our last chance at the Nationals, and you are not going to wimp out on me."

Angry little lines appeared around Caroline's mouth, but Misty cut her off before she could say something that would get her fired. "I'll be fine, Mother." But she was looking at Caroline. "We'll wrap it and ice it and it's only one more class. I can stay on him for ten minutes."

"That's right. You are getting on that animal tonight, you are riding that class, and you are going to win it. I haven't busted my ass dragging you all over the countryside this year for nothing!"

Vulcan's ears went back at the rising shriek and he growled, strained against the cross-ties, digging with his hooves in the hard-packed dirt of the stall. Caroline said "We're making Vulcan nervous, Mrs. Bell. We should get Misty into the trailer and elevate that knee."

"You do that." She glanced at her watch, encrusted with pink diamonds. "Oh God, now you've made me late. Look, I'm meeting Harvey to talk about your publicity photos over lunch, and then I'm going to get my hair done. I'll see you at the gate at seven." She strode out toward the parking lot, calling over her shoulder "And I'd better not get another call from the show office!"

Misty looked around for the ice pack and saw it lying in the dirt, just out of her reach. "Can you get that for me?" Caroline leaned over and retrieved it, her lips pressed together in a hard white line. "Go ahead and say it," Misty prompted.

"Why bother? All it would do is make you have to defend her. And hearing you defend her is worse than watching how she treats you."

Misty sighed. She didn't know which would be worse—arguing with Caroline, or admitting that she had a point. "She's my mother, Caroline."

"Only genetically. Now let's get you inside. Can you hop, or do you want me to carry you?"

"I'll hop." But even straightening up was agony, and Misty didn't protest when Caroline carefully scooped her up, one arm warm behind her shoulders and the other under her thighs. Misty opened the trailer door and Caroline set her down on the bed in the back.

Misty looked down at the toes of her pink Ropers, dreading the thought of pulling them off. "If we cut those, Mother will kill me."

"Let me try." Caroline worked one hand up Misty's pant leg to her calf. She cupped the heel of the boot in her other hand and started to ease it off. Misty gasped in pain, but a moment later the boot slipped off. "Good girl. Now the other one."

But when both boots and the socks were off the situation got even scarier. Misty's left foot was as white as her mother's leather skirt. "It's the swelling," Caroline said. "It's cut off the circulation. We have to get those jeans off."

Pulling the jeans down was absolutely out of the picture. Caroline went to the kitchen cabinet and came back with a pair of shears. Misty trembled, but said nothing as Caroline began to work her way up the outside seam. When she reached the knee, the scissors burned like ice against the hot skin and Misty bit her lower lip hard. Then, as the fabric parted, she thought she might faint from relief as the pressure released.

Caroline paused, her hand warm on Misty's inner thigh, after she had cut well past the knee. "They've got to come all the way off sooner or later. Do you want me to keep cutting?"

Misty's heart thudded in her throat, and she had to swallow before she could reply. "Might as well," she managed faintly.

Caroline seemed to be having trouble speaking as well, but she took a deep breath and resumed cutting. The cold scissor blades crept along Misty's thigh, and she felt the tip slip under the elastic of her panties. "Um, you got more than the jeans there."

"Sorry," Caroline squeaked, then cleared her throat and readjusted the scissors. "Sorry," she repeated in a more normal tone.

The bunched fabric at Misty's hip was awkward to get past. Then she had to wiggle out of her belt, and even with the belt gone the heavily layered waistband was a formidable obstacle. But Caroline sawed through it, and finally Misty was free. Both of them were panting from the effort. "Well, here I am, a seventeen-year-old virgin with no pants," Misty quipped in a trembling attempt at humor. "I bet there's a thousand boys who'd love to be you right now."

Caroline licked her lips. "Uh. Yeah." And she glanced up at Misty, her brown eyes half-hidden by her eyebrows, her face gone all serious. Misty swallowed, but returned Caroline's gaze for a long, awkward moment. Caroline was bent over her in the confined space, her calloused hand pressed between Misty's thighs. Misty had seen Caroline in nothing but a bra and panties plenty of times, living in the same trailer with her for what felt like a thousand shows. They'd been best friends since they were both eight, but she'd never wondered before what Caroline's skin felt like.

Then Caroline broke the contact to look down at Misty's knee. "Shit, girl. You aren't going to be standing up on this any time soon, much less getting on a unicorn." She was right. The knee was the size of a cantaloupe and an evil mix of purple and black.

Tears pinched at the back of Misty's throat. "I've got to, Caroline. I've just got to." If Misty didn't ride tonight, her mother would unleash her wrath on the nearest available object, and that was Caroline. Mother would make sure she never worked again.

Caroline sat back on her haunches, leaning her back against the bad imitation woodgrain of the wall. "I don't see how."

Misty licked her lips. "What about that healing touch of yours? It works on Vulcan."

"That's just a little hedge witchery. I don't practice on *people*! I don't have any experience, I don't have a license... hell, I wouldn't even do it on myself!"

"But Caroline, back in the arena..."

"I completely missed how badly you were hurt. If I mess up your knee healing it, they'll have to do surgery to put it right! You could be out of commission for six months!"

"So? Six *hours* is enough to lose our shot at the Nationals. I won't let my stupid mistake mess up your career."

"Screw my career!"

"Please, Caroline!" She reached out and took Caroline's hand. "Please."

Caroline didn't pull away. Her hand was very warm and moist in Misty's; her long strong fingers almost overwhelmed Misty's tiny delicate ones. "Okay," she said at last. "But only if it's what *you* want. Not your mother."

Misty held Caroline's hand tighter. "This is what I want."

The two of them rearranged themselves in the tiny space so that Caroline could lay both hands on Misty's knee. They were trembling. Misty put her hands over Caroline's. "It's okay," she said. "I trust you."

"I know. But if I hurt you..."

"If you do, it'll be because I asked you to."

Caroline nodded and took a deep breath. Then she began to murmur, words as soft and convoluted as the inside of a unicorn's ear. At first Caroline's hands were cool on the heat of the injured knee, but then they began to warm — a deep thrumming warmth that resonated in Misty's bones. The heat of the injury was absorbed in that warmth, the shards of hot glass cooling and softening as Misty's knee relaxed back to normal. It was like music — the harsh jangled vibrations caught up and subsumed in the melody of Caroline's magic — a melody woven of Caroline's hands and her soft voice. It echoed low in Misty's belly. Misty sighed and closed her eyes.

As the swelling subsided, the warmth spread up Misty's leg and across her torso until it reached her heart and flowed to every part of her. She felt the rhythm of Caroline's words in her own pulse—each stronger for the other's presence.

"Misty...?"

Caroline never called Misty by name... "blondie," "shorty," but never, ever "Misty." She opened her eyes.

Caroline was looking at her with bottomless dark eyes. Her hands were wrapped around Misty's knee, almost reverently. She was trembling again, and a sheen of sweat glistened on her face. "Misty... are you all right?"

"Better than all right." She leaned forward and slid her hands around the back of Caroline's neck, sliding forward until their bodies meshed. "Caroline..."

Caroline began to pull away. "I don't want to hurt you."

"This is what I want." And she kissed her.

03

Misty drifted slowly awake to Caroline's warm clean smell and the softness of her breast against Misty's cheek. The whole length of Caroline's long lean body was fitted smoothly against her, skin touching skin, and her arms enclosed Misty with gentle protectiveness. Misty sighed in contentment... but when she moved, like hitting the sand in the arena, it was going to hurt. Caroline would wake up, and the moment would be over, and Misty couldn't stand the thought of it.

The general public had a lot of misconceptions about unicorns, but the virginity trip was the real deal. Unicorns didn't share. The women around them were their herds, and they would brook no competition or threat to those they loved. Anyone not a virgin who tried to mount a unicorn was taking her life in her hands.

Misty's career was over.

Caroline's arms tightened around her. Holding on. Misty tipped up her head to look at Caroline's face, and saw tears in her eyes.

In all the years they'd lived together in trailer after trailer, Misty had never seen Caroline cry. No matter what cruel, horrible thing Mother said to her, Caroline pinched her lips together and sucked it down.

Misty brushed the tears off Caroline's cheek. "Don't cry, Caroline. It's okay."

Caroline squeezed her eyes shut and buried her face in Misty's hair. "It's *not* okay," she whispered, her voice broken. "I've ruined your whole life."

"It's only my life so far." Misty shifted so she could look Caroline in the eye. "And you didn't do anything to me. I'm the one who started it, remember? I think I've wanted this for a long time, even if I didn't know that until today." And she kissed her — trying to show Caroline that it really was all right, even though she wasn't sure herself.

Caroline kissed back with a desperate edge she hadn't shown before. She tasted of salt. She smelled of Misty.

Misty stroked Caroline's hair, gentling her down from desperation and murmuring vague reassurances. "We'll be all right. We'll be all right."

"How?" Caroline's voice was muffled against Misty's breast. "What do we do now?"

Misty took a deep breath. "Right now we're going to get up and take Vulcan a drink. He's been tied out there for three hours without any water. Then we're going to both get through the shower before Mother shows up."

"And then what?"

"I'll handle Mother. She's not your problem any more."

Caroline swallowed. "Okay. I'll take care of Vulcan while you hit the shower." She gave a rueful little smile. "Too bad there isn't room for both of us at once." Then she kissed Misty on the neck and slid out of bed, leaving a cold vacancy behind.

Once she was alone, Misty gathered the sheets into a wad in her lap, hunching herself into a tiny ball and rocking back and forth.

Her career was over.

No more trophies. No more spotlight. No more photographers. No more reporters watching her.

Imagine that.

No more having to act twelve. No more biting back what she wanted to say because it wasn't "nice." No more of Mother dressing her in fucking *pink* Wranglers.

And no more Caroline.

Even if she couldn't train unicorns any more, Caroline could make a perfectly good living working with horses. Once she realized what Misty had done to her, she wouldn't want to hang around a short, skinny ex-unicorn-rider who'd cost her a good job.

Misty'd always tried not to think about what would happen when she couldn't ride anymore. The very few riders who didn't grow up and get married became trainers, living like sisters in a closed monastic order. That never had been attractive to Misty before—she didn't have the patience for training—and it sure as hell wasn't an option now.

She didn't want to pop out babies for some goat-roper, and she didn't want to move to Dallas and marry the rich son of one of Daddy's friends.

She wanted Caroline.

But she didn't want Caroline to see her like this. She dried her eyes on a corner of the sheet, pulled herself together, and headed for the shower.

Three minutes later the water was turning lukewarm, and Misty shut it off to leave a little for Caroline. She poked her head out of the closet of a bathroom. Caroline hadn't come in yet.

How long could it take to get a pail of water?

Heart in her throat, Misty yanked a clean pair of jeans out of the drawer and struggled to pull them up her damp legs. Had Vulcan mauled her? Caroline was the best, but she'd never dealt with unicorns in a less-than-virginal state before. Misty fumbled with the buttons on her shirt as she headed for the door, afraid she'd find Caroline bleeding into the sawdust on the stall floor, but as she put her hand on the latch the door opened under it. It was Caroline.

"What took you so long?" Misty shouted. "I thought you were dead!"

Caroline pushed Misty gently back and closed the door firmly behind her. "Misty, maybe it doesn't count."

"What?"

"What we did. I'm not sure it *matters*."

"Well it mattered to me!"

"Me too, but I meant *Vulcan*."

"Oh." Misty paused. "Huh?"

"He was really snappish, but he let me water him and feed him."

"What do you mean 'snappish'?"

"He growled a lot, and pushed me into the wall, and he tried to bite me twice. But he could just be pissed at being locked up all day."

"Did you try to get on him?"

"I..." Caroline looked down. "No."

"Did you even take off the cross-ties?"

Caroline shook her head and didn't look up. "No. Didn't have the guts."

Misty sat down hard on the dinette bench. She didn't know what to think... didn't know if she could afford to hope... didn't even know if she *wanted* to hope.

And then came a familiar screech of "Misty!" The door slammed open, revealing Misty's mother beaming in carnivorous glee. "Misty, you'll never guess!"

Misty's heart tried to climb up her throat. "Mother!" she squeaked.

But Mother was on a roll, and didn't notice that half the buttons on Misty's shirt were in the wrong buttonholes. "Mary Frances

Schwartz got herself gored!"

Caroline paled. "Omigod!"

Misty said "Is she okay?"

"Oh, she's at the hospital, I'm sure she'll be fine. The point is, *she can't ride*! Probably not for months! And with her out of the way, all you have to do is not fall off the stupid animal again, and we'll win the Nationals!" She grabbed Misty by the cheeks and pinched hard. "We'll win!" she sing-songed, bouncing on the balls of her feet. "We'll get our first National championship!"

Misty couldn't keep the image of little Mary Frances torn open and bleeding out of her mind. It was too close to what she'd visualized happening to Caroline. "How did it happen?"

"The stupid little tart kissed a boy. Can you believe it?" She shook her head, and over her shoulder Misty saw Caroline's face drop into an expression of anxiety and dismay. "Now look, we have to get you into your outfit right away. There are going to be lots of photographers waiting in the warm-up arena and my little angel will have to be *perfect*." She turned to Caroline. "And so does Vulcan, so *you'd* better get to work instead of loitering around the trailer." But her habitual nastiness lacked its usual edge—blunted by the thought of Misty's ensuing triumph. She began to fuss at Misty's hair. "What, you've only just showered?" She made a sound of tried patience.

Caroline didn't move. She just stared as though she was afraid she'd never see Misty alive again.

Without turning, Misty's mother said "I thought I told you to get to work."

Caroline blew a shaky kiss to Misty and headed for the barn. Misty opened her mouth to call Caroline back, to say "don't go," but Mother started to unbutton Misty's shirt.

"Good God, child, you're all crooked!"

In her panic over Caroline, Misty hadn't had time to put on a bra. She snatched the front of her shirt closed, backing towards the bedroom. "I can dress myself, Mother."

"Well, you can't prove it by me! Now hurry up, we have to do your hair."

Misty shut the folding door and swallowed her heart back down to its proper position. Her show outfit was hanging on the wall in its protective bag, and the white hat with its pink rhinestone hatband was still in its box on the shelf. She dressed in a daze, more out of habit than conviction.

What could she say? What could she do? What *should* she do? Would Vulcan even let her mount? She wasn't sure which she feared more—Vulcan's horn or her mother's tongue. At least if Vulcan attacked her she'd be dead.

At last she emerged, fully decked out in gleaming white and glittering pink. Her mother looked up from polishing Misty's pink Ropers. "There's my angel!"

Misty thought she might throw up.

Her mother took her by the shoulders and looked seriously into her face. "You're gonna make me so proud."

Misty wanted to say "let's just get this over with." But she put on the best smile she could muster and said "Thanks."

Caroline had Vulcan saddled and ready to go. He tossed his head and sidled, ears back and lips taut. Misty reached out to stroke his neck and he snapped at her. "Easy," she crooned, but he twitched away from her touch.

Misty's mother cast a disgusted eye at Vulcan. "What on Earth is wrong with that animal?" He growled and snapped at her. Mother backed away and turned to Caroline. "You keep him under control, do you hear me?"

"Yes, ma'am." She didn't sound at all certain.

Mother turned back to Misty, her face aglow, and squealed "I'll see you in the ring!"

Once Misty's mother had left, Vulcan sniffed and snuffled Misty all over. She was used to that—she was covered in hairspray and powder for the show ring—but today his examination seemed more intrusive, more urgent. "What do you think, big fella?"

He snorted, which wasn't exactly an answer.

Caroline said "Don't do this, Misty. Mary Frances got gored just for *kissing* a boy."

"You're not a boy." She reached for Caroline's hand, but before she could touch her Vulcan tossed his head and growled. "Whoa! Easy, boy!"

Working together, with pats and whispers and lumps of beef jerky, they managed to get him calmed down a bit. Eventually he let Misty rub his ears and scratch at the base of his horn.

"I don't know..." Misty said, stroking Vulcan's warm cheek. "Maybe he's just a little out of sorts. I think... I think I could ride him."

"And you could get killed trying." Caroline's eyes glistened. "I don't want to lose you!"

"You won't." Misty drew herself up to her full four-foot-eleven. "Not ever. But I have to do this, Caro. I have to try." She started walking.

After a moment Caroline followed, with Vulcan in tow.

They walked Vulcan up to the gate and checked in with the gate steward. He winked and gave them a thumbs-up. Misty smiled weakly back at him.

"Good luck." Caroline's voice was trembling as she handed Misty the reins.

Their fingers met briefly on the reins, and Misty stood abruptly up on tiptoe to kiss Caroline on the cheek. Caroline looked surprised, then a smile spread across her face. The expression made Misty's throat close up and her heart turn over. Flashbulbs stabbed through the semi-dark at them.

Caroline turned toward the stands, stroking her kissed cheek as she walked away.

Misty stood alone in the crowd of unicorns and riders, waiting in the shadow beneath the announcer's booth. A pall of apprehension hovered over them, riders pale and unicorns skittish—the usual pre-class jitters amplified in the wake of Mary Frances' accident. No one spoke.

The loudspeaker boomed and the first rider walked her unicorn out into the floodlights' scrutiny to mount in front of the judge. One by one they trickled away, in ascending order of points for the year, until only Misty remained.

"And finally," roared the announcer, "with four hundred and eighty-seven points, Miss Misty Bell and B.R. Vulcan's Golden Hammer!"

The gate steward swung the gate open and smiled at her.

Vulcan gently nudged her shoulder with his muzzle. They had done this hundreds of times, and he knew the routine. They should move forward into the glare of the arena.

And she knew. She knew that she could ride him.

She licked her lips and took one step forward. And stopped.

The announcer's voice came again. "Miss Misty Bell. Two minutes."

The gate steward looked at her quizzically. Vulcan reached under the brim of her hat to touch her face with his muzzle. His breath was sweet with oats and alfalfa.

All she had to do was walk in, mount, ride this class, and she would win it.

And then she'd win the Nationals, and next year she'd be back here doing it again. And every year after that, as long as her mother's ambition held out.

Her mother's ambition. Not hers.

"Scratch," she said quietly.

"Beg your pardon, Miss Bell?" said the gate steward.

"Close the gate, Harry."

And the ring steward closed the gate, giving the judge a go-ahead wave.

Misty turned and led Vulcan away from the lights of the show ring and out into the peaceful darkness of the fairgrounds. Behind her, the announcer's voice called out "Miss Bell scratches." A mutter of consternation and curiosity ran through the stands, but she just kept walking, putting one pink boot in front of the other, in no particular hurry as she headed back through the evening to the barn.

Her mother caught up to her in the fringes of the barn lights, her face half-lit like a bright half moon. "*How can you do this to me?*" she screeched, face dark with rage above the white leather of her Show Mother suit.

"I'm not going to ride tonight, Mother," she said, her boots firm on the packed earth. She'd expected to be afraid, but she wasn't.

"Listen, little girl..."

"I'm not a little girl, Mother. That's the point."

Caroline pounded up behind Misty's mother. "What happened? Wouldn't he let you mount?"

Misty's mother froze, staring at Misty with dawning understanding and rage. "You. Little. Slut." She clenched her fists, and Vulcan growled a warning. "Who was it?" she hissed.

"That's none of your business."

Misty's mother whirled on Caroline. "You were supposed to watch her! How can you let this happen after all I've done for you?"

Caroline opened her mouth, but Misty cut her off. "You've never done anything for her, you platinum-plated bitch."

Misty's mother gawped at Misty, sputters and gasps of frustrated fury choking in her throat.

"You should go back to the hotel, Mother. Have a drink. We'll talk about it in the morning. And my knee's fine, thanks for asking."

"We'll see how fine you are with no money, you ungrateful little whore."

"Good night, Mother."

Left with nothing else to do, Misty's mother stalked stiff-backed toward the parking lot. Misty felt the muscles in the small of her back unclench.

Caroline could only stare. "Misty... what did you do?"

"I..." Misty slumped. "I think I just got you fired. Oh, Caroline... I'm sorry."

"I won't have any problem finding another job—Jack Thornton's been begging me for two years. But what about you? She's your mother!"

"I couldn't let her treat you like that any more. If I hadn't done something, neither of us would ever have gotten away."

"Misty, what'll you do?"

Misty shrugged, shook her head and couldn't make herself not smile. "I dunno. Maybe Jack Thornton'll let me shovel stalls for him or something." She put her foot in the stirrup and swung up into Vulcan's saddle. He purred and reached around to nuzzle her boot. "I'm going for a ride to clear my head. Will you still be here when I get back?"

Caroline squeezed Misty's knee. "You know it, shorty."

Misty pulled off the pink-rhinestoned hat and flung it into the darkness. Then she nudged Vulcan with her knee, and as they ambled down the quiet aisle between the barns, she shook her hair loose into the cool of the evening.

Ψ

The Ecology of Fairie

THE STAINED ALUMINUM SCREEN DOOR was cold in Dora Huntleigh's hand as she waited in the cool summer night. She stood still for a long time, listening. She heard the hum of the light over the door, the soft rush of traffic on 82nd Avenue, the distant barking of a dog. But no frogs.

Dora worried about her frogs. She enjoyed their soothing, rhythmic *bredeep-bredeep-bredeep*—it reminded Dora of the peaceful suburban nights at the old apartment. When she listened to the frogs she forgot the peeling paint here, the noisy neighbors, the Burgerville grease that clogged her pores. Sometimes she could even forget about Mom, wasting away in a bright sterile room on Pill Hill.

It used to be that the frogs' chirping chorus would pause for only a few moments as she walked across the parking lot past the drainage ditch where they lived. It was as though there were some invisible line at the third parking place, where the woman from 3A always parked her rusty green pickup, and once Dora had crossed that line it was safe for the frogs to resume their song.

But two weeks ago, Dora had noticed that the frogs didn't start up again until she was well past the blue Toyota next to the pickup. Last week they had remained silent almost until she reached her own front door. And tonight...

Just then a single voice called out *bredeep*, then repeated itself. Soon it was joined by another, and another. But they wove a thin fabric of sound, a patchy thing that felt as though the lightest movement would tear it in half.

They're frightened of something, Dora thought, then rolled her eyes at herself. She pulled the screen door open, the harsh rasp of its hinges startling the frogs into silence again, and rattled her key into the lock.

The phone machine's red light blinked at her from the little table beside the door. Her chest tightened at the sight—any phone call could be bad news—but it was only Jenifer, from her old school. "Hey Dora, it's Jen. Haven't heard from you in a while. Give me a call, OK?"

Dora paused with her finger on the button. Jen had been her best friend, and it would be nice to see her again. But it would take an hour and a half on the bus, and then, inevitably, she would have to face The Question: "How's your Mom?"

"Message, has been, erased," said the machine's crisp Japanese-accented voice.

Dora took a shower and scrubbed her face hard, trying to remove every tiny particle of Burgerville from her pores. Then she wrapped herself in her favorite fuzzy bathrobe and opened the freezer, where a Marie Callender's Apple Cobbler waited among the Healthy Choice frozen dinners. "Thanks, Dad," she said aloud, then pulled the cobbler from its box and popped it in the microwave, ignoring the Healthy Choices.

While the cobbler heated, she sorted the mail that lay piled just inside the front door. That was one of her jobs. Bills went in the folder on the kitchen table. Junk mail went straight into the recycling bin. Letters, or anything that might be important, went on Dad's chair where he'd see it when he got home from his four-to-midnight shift at the phone company.

Here was a fat envelope from the hospital. Dora flexed it; was it something important, like test results, or just another bill? She finally put it on the chair unopened — she had already learned more than she wanted to know about alkylating agents, and glucocorticoids, and all the other painful and expensive things they were doing to Mom in the hospital.

The microwave's single clear note, so unlike the calming rhythm of the frogs, jerked Dora from her thoughts. She ate the whole cobbler, washing it down with Diet Pepsi and an ancient re-run of The Cosby Show. She would rather have watched The Sopranos, but that was on HBO and they didn't have cable here.

Leukemia was a bitch.

Soon the cobbler and the Cosby Show were both finished. It was ten o'clock and she was supposed to go straight to bed, but she turned around on the couch and stared out the window instead.

She saw her own reflection — a sixteen-year-old girl with freckles, straggly dark brown hair that refused to behave, and a nose that was too long and had a stupid little bulb at the tip — and the reflection of the TV, and blackness. Dora listened hard, but if her frogs were singing they couldn't be heard over the TV.

She got up and turned off the TV and the lights, then returned to her post, resting her chin on the back of the couch. It smelled dusty. With the lights off she could see the parking lot — cracked asphalt covered with yellow lines and rusty, outdated cars -- and the line of reeds and cattails marking the edge of the drainage ditch. Beyond that, silence and darkness.

No — not quite darkness.

A light was moving among the cattails. A very faint greenish-blue light. Could it be a firefly? She had never seen one before; she didn't think there were any in Oregon — or not any more. She had read that they were dying out because of insecticides and global warming. Like the frogs.

Anyway, the light didn't *move* like an insect. It traveled in a straight line, three or four feet at a time, then stopped dead for a moment before moving off in a different direction. Up, left, right, left, down. And it didn't blink on and off—it flickered, like the light of a TV seen from very far away.

Sitting backwards in the dark, watching that strange faint quivering greenish light moving outside the window, Dora suddenly got a chill that started at the back of her neck and ran all the way down to her tailbone. There was something about that light, about its pale luminescence and deliberate motion, that made her feel very small and defenseless. She felt *watched*.

Dora closed her eyes and shook her head. She was just spooking herself.

But she drew all the curtains and made sure the door was locked before she went to bed. And then she pulled the covers up over her head like she used to do when she was little.

Just before falling asleep she realized she had forgotten to brush her teeth. But even the knowledge that Dad would be disappointed in her wasn't enough to get her out from under the covers.

଼

Dora hated the paper mask she had to wear when she visited Mom. The little metal strip over her nose always pinched somewhere no matter how she adjusted it, and the mask filled up with her breath and smelled like tears, even when she wasn't crying.

Mom didn't look too good today. Her eyes were rimmed with red and black, and they didn't seem to quite focus on Dora when she came in. A few remaining wisps of hair poked out from under her Cubs cap. Why did she want to identify with a team that always lost—especially now? "Hey, sport," she said. "How's my

Theodora?" She reached out a hand.

"I'm OK, I guess," she said. "I'm worried about the frogs."

"C'mere, you. Don't be such a stranger."

Dora took a step toward the bed, but stayed out of reach. Mom looked so fragile, with all the tubes and wires attached to her, and between the disease and the treatment she had almost no immune system. Early in her illness she had caught a cold that Dora brought home from school, and it had nearly killed her. "They're getting so quiet, Mom. It's like they're afraid of something."

"It could just be the weather changing," Dad said, his voice muffled by the mask. "They don't sing when it's too warm."

"Already?" said Mom, and sat up a little. "Where did the spring go?" Dad and Dora shared a quick glance over their masks. Mom had been in the hospital since February. It seemed like a year ago. A lifetime. "I wish I... uh... oh God..." Mom groped for the kidney-shaped plastic dish on the table by the bed, barely getting it into her lap in time to throw up into it. Dora smelled the vomit, even through her mask, even through the smell of tears.

She left the room and sat on the hard plastic chair in the hall outside, knees drawn up under her chin and arms wrapped tight around her legs. She couldn't stand to see Mom throwing up. Through the door she heard the retching, and Dad's voice murmuring reassurances. Dora shivered, though it wasn't particularly cold in the hall.

"You OK? Can I get you something?" It was Nina, one of the nurses. She was Vietnamese and even shorter than Dora, who was small for her age. "How about some cranberry juice?"

"Uh... sure."

The nurse came back with a clear plastic cup. "Here."

"Thanks."

Nina stroked Dora's shoulder while she sipped the juice. "Your mother's a fighter, Dora. She'll come through. She's motivated."

"You really think so?"

"She wants to see you grow up."

"Is that enough to make a difference?" The last word came out half-choked with tears, and Dora was ashamed. She needed to be strong.

"It really is. But she needs to know you're there for her."

Dora finished the juice and handed the empty cup back to Nina. "Thanks. For everything."

But she didn't go back into the room.

Eventually Dad came out and said "She's sleeping now. Let's go home."

၃

In the afternoon Dora visited the drainage ditch with her ecology notebook. So far she had seen water bugs, minnows, dragonfly nymphs, snails, and of course tadpoles and frogs. She had tested the water for some common pollutants. But she still hadn't figured out what was making the frogs so quiet and nervous. She'd done research at the library and had learned that amphibians were dying out all over the world, but nobody knew why for sure, and that wouldn't explain what had changed just in the last few weeks.

She pushed through the reeds at the edge of the parking lot and squidged down into the marshy area by the water. It smelled warm and moist and earthy here—a little icky, but natural and real, not like the sterile artificial smell of the hospital.

There was something strange at the edge of the water—a slippery translucent thing, like a used condom but much smaller. She poked at it with a stick, spread it out so she could see what it was.

It was the skin of a frog, about two inches long. Complete with eyes, toes, and mouth. The frog's stripes and spots were barely visible on the thin translucent surface.

Dora knew that frogs shed their skin, though she'd never seen one do it. But she also knew that they usually ate the skin after shedding it. And this skin didn't seem to have an opening where the frog had taken it off. It was more like something had removed the frog and left the skin behind.

Dora got a nervous feeling and turned quickly around. But there was nothing behind her.

○3

After work that night, Dora went back to the ditch. She brought her flashlight, but she didn't turn it on—instead she waited at the edge of the parking lot until her eyes adjusted to the dark. Whatever was happening to her frogs, and whatever was the source of that strange greenish glow, it was a thing of the darkness, and if she blundered around with a flashlight she'd never see it.

Moving slowly, as silently as she could, she crept through the rustling reeds and squatted down at the water's edge. The frogs shut up as soon as she came near, but after a long time they started in peeping again.

A three-quarter moon illuminated the scene with a cold fluorescent light. Dora's knees started to hurt and the wet ground chilled her feet and her butt. But she remained still. Waiting. Watching.

A *plip* sound in the water to he left gave her a start, but it was just a frog jumping. She settled down and waited for her heart to stop pounding.

Then the frogs shut up again, though she hadn't moved, and she thought she saw something off to her right. Slowly she turned her head. There was a pale, flickering, greenish glow, right at the water's edge maybe three feet away. And at the center of it was something that made her heart contract into a hard cold lump.

It was a tiny human figure, maybe five inches high. Its arms and legs were long and thin, and it had translucent wings like a dragonfly's. It crouched at the edge of the water, slowly raising one arm—getting ready to pounce on a frog, which floated stupidly just a few inches away from it.

Dora flicked on her flashlight to get a better look at the thing.

She wished she hadn't.

Whatever it was, though it was shaped like a human being it had nothing else in common with Dora. Instead of skin or fur it was covered with something hard, glistening, and iridescent—black with purple-green highlights. Its limbs were skeletally thin, with harsh mechanical joints like an insect's; its hands were as disturbingly inhuman as a mouse's clawed feet. The raised hand held a three-inch spear, thin as a needle, with a wicked-looking barb on the end. On its head it wore a leaf, twisted into a cone.

But what really made the breath catch in Dora's throat was its face—huge black eyes and a wide mouth bristling with curved, ragged teeth like fingernail trimmings.

The creature opened its mouth and screeched—a thin sound like two pieces of broken glass scraping together—then it flew into the air. The water riffled in the wind from its wings, which made a rattling hum like a big beetle. Dora kept the flashlight beam on it. It screeched again and flung the spear at her with vicious force.

Dora raised her left hand to ward off the tiny spear. It plunged into her palm with a terrible sharp sting, and stuck out the other side. Dora cried out in pain, but she didn't take the light off the thing.

And there in the light of the moon and the flashlight, in plain sight, it vanished like a candle flame guttering out. One moment it was there, then it flickered and faded and then it wasn't.

Dora darted the flashlight around, trying to tell herself that it had just moved out of the beam. But it wasn't anywhere. It had disappeared. She had seen it go.

She realized she was holding her breath. She let it out with a shuddering rush.

All was silent.

cs

Dora's mouth was dry and she fought to control her breathing. In the warmth and light of her own bathroom it was possible to imagine that she had not just seen a tiny human figure fly and vanish. This spear thrust through her bleeding hand was just a thorn, she had stuck herself by accident, and she would break off the barb and pull it out and put a Band-Aid on it and then it would all be better.

But when she snapped the spear in half it melted away like a tiny flake of ice. She whimpered as she felt it evaporate from her injured hand.

Trembling, she washed her hands thoroughly with soap and water, put antibiotic ointment on the wound — it smelled like the hospital — and stuck a Band-Aid on each side of her hand.

Then she turned on every light in the house, and the TV, and the radio. And she closed all the curtains and huddled, shivering, in her bed.

cs

She shrieked when she felt a touch, but it was only Dad. Somehow she had fallen asleep. The clock said 12:53.

"Hey, tiger. What's with the lights?"

Dora opened her mouth, then closed it again. Swallowed. "I... I had a bad dream. A really bad dream."

Dad sat on the edge of the bed. "Must have been. You OK now?"

She wanted to hug him. "Yeah. Now that you're back."

"I'm back." He looked like he wanted to hug her too. "Want to talk about it?"

"Huh?"

"The dream. Was it about Mom?"

"Uh... no. No. It was... it was bad." A twinge ran through her.

"Hey, what happened to your hand?"

"I, uh, stuck myself making dinner. Don't worry, I cleaned it off and I put on antibiotics."

"That's Daddy's girl." He yawned broadly. "'Scuse me. Sleepytime for Daddy." She hated it when he talked like that, like she was just a little kid, but at the same time it was kind of comforting. "You gonna be OK?"

"I'll be OK."

But she didn't get back to sleep until after three.

❧

"May I help you?" The librarian had a salt-and-pepper beard and a button that said PERFORM A SUBVERSIVE ACT: READ.

"Um, I'm looking for some information on... um, fairies?" Suddenly she felt extremely stupid, but she pressed on. "I mean, you know, little people with wings. Only not Disney."

"Fairy tales?"

"No. Non-fiction."

"Hm." The librarian tapped at his computer. "Let's see what we can do for you..."

Dora left the library with a stack of eighteen books about folk tales, mythology, and Victorian England. There was much more to this whole fairy thing than she'd ever dreamed. She wasn't the first to see one. Sir Arthur Conan Doyle, the author of Sherlock Holmes, had even photographed them!

But once she got on the bus and began to read, she began to doubt herself again. Arthur Conan Doyle had been duped. The books on folk tales and myths were all about psychology or literature—none of them seemed to consider the idea that fairies might actually, literally, exist. The Victorian fairies were cute, frilly, Disney things, not at all like the frightening being she had met. And the one book of "Faery Magick" that seemed to take fairies seriously was full of meaningless woo-woo about "earth spirits" and "focused energy."

She thought about taking a different tack—going back to the library tomorrow, researching insects and other small creatures. She knew that love-starved sailors had once thought that manatees— those huge cow-eyed sea mammals—were mermaids. Maybe what she had seen was really nothing more than a big bug. But the thought of asking the bearded librarian for more help was daunting, and she couldn't really convince herself that any bug could have done what the creature—the fairy—had done.

The one thing she read that resonated with the experience she'd had was that the term *fairy*, or *fair folk*, was a euphemism—like when Mom called the President "our glorious leader." It was a way of talking about them without revealing just how much you hated and feared them.

The really scary thing about that statement was what it implied: that you never knew when they might be listening. They could be anywhere. Even on a noisy smelly bus full of chattering adolescents. And like some invisible carcinogen, they might bide their time for years before deciding to strike.

Unconsciously, Dora clutched her backpack hard to her chest.

 C8

For the rest of that day Dora tried to forget all about the fairy, or whatever it was. She sorted the mail; she washed dishes; she even vacuumed, for the first time in months, and found the missing half of her favorite pair of green socks under the couch. But when the sun went down she made sure the door was locked and kept the lights on and the curtains shut tight.

She went to bed at ten. But at 10:57 she was still awake. Finally she could bear it no more. She kneeled on her pillow and peeked through the curtains over her headboard, peering across the parking lot.

At first she saw nothing unusual, but then as she sighed and started to let the curtain fall she thought she saw movement. Clutching the curtain, its rough weave harsh against her cheek, she blinked hard, then looked again.

Faint, bluish-greenish lights. Not just one. Dozens.

They were moving toward her.

"Oh shit," she whispered, and pushed the curtains closed.

She clutched herself into a little ball with her back against the headboard of her bed as the sounds started. Faint but undeniable, tiny scratching scrabbling sounds that she felt as much as heard through the wall behind her back.

It's mice, she told herself over and over. *Mice mice mice.*

But she knew it wasn't mice. She knew it was malevolent little inhuman claw-hands, and faces with huge black emotionless eyes and mouths full of teeth.

Finally she had to *do* something. She jumped from her bed, turned on the bedside lamp and the radio and the overhead light and the desk lamp. Twisted the desk lamp to shine its seventy-five watts out the window. Flung open the curtains.

There was nothing there. Nothing but the reflection of a terrified sixteen-year old girl.

But in the morning she found hundreds of tiny scratches on the aluminum window frame. Right next to the latch.

೫

"You look *terrible*, sweetie."

Mom didn't look too good herself, but Dora didn't mention that. "I've been having trouble sleeping. Bad dreams." She had sprayed bug repellent all around the window, and that seemed to slow them down some, but they still came every night.

"I'm sorry." Mom reached out a hand. The hospital bracelet was loose on her thin wrist, and catheters were held in place with hospital tape that pulled at her pale skin. "C'mere, honey. Let me give you a hug."

Dora took the hand, but she knew that any contact or pressure hurt terribly, aggravated the pain of the cancer that scraped at the insides of her bones and veins and arteries. She didn't squeeze the hand, didn't move any closer. "I'll be OK, Mom. Don't worry about me. You need your strength."

"I do worry about you, you know. I can't help it. It's part of my job." Mom tugged at Dora's hand, urging her closer, but Dora stood her ground. She didn't want to give her any pain, didn't want to risk infecting her again with some simple little virus that could kill her. A glance passed between them — a brief complex moment of defiance and concern from Dora, of release and resignation from her mother — and the tugging stopped.

"I'll be OK," Dora repeated, though she wasn't at all certain of that.

Mom gripped her hand tightly. "If there's anything I can do, you just ask."

cs

Dora was sorting the mail again. Junk mail. Bill. Letter from Aunt Jacquie. Junk mail. Bill. Junk mail. What's this?

It was junk mail, no doubt, with a bulk rate stamp and addressed TO OUR FRIENDS AT Dora's address, but the colorful envelope caught her eye. It bore a cartoon of a grinning ladybug and the words DEVOURS UP TO 60 APHIDS A MINUTE! ONLY $24.95 PER PINT! FREE DELIVERY!

Dora smiled at the cartoon, and at the thought of buying bugs by the pint. She briefly imagined ordering a pint of them, setting them free in her drainage ditch. The cheery red-and-black insects would swirl around her like the little plastic flakes in a snow-globe, beneficial predators to eat aphids and other harmful pests.

Not that aphids were her problem.

But...

She set down the rest of the mail and sat cross-legged on the floor, staring at the envelope in her hand.

What if...?

cs

She attacked the library books again, with a new agenda. Reading between the lines. Searching for the deeper truths beneath the myths, the legends, the Disney versions. Looking for the manatees behind the mermaids.

There were many kinds of fae creatures, she learned, with different names in different cultures. Fairies. Pixies. Goblins. Leprechauns. Each had its habits and habitats, its preferences and weaknesses.

Its predators and prey?

The information was sketchy, contradictory, unreliable. But there were certain themes that cropped up over and over. Goblins were malicious. Pixies were self-centered and fickle. Fairies could be helpful or hurtful, and appeared at times of transition: birth, puberty, marriage...

And death.

No!

But there was another type of fae, called a hob—a guardian earth spirit, protector of the home, drawn to generous and caring people, and fond of a saucer of milk.

If she just put out a saucer of milk, the only thing she would attract was the neighbors' cat. There had to be something more direct, more concrete.

Most of the spells in the book of Faery Magick were inapplicable, or vague, or unreasonable — where was she supposed to get garnets, or a dram of dragon's blood? But here and there she found a paragraph or a sentence that made sense, a rhyme that resonated with something inside her, a list of ingredients that she could obtain. From these she cobbled together a ritual that felt right.

She couldn't be sure. It wasn't much to go on. But she had to do *something*.

CB

Dora stood barefoot at the edge of the drainage ditch, wearing only a clean cotton nightshirt and carrying a shoebox. The cold mud squidged between her toes, and the light of the full moon rippled on the water.

This is the stupidest thing I have ever done, she thought.

She set down the shoebox on a rock, and from it she drew three shot glasses. She'd found them way at the back of a cabinet and she hoped they wouldn't be missed. Squatting down, she placed them in an equilateral triangle at the water's edge, pressing each one into the mud so it wouldn't tip over. Then she brought a Tupperware container from the box, containing a few cups of milk with several tablespoons of honey mixed in. As she poured an equal quantity into each shot glass, she hoped that 2% milk would be good enough. Finally she poured a line of salt around the three glasses, forming a triangle, careful that it be continuous and connected.

She folded the little metal spout back into the canister of salt and put it back in the box. She stood, facing the moon, and drew in a breath. Then she let it out again.

This is ridiculous, she thought. I can't do this.

But she took another breath, licked her lips, and read from a square yellow Post-It:

"Guardian spirit,
Gentle one,
To my aid
I bid thee come.
Share your wisdom
And your power,
Seek the evil
And devour.
By the Moon's
Magick light,
Come to me
This long sweet night."

Her voice quavered a little, especially on the part about the Moon's Magick light, and she hoped fervently that none of her neighbors could hear or see her, but she got all the way through without stumbling over any words.

She waited.

Nothing happened.

Finally she blew out the breath she hadn't realized she was holding. Well, that was stupid, she thought; I should get inside before I catch my death of cold. She bent and picked up the box.

She was about to gather up the shot glasses as well. The book said they should be left out overnight, but at this point it just felt like compounding her own foolishness. At the last moment, though, she decided to leave them. What harm could it do?

And then, as she was walking away, the asphalt rough under her dirty bare feet... the frogs began to sing. It was a thin chorus, to be sure, but still stronger than she'd heard in a week or more.

Dora washed her feet, put away the Tupperware container and the salt, and crawled into bed.

She fell quickly asleep, and slept undisturbed all night.

CB

One of the boxes at Mom's bedside was beeping when Dora and Dad arrived, a high harsh tone, and Nina was fiddling with her catheters. Finally she did something that made the box shut up. "Thank you," Mom mouthed, but no sound came out. Nina smiled and touched Mom lightly on the shoulder as she left the room.

"Hi, Mom."

"Hi." She had to try a couple of times, and even then it was little more than a croak. "Sorry. I had a rough night." Dad took her hand.

Dora sat on the edge of the bed, wondering what to say. Finally she asked "Is there anything I can do?"

"Just be here with me."

The three of them sat together, watching clouds scud by over the city outside the window and talking about nothing in particular, until suddenly Mom lurched upright, reaching past Dora for the dish on her bedside table.

I coped with fairies, I can cope with this.

Dora grabbed the dish and gave it to her mother, then held her shaking shoulders while she vomited. Dora was shaking too, but she thought over and over: *Guardian spirit, gentle one, to my aid, I bid thee come.* It helped, a little.

Eventually, the episode passed. Dad took the dish away, and Dora brushed the wispy hair from her mother's cold and sweaty face. Her eyes stung with tears, but she sniffed them back.

"Thank you," Mom said after a while. "Thank you for being here."

"It's part of my job."

CB

After that there were good days and bad days, surgeries and therapies, a new school year to prepare for, dishes that still had to be washed... somehow, life went on. But the frogs' song grew stronger and stronger. And once, just once, as she was setting down a paper cup of milk at the edge of the water on a moonlight night, Dora saw something. It was toadlike, a brown and hairy thing the size of a football, with large black eyes and a broad mouth. It smiled at Dora and slipped silently into the water.

She remembered what she had read about hobs, and so she did not thank it.

☙

At the Twenty-Fifth Annual Meeting of Uncle Teco's Homebrew Gravitics Club

MIRABELLA MCALLISTER ARRIVED AT THE meetpoint in Low Earth Orbit by submarine.

One of the new kids, a fifteen-year-old who went by the name Striker, was the first to spot her, a bright brassy glint rising from the deepening blue of the Earth so far below, just as the terminator crossed the U.S. Pacific coast. Typical Mira, to time her ascent for the most spectacular entrance. Striker called out "Hey, I think that's her!" and soon the habitat's viewing lobby fluttered with excited confirmations and speculations. Would Mira's ship be as outlandish as the dragonfly with the sixty-meter wingspan, or as ethereally beautiful as the abstract she'd called *Aurora Occidentalis*? Could her suit possibly outdo last year's feathery vacuum flower, or her co-pilot outshine the blonde who'd accompanied her back in '53?

The whole ensemble would be something spectacular, we all knew that. After all, this was TecoCon 25, and Mira was not one to let a major anniversary pass without a major observance. Which is why none of us had expected Gary to appear.

But, of course, that's exactly why he did.

Gary Shelton had arrived six hours earlier, at exactly 1200 hours Pacific time, exactly 400 kilometers above the summit of Mount Hood, exactly as he always had before *Chimera*. He was still flying the same silver-blue tetrahedron, the *Edison*, its every angle laser-sharp and its four faces still mirror-perfect. Sometimes it vanished from sight for long moments; other times it reflected a bright triangle of swirling clouds among the stars, or formed a hard-edged polyhedron of night against the Earth below. Technically brilliant, mercurial, and showing more of its surroundings than it did of itself; that was the *Edison*.

An uncomfortable silence fell across the airlock lobby when Gary removed his helmet and his beard unfurled into free-fall like a slow explosion. The beard had turned completely gray, and the hair that had been thinning the last time we saw it was now all but gone. Perhaps that reminder of our own mortality was what subdued us all, or perhaps it was the ten years of unanswered questions that came flowing out of his suit along with the beard.

I was the first to break the silence. I excused myself from the conversation I'd been in and kicked off the wall, bringing myself to a halt at a stanchion next to the suit locker where Gary was carefully folding and stowing each segment as he removed it. "Let me help you with that" is what I said, though it's not the first thing I thought.

"Thanks, Ken," he said, and turned his back to me so I could undo his airpack. It was still the same, a fifteen-year-old design but just as elegant and functional as the day Gary designed it. Without a word, I undid the catches as he had silently requested, both of us relying on functional routine to carry us over the awkward chasm of a friendship too long divided. Hilton and Luxus habitats have valets to help with unsuiting, but at the shabby Black Lion Inn where TecoCons were held it was strictly do-it-yourself, and helping friends unsuit is one of the convention's traditions.

After Gary's suit was removed and properly stowed, we shook hands as though we were business people meeting at a professional conference—which, in a sense, we were. Things had changed a lot since the days when we were both "tickling Uncle Teco's feet."

"So..." I said, and at the same time he said "Well...", and we both stopped, and then we laughed a strained little laugh.

I tried again. "So where're you living these days?"

"Boulder," he said, with all that implied.

"Working for Gradient, then? What division?"

"No division. I have my own company now, and five employees. Most of our contracts are with the Big G, sure, but they aren't the *only* game in town."

"Probably doesn't leave you a lot of Up time."

"I get Up every now and again. But I didn't see *your* old rattletrap floating in the parking lot. Flying something new?"

His eyes brightened a bit as he asked the question, and I had to look at his chest. "No. I, uh... I flew Skylark."

"Ken Griswold, taking a *commercial carrier*? How are the mighty fallen!" He said it with that lighthearted mock-seriousness of his, but I heard the true disappointment behind the feigned disappointment.

"I still have *Michelangelo's Dream*," I said with defensive haste. "It's just... I've been too busy to maintain it properly." I swallowed, and looked out the window. "Hey, it's the Northern Lights."

He leaned in toward the glass. "Beautiful," he breathed. No matter how many times Gary came Up, he was one of those for whom the view never palled.

I had pointed out the aurora to Gary so I wouldn't have to admit that my ship hadn't been out from under its tarp in over five years. Unlike him, I'd fallen into the gravity well of the Big G, and now I flew spreadsheets sixty hours a week. But the sight was enough to raise even my spirits. Pale shimmers of pink and blue and gold streamed over the darkened polar horizon, fluttering silently like ribbons in the solar wind.

"This is why we come Up, isn't it?" I said, still looking out the window.

"Partly," he replied, and turned his head so that his reflected eyes met mine. "But mostly it's the people."

Gary's reflection and the aurora blurred together for a moment. "Damn, it's good to have you back."

"It's good to be back."

Six hours later, though, with Mira rising to the meetpoint, I wondered whether he still agreed with that assessment.

I was at the bar, in a crowd of old-timers catching up with Gary (but carefully avoiding the tender spots in our shared history), when Striker called out the news of Mira's approach. Immediately we floated up to the bar's big viewing window, a jostling flock of graying, overweight gravity hackers bumping lightly against each other like a school of tuna. Connie, a New Yorker whose ship looked like the Chrysler Building as a baby, had an image amplifier in her thigh pocket, and it got passed around in a flurry of impatient demands and gawps of wonder. Finally I snatched it from someone's hand and peered through the eyepiece at Mira's rising ship.

It was done up as a submarine. Not just any submarine, either — Jules Verne's *Nautilus*, a Victorian confection of brightly polished copper and brass, sparkling with glass and bristling with filigree and gingerbread. Soft blue and green light rippled from its portholes, adding to the underwater effect. As the ship approached, details became apparent: spiraling sea shells and sensuous mermaids encrusted its hull, and for a figurehead it sported a huge brass narwhal, its unicorn tusk thrusting forward through the vacuum.

"She's still got it," I said, and offered Gary the image amplifier.

He waved it away. "Mira always said her work is best appreciated with the naked eye." The expression on his face was subtle as a fine wine — sorrow and regret and anger mixed together, filtered through the mind of an engineer, and aged for ten years.

Gary and I floated side by side watching the sub grow from a fingerling to a whale. It was easily twice the size of any other ship in the parking lot, and the waves of light from its portholes made that collection of flying teddy bears, Christmas trees, and DeSotos look as though they too were under water. The force of Mira's personality transformed those other ships into mere setting for her latest creation.

Finally, majestically, the sub drew to a halt, and there was a scattering of applause. But Gary and I exchanged a knowing glance. A moment later, the crowd gasped as an enormous chartreuse tentacle came curling up from behind the sub, followed by another, and then another, and then the saucer-eyed head of a giant squid rose into view. The squid wobbled a bit as it inflated, but the illusion was otherwise nearly perfect, and the crowd applauded with greater and greater enthusiasm as the tableau stabilized. Fully inflated, the squid was even bigger than the sub itself; its eyes leered with menace as its tentacles held the sub in a death grip.

Gary applauded as hard as anyone. But his eyes shone with tears.

We moved into the airlock lobby as the applause dissolved into a babble of discussion and speculation. Was that real brass plating over the structural foam, or just paint? Were the squid's seven tentacles an error, or a reference to a movie from the last century? And who was her co-pilot du jour? Gary floated in the middle of it, saying nothing, his expression neutral. Connie came up to him and seemed about to speak, but her unspoken question collided with the look in his eye and she just shook her head and turned away.

Then came the whir of the inner door, and Mira floated into the lobby to thunderous applause. Her suit was done up as a diving suit, of course; a fantasia of a suit with a brass airpack as rococo as the ship. She undogged the helmet, red hair spilling into the air, and smiled her appreciation at the crowd, acknowledging old friends with blown kisses. And then she turned and gestured into the airlock.

Mira's co-pilot poked her head out of the airlock as nervously as a guppy in shark-infested waters, but with Mira's encouragement she slowly drifted into the lobby. "Everyone," Mira announced, "this is Babette."

Above the waist Babette's suit was close-fit, painted to match her own pale skin except for the twin scallop shells over her breasts; the helmet was a transparent bubble that almost wasn't there. Below the waist she wore a fish's tail, encasing both legs and shining with metallic scales in iridescent green. It wasn't much of a handicap in free fall.

I've never understood where Mira keeps finding such gorgeous girlfriends. This one was a blonde, slim and willowy as Mira always preferred, with large expressive eyes and perfect high cheekbones. She looked to be about twenty-five.

Mira herself, as even she would admit, was no beauty, having a long face and a substantial nose. She was fifty-one, the same age as me and a year younger than Gary. But she was a genius with clothing and make-up, her blue eyes crackled with intelligence, and her petite body hummed with creative energy. The substantial inheritance that supported her gravitics hobby didn't reduce her allure, either. But she was a woman of powerful opinions and her temper was legendary. Perhaps that was why her girlfriends rarely lasted a year.

Most of the crowd focused on Babette, who swam through the air with a lithe unconscious grace as she unscrewed her helmet, but Gary ignored her; his eyes were locked on Mira as though she were a closing door between him and Paradise. Mira, in turn, divided her attention between admiring Babette and enjoying the crowd admiring Babette. She contained herself well when she noticed Gary, I'll grant her that; she only nodded to him as she had to so many other old friends. But her eyes kept creeping back to him, then flicking away as she noticed he was still watching her.

Gradually the crowd broke apart, people forming knots of conversation, heading off for technical presentations, or wandering toward the bar. A few hours later I found myself at a gravity table in Foster's, the habitat's most expensive restaurant, with Mira, Babette, Connie... and Gary. I was surprised that Gary had wound up in Mira's dinner group; perhaps one of their other old friends had nudged the two of them together.

The conversation was light and witty, focusing on the latest gravity hacker gossip and the details of the *Nautilus's* construction, but the tension between Mira and Gary was palpable. Have you ever broken a magnet in half? The two halves, once a single unit that not only held itself together but drew other objects to itself, now repel each other. Mira and Gary were the same.

Service in Foster's was abominable, as always, and we'd already finished a bottle and a half of wine when the appetizers came. Connie celebrated the waiter's arrival with the traditional toast to Uncle Teco.

As we sipped, Babette asked "So where is Uncle Teco, anyway?" Her voice had a cultured Southern sweetness, a slow expensive cadence that brought to mind cotillions among the magnolias.

Mira raised her glass to her lips, to hide her expression, and looked at Gary, who smirked and looked at me. It all took less than a second, and Babette didn't seem to notice.

I cleared my throat and said "Uncle Teco is a very busy man. I'm not surprised he wasn't able to be there for your arrival, but I'm sure he'd love to meet you."

"Probably stuck in a meeting with the habitat," said Connie.

"Oh, that's all right," Babette drawled. "I'd hate to make a big important man like him waste his time with insignificant little ol' me."

"No, he's a real sweetheart once you get to know him," I said.

"In fact... tell you what." I reached in my pocket and found a data chip. "I meant to give him this the next time I saw him. Why don't you give it to him for me? That'll give you an excuse to introduce yourself. Oh, and it's pronounced 'Teeco.' Only earthworms say 'Tecko.'"

Babette's eyes didn't budge from mine as she tucked the chip in her décolletage. "That's mighty considerate of you, Ken. But tell me now, what does he look like?"

Gary stepped into the gap. "Just ask anyone, they'll tell you where he is."

Babette nibbled her salad. "I can't wait to meet him. There are so many people here that Mira's told me all about, and they're all so friendly." She took a sip of her wine. "But Gary... you seem to know all the same people as Mira, but she's never mentioned you. Isn't that funny?" The statement seemed perfectly innocent, but in her eyes I saw a glint of the steel behind the magnolia. "And I keep hearing the name Janet Stein. Who's she?"

Gary seemed to crystallize, his expression becoming cold and brittle. Connie's mouth dropped open. Mira reached for the wine, but misjudged and knocked the bottle over. It rolled out of the table field and spun away, leaving a spiral of red droplets wobbling in the air behind it.

Gary didn't notice the wine. "I can't believe you didn't even tell her," he said to Mira. His words were ice-cold, but they boiled at the same time, like water leaking into vacuum.

Mira stared into her empty glass, clutching it with both hands. "I was going to. When the time was right."

"How long have you known her?"

"Eight months," said Babette.

"Eight months," Gary repeated, still looking at Mira, "and you just couldn't be bothered. Too busy with the present to acknowledge the past. How typical."

"*I* couldn't be bothered?" Mira's voice didn't get any louder, but her teeth were clenched. "Who *vanished* for ten years and then came waltzing back as though nothing had happened? Who left me and all our friends to pick up the pieces and move on?"

"It took me ten years to steel myself to see you again." He stood up. "I see it wasn't enough." He stepped out of the table field too quickly and went into a tumble, splashing into a glob of wine the waiter hadn't yet vacuumed up, but he caught himself on the floor with his hand, kicked off against a railing, and shot out of the restaurant.

The four of us stared at each other for a time. Then Mira raised her empty glass. "To *Chimera*." Her voice barely quavered. Connie and I touched our glasses to hers, and they rang in the silence. There was still a little wine at the bottom of mine.

"Mira, honey," said Babette, "Is there something you want to be telling me right about now?"

Mira rolled her glass around on the table with one finger. "Janet Stein died ten years ago," she said at last. "Ten years ago this weekend, at this very habitat. TecoCon 15. *Chimera* was the biggest thing we'd ever done, the biggest thing anyone had ever done. It was too big. It fell apart." She put her head down on the table. "Everything fell apart when Janet died," she muttered into the tablecloth.

"Janet was..." I began, then backed up and tried again. "Janet and Mira and Gary, they were the greatest ship design team TecoCon ever saw, and *Chimera* was their masterpiece. It was like they were one person. Gary was the brains, he pushed the technological envelope. Mira was the heart, she had the artistic talent. Janet... Janet was the soul. The fulcrum."

"I loved her," Mira said almost too softly to hear. The tablecloth under her cheek was dark with moisture.

"Gary loved her too," I said nearly as softly. "And she loved you both."

"She had too much love for just one person." Mira might have been talking to herself. "She had enough love to keep the three of us together. But with her gone, Gary and I spun off in different orbits."

Connie poked at her French onion soup, which had cooled and congealed. "I can't believe he came back after ten years."

The waiter, who had been drifting nearby for some time, cleared his throat. "Would you like your entrees now, or would you rather wait for the gentleman to return?"

"Just bring us the check," I told him. "I don't think any of us are hungry any more."

I went straight to my room after that, where I stayed up too late, emptying expensive little bottles from the mini-bar and staring down at the Earth, a clouded blue eye that blinked away tears every ninety minutes. But the next day, when I dragged myself to breakfast, *Edison* was still in the parking lot and Gary was giving an impromptu technical talk in the lobby. A bunch of new kids orbited around him like so many moons of Jupiter, enraptured by his history of the Yamaguchi coil.

A little while later he tracked me down in the Badger Hole, the habitat's casual restaurant, where I was holding my head and trying to convince myself the habitat's attempt at free-fall eggs was preferable to going hungry. "I suppose you're surprised to see me still here," he said.

"I have to admit I am, but I'm glad."

"It was what Mira said about leaving our friends to pick up the pieces. She made me realize I would be hurting more than just her and myself if I went away again."

"TecoCon really hasn't been the same without you," I said. "Join me for coffee?"

He attached himself to a sticky-strip next to me — no gravity tables in the Badger Hole — and we sat shoulder-to-shoulder, talking earnestly about old friends and looking out at the broad expanse of the viewing lobby. We had a good view of the Earth rolling by, the parking lot full of ships of all sizes and descriptions, and the members of the convention moving between program items or just drifting and talking.

"Hey, there's Babette," I said *sotto voce*, indicating her with a slight motion of my chin.

She was earnestly going from one group to another, her native grace warring with her obvious inexperience in free-fall, asking each the same question. Younger people shrugged or just looked puzzled; older ones gestured emphatically in different directions, and grinned at her back after she left them.

"Still looking for Uncle Teco," Gary said.

I watched her pilgrimage for a while before replying. "I feel a little bad about it."

"Maybe it's time to call off the snipe hunt."

"Yeah," I said. "Maybe it is."

We paid our tab, then looked around to see where Babette had gotten to. I spotted her first; she was pacing back and forth on the gravity landing in front of the men's restroom. She waved at us, rather frantically, and we pushed off from the Badger Hole and headed in her direction. As we floated toward her I wondered what the trouble might be.

Then Mira emerged from the women's restroom, and greeted Babette with a peck on the cheek. She hadn't spotted us yet, but she would in a moment, and I really didn't know what would happen then. Gary had calmed down quite a bit since last night, but there was no telling what Mira might do—I'd hoped to be able to talk with the two of them separately before trying to bring them together again.

So I was thinking more about interpersonal than orbital dynamics when the impact occurred.

We later learned it was a piece of the old Prosperity station, thrown out of its orbit by a close encounter with an unauthorized heavy tripper. If we'd been at the Hilton it would have been vaporized by antimeteorite lasers, but TecoCon didn't have the money for the Hilton, and the Black Lion Inn was too old and too cheap for a comprehensive space junk defense. So a couple hundred kilos of plastic and metal slammed right into the lobby's big viewing window, splaying a white spiderweb of cracks all the way across it.

The sound of the impact was like five crystal chandeliers all crashing to the ground at once. For a moment after that there was a breath-holding silence, but then came a sound I hope never to hear again—a groaning, creaking, and crackling, accompanied by a sharp increasing hiss of escaping air, as the fractured window began to bulge outward.

"Oh, shit," Gary said, just before the klaxons started.

Most of the TecoCon people were experienced space hands. They reacted quickly and with minimal panic, scrambling quickly for exits and refuges as emergency doors began to slide closed. But Babette and Mira stayed right where they were, arguing over something. We would be there in just a few more seconds, but by the time we arrived it might be too late to make it to the nearest exit before the doors sealed.

Gary reached over and gave me a shove, propelling himself toward Babette and Mira and me toward the nearest emergency door. I had enough velocity to reach it before it closed.

Leaving Gary, Mira, and Babette behind.

I grabbed an aluminum cross-brace and reversed my course. A moment later I was stumbling into the gravity field of the men's room landing.

"Couldn't reach it," I said.

I never could get a lie past Gary. "Damn fool," he said, and shook his head.

Mira pounded on the men's room door actuator with the heel of her hand. "Someone's trapped in there," she said, "and the door's stuck!"

"Leave it!" said Babette, tugging at Mira's sleeve."There's no—"

Gary pushed both women away from the door. "It's the

pressure drop." He licked his palm, slapped it over a grille on the door's control panel, and pressed hard, pushing the actuator with his other hand. The door slid open—he'd fooled it into opening by raising the pressure at the sensor. "Hello!" he called, holding the door open, but no answer came back.

"We'll have to get him out!" said Mira, and ran inside.

Babette's panic only deepened. "Mira! Come back!"

Gary looked back at the shattered window and closing emergency doors. "No more time!" He grabbed Babette's arm and ran into the bathroom with her. I followed.

The door slid shut. A moment later came a sound like a greenhouse being torn in half, and then—silence.

The silence of vacuum.

The door strained against its seals as though someone large, heavy, and invisible were leaning against it from this side. It was airtight, like any door in an orbital habitat, but this restroom wasn't a designated blowout refuge so there was no guarantee it would stay that way.

Gary, Mira, and Babette lay gasping in a heap on the tile floor. I leaned heavily against the wall and slid down to a sitting position, clutching my knees to my chest to keep my hammering heart from bursting right out of my ribcage.

"That was too close," I said at last.

"Everyone all right?" asked Mira.

Gary said "I'm okay, but my phone's dead. The local repeater must have been damaged in the blowout."

While Babette and I checked our phones—equally dead—Mira peered under the partitions into the stalls. There were two of them, and two urinals; there was no other exit, and no place for a person to hide. "Where is he?"

I had a horrible thought. "Mira, did you actually see anyone go in here?"

"No, but Babette told me she was waiting for someone to come out..."

Gary's face showed he'd had the same thought as me.

We all looked at Babette. Her face was stony. "Yes. It was Uncle Teco."

"Oh God," said Gary, and he shook his head slowly. Mira sighed heavily and put her face in her hands. Her shoulders shook, but I couldn't tell if she was laughing or crying. Maybe both.

Babette gave me a look as hard and cold as the vacuum outside the door. "This is all your fault! You sent me on a wild goose chase!" She pulled the chip from her cleavage and threw it at me.

I let it bounce off of me and land on the floor. It clattered lightly across the tiles. "Guilty."

Babette sat down on the floor and pushed back her hair with both hands, holding her head as though she were trying to keep it from exploding. "I *tried* to tell y'all... Why wouldn't y'all just save yourselves?"

Gary and Mira looked at each other across Babette. Their shared history stretched between them like a strand of barbed wire wrapped around both their hearts. "Babette," I said as gently as I could, "nothing you could have said would have kept either of them from trying to help someone in a vacuum emergency."

"Janet's faceplate blew off when *Chimera's* hull gave way," Gary said in a voice that echoed from a well ten years deep. "There was nothing we could do but watch her die."

"If only I had taken as much care on her suit's seals as I did on the paint job..." Mira whispered.

"It was my spaceframe design that failed," said Gary. "The suit would have been fine if the hull breach hadn't been so catastrophic."

"The inquest held that it was faulty materials in both the frame and the suit," I explained quietly to Babette. There was no point in repeating the fact to either Gary or Mira; I knew that facts alone could not open the locks of their personal hells.

Mira crumpled into a ball under the sinks. "I can't believe how much it still hurts," she muttered to her knees, then raised her head to Gary. "How could you bear to see me again, after the pain I've caused you?"

"I hoped that ten years might be enough time for you to learn to forgive me. Besides, I couldn't pass up the twenty-fifth convention." Gary's throat worked, and two little wrinkles appeared between his eyebrows. I thought it meant he was about to cry, but then I swallowed too.

My ears popped.

"The pressure's dropping," I said.

It didn't take us long to find the problem; the seal at the bottom of the door was hissing audibly. "Damn it," I said, "when will people learn not to step on the floor seal!" We stopped the leak with wet paper towels, but it had obviously been going the whole time we'd been in here. Gary and I both knew what that might mean.

"Do either of you have a gavel?" he said.

TecoCon had been using the Black Lion Inn for almost twenty years now, and some of us had managed to wangle key cards with staff access privileges. For reasons unknown, the staff called them "gavels." But neither Mira nor I had one on us.

"I do." Babette dug in her little purse and handed the card to Gary.

Before I could ask her where she had gotten it, Gary slotted the card into the maintenance panel next to the light switch, which obediently popped open. "Damn." He tapped the oxygen meter. "Empty."

"How can we be out of air already?" said Mira. "We haven't even been in here for an hour!"

"In an interior room like this," Gary explained, "the emergency air system is only designed to maintain the balance of oxygen and carbon dioxide if the ventilation goes. With the overall pressure dropping, the stupid thing did its best to maintain the partial pressure of O2 by releasing more oxygen. That masked the larger problem until its little tank was empty."

"So how long do we have?" I asked.

Gary eyeballed the room. "Call it 50 cubic meters, standard orbital pressure, four people... maybe five hours."

"We can't just wait for help," said Mira. "I was stuck for more than five hours when we had that airlock problem back in '51, and that wasn't even a full-blown emergency."

We explored the space, but there wasn't a lot to work with — even the storage for paper products was outside the room. "Maybe there's frost on the outside of the door," Mira said. "We could warm it with our hands, thaw out a message."

Gary brought a hand to within a centimeter of the door, then drew it back. "Our fingers would freeze first."

"What if we poked a little hole in the door seal, sent out a streamer of cloth?"

The two of them batted ideas back and forth like Ping-Pong balls for the next couple of minutes, falling into an old familiar rhythm — Mira coming up with wild, offbeat ideas and Gary figuring out how they could be made practical. Or, unfortunately, determining that they couldn't.

"If we all yelled together..." said Babette.

I looked around. "Not much point. There's vacuum outside those two walls, and on that side is the women's room — even if there's anyone there, they're in no position to help us. What's back there?"

Mira had been the convention's liaison with the habitat for a couple of years and knew the floorplans by heart. "The bar. But it opens to the lobby, and I don't think it had an emergency door."

Gary pounded on the back wall and got the tinny thud of sound vanishing into a void. "Vacuum. How about above and below?"

"The whole lower level is air and water tanks. Above..." she pondered for a moment. "I think it's the Mueller Ballroom."

Gary looked up. "That explains why the ceiling is soundproofed."

We all stared at it. Thick tiles of acoustic foam, and above that probably half a meter of ducts and lights. All of us shouting together wouldn't be enough to be heard through that. But on the other side would be people who could help us.

We tried shouting, anyway. We tried standing on the toilets. We tried standing on the sinks. Gary tried lifting Mira up. Nothing got us through the foam. The closest we came was when Gary and I together lifted Babette, who scratched at the ceiling with her fingernails for a few moments before we all collapsed in a heap.

We lay gasping for a while, considering our options. They didn't look good.

"I'm sorry about the Uncle Teco thing," I said to Babette. "If I hadn't sent you off on that snipe hunt none of us would be here now."

"I just don't understand it," she said. "Y'all're so smart—why'd y'all have to go and play a dumb prank like that?"

"Sending new kids to look for Uncle Teco is an old tradition," Gary said. "It's a way of making sure they meet everyone and visit every part of the convention. And helping to pull the same gag on the next one in line makes you feel like you're part of a secret society."

"But if there's no Uncle Teco... why is the convention named after him?"

Mira sat next to Babette and put an arm around her shoulders. "The convention's named after an old Internet mailing list," she said. "Uncle Teco's Homebrew Gravitics Club. Most of the people who started TecoCon met through the list. But there was never anyone named Uncle Teco. I don't know why it was called that."

"It was before your time," Gary said. Though it was easy to assume Mira had been with us from the beginning, she hadn't

shown up until TecoCon 3. "Babette, do you know what a
Yamaguchi coil is?"

"It's the... whatsit that makes ships go Up. Gradient makes
them."

"Close enough. Back in the Twenties it wasn't just Gradient—
there were dozens of companies making coils. The technology was
still fresh; every couple of months someone would bring out a new
improved model and we'd all jump on it. And there was a period of
about six months in '23 when the best and hottest coil was a
Shreveport Gravitics semi-super with part code NCATCO. We
called it Unca' Teco."

"It was a bitch to stabilize," I said, remembering the smell of hot
solder and cheap beer. "I once stayed up until five in the morning
'tickling Uncle Teco's feet' and even so the damn thing flipped right
over the first time I took it Up."

"Ken and I started the list in May of '23, so the name was
obvious. But by the time of the first TecoCon the hot coil was the
Lift Systems GravBlazer and Uncle Teco was already forgotten. We
kept the list name out of nostalgia, but I bet there aren't five people
at this convention who remember who he really was. Not even you,
Mira."

But Mira wasn't listening to Gary. Ever since I'd told my last
story her eyes had gone all distant. "We've been going about this all
wrong," she said. "We have to turn the problem on its head. Can
you rewire it, Gary?"

I didn't follow her at first, but Gary's face lit up. "I think so, but
it'll be a heck of a drop."

"Better a broken leg than asphyxiation. But what if we all stood
on *our* heads first?"

A few minutes later Mira, Babette, and I were on our heads,
with our backs against the walls and our feet in the air. Gary,
having tried several ridiculous positions, had finally given up and
was simply standing by the maintenance panel. "This is going to

hurt," he said, and reached in and twisted a control.

With a stomach-wrenching jerk, the room turned over — or rather, the gravity field provided by the room's Yamaguchi coil did.

We fell two meters to the ceiling, crashing through the foam and winding up in a tangle of ductwork and electrical wiring. The two toilets flapped open, drenching me with water, but Mira and Babette were against the other wall and stayed dry. Gary landed on his side; he said he was "in a world of hurt" but nothing seemed broken.

We struggled to our feet, as disoriented by the sight of sinks and toilets above us as by the gravity shift. The few undamaged lights shining up from our feet gave the whole scene a surreal quality. But we soon cleared a square meter of ceiling and began stomping out an SOS.

It turned out the Space Guard was setting up their command post right there in the ballroom. They cut through the floor and had us out of there in less than an hour.

಄

I brought Babette a cup of Red Cross coffee, with cream and sugar, and we sat side by side on a folding cot. All around us people bustled, pointing at charts and yammering into communicators, while on another cot nearby a medic was splinting Gary's sprained wrist. Mira was sitting with him.

"So," I said to Babette, "when did you figure out that Uncle Teco was a wild goose?"

"As soon as I saw the look Mira gave you when I asked about him."

That took me aback. "You knew all along? So why did you go around looking for him anyway? And why did you tell Mira you thought he was in the bathroom?"

"Well... getting the two of them together at dinner didn't work because Gary just ran away again, but I figured if I could lock them into an enclosed space for a while they might work things out. And a 'dumb blonde' on a snipe hunt can learn an awful lot about a habitat, like which bathrooms have only one entrance and which of the staff can be sweet-talked out of a gavel card." She glanced over at Mira, who was talking quietly with Gary. "It worked, too, though not at all the way I'd planned."

"Why?" I asked at last.

"The only way she and I could ever have a future together was to lay Janet's ghost to rest, and the only way to do that was to reconcile her and Gary."

I thought about that for a long while. "My hat's off to you." I raised my paper coffee cup. "To forgiveness."

She tapped her cup against mine. "To the future."

ᚳ

Mira came back the next year with a ship called *Uncle Teco*, a huge Macy's Thanksgiving Parade balloon of a ship in the shape of a roly-poly man with big feet. Gary helped her out with the engineering, though he admitted to me she didn't really need his help any more. That was a good thing, because he was so busy helping to put together the convention's technical program he didn't have a lot of time to work on art ships.

Babette came back with her. Many people were surprised, but a few of us knew just how much steel there was in that magnolia. And Mira was happier and more creative than she'd been in years.

And me? I fixed up *Michelangelo's Dream* and came to the convention under my own power.

The view from the pilot's seat was spectacular. But, as Gary said, it was mostly the people that made the trip worthwhile.

ᚳ

Love in the Balance

THEOPHILE NUNDAEMON CLOSED THE book, shaking his head over the images he'd found therein. So sad, so mad... he closed his eyes and set the book aside, a few maroon particles of the decaying cover dusting the ormolu surface of the table.

Unobserved, a cleaner descended silently and snuffled the debris away. It sniffed at the book as well, but Theo's scent on the cover indicated this was no discard. The little creature puffed itself up to grapefruit size and drifted off to its nest in the corner of the room. Immature cleaners peeped supersonically and opened wide their jaws.

Theo opened his eyes and stared out the window. Beyond the glass loomed the fog of endless night, and bulbous shapes drifting. Here and there a spotlight picked out the sigil of one or another House on a pennant or tail fin. The red bat of the Unknown Regalia... the silver spoon-and-circle of Theo's own Guided Musings... and there, the gilded fish of the Pulp Revenants. Angrily Theo twisted the brass and crystal handle beneath the worn sill, and wooden slats snapped shut over the view.

How *dare* Kyrie summon the zombies again — on this day of all days, and upon the Musings of all Houses? How *dare* she?

Theo picked up the book and shoved it back on the shelf. That compendium of ancient lore and legends was nearly as useless as the endless mutterings of the House Fathers. He paced before the shuttered window, heedless of the books' shuffling and muttering as they rearranged themselves alphabetically, and lit his pipe. Then a low familiar foghorn sounded outside the window, and Theo sighed and opened the shutters.

Looming from the dark and fog came the nose of the *Grand Edison III*—the personal airship of Kyrie Strommond, the flagship of the Revenants, and the long-estranged lover of Theophile Nundaemon.

Theo still felt fondly toward the *Edison*, and he knew that, despite everything, she still held some warmth in her engines for him. But those cooling ashes of love would be no protection at all from the zombie warriors the *Edison* now bore within her gravid silver hull. For fluttering from the foremast was Kyrie's own sigil— Capricorn on a field of stars.

That damnable goat.

A tear gathered in the corner of Theo's eye. "Zenobia," he called to his personal servant. "Prepare my zeppelin gun."

Not waiting for a response, Theo strode from the library and descended the brass-railed oak spiral stair to his quarters. There he shrugged on his black wool overcoat, with the high, stiff collar and gold-braided epaulets of a Commander of the Musings. He descended two more flights, then took a long corridor—his thudding boots raising dust from the worn carpet below portraits of long-dead zeppelin captains—to the reception bay, where the house slaves had already opened the doors and extended the boarding ramp to meet the descending *Edison*. A cold, damp breeze blew in from the endless night. Theo fastened his top coat button.

Theo stood silent, marinating in memory and regret, as shouting slaves tossed lines to the *Edison* and made her fast. Then her hatch opened, the boarding stair unrolling itself like a great slatted tongue, and Kyrie Strommond descended to the ramp, majestic in the green uniform of a Commander of the Revenants.

Though the threads of gray in her hair now outnumbered the black, Kyrie was still a handsome woman, with keen, intelligent green eyes and clear, pale skin. But the mouth tightened in a hard line as she saw who had come to meet her. "Honor to you, Theophile," she said, "and honor to your House."

"Honor to you, Kyrie," he replied, "and honor to your airship."

It was a calculated insult, barely within the bounds of protocol, but his only reward was a single blink. Despite himself, Theo had to admire her steel. It was a shame they could never be friends.

"I require quarters for my troops," she said, "as stipulated by the Compact."

"That may be... difficult. At this time of year. How many?"

"Three hundred." At that, Theo blinked. So large a contingent had not been seen in centuries. What could the Revenants be planning? "But they require no food or water, and only the minimum of space."

"Of course." He escorted her to an alcove in the wall, where a wooden model of the House of the Guided Musings floated in the air. He touched one of the brass knobs that studded its surface, and the model obediently split open, revealing the warren of rooms and corridors within. Thousands of tiny wooden pegs populated the spaces — mahogany for men, maple for women, fir for slaves — their fitful motion reminding Theo of a disturbed anthill. "As you see," he said, "the Reunion Day crowds have already arrived."

Naturally, since this model was in a public space, much of the information was lies. But Theo's lip quirked in amusement at the two pegs, maple and mahogany, that stood by the alcove in the model's reception bay.

Theo turned the model this way and that, opening and closing its various sections. "Ah, I believe the children's squander-ball games can be moved from the lesser gymnasium. Would that do?"

Kyrie pondered the model gymnasium, as though trying to discern its size. The model did not show the steel doors and mantraps that surrounded it, of course, but Kyrie would be looking for tell-tale voids and discontinuities. Theo sweated under his heavy coat. He had supervised the reconstruction of the Red Diamond section himself, and the model's complex of feints and deceptions was superb, but Kyrie was a formidable strategist.

"Yes," she said at last, "that will suffice."

Theo pointed out the route from the reception bay to the gymnasium. "Your troops will be escorted, to prevent them losing their way."

"Thank you." She gave a smile that appeared nearly genuine.

As Kyrie returned to the *Edison*, Theo climbed an aluminum ladder to the glass-enclosed mezzanine. There he stepped to a brass trumpet set in the wall and pulled the chain for privacy. Immediately the reception bay's clatter and banging were stifled to a dull mutter, accompanied by a feeling of pressure in Theo's ears.

The grating voices of the House Fathers emerged from the trumpet. "What does Kyrie plan?" they demanded without preamble.

"There can be little doubt she will attempt to take the House, most likely tonight," he replied. "I have quartered her troops in the lesser gymnasium."

"Excellent. We will transfer Cherub and Centaur divisions to that section immediately."

"You must also prepare to cut the section loose, if necessary. Even with all our preparations, three hundred zombies are a formidable force."

The Fathers muttered in consternation, but finally replied "We will begin the calculations. We hope it will not come to that."

"As do I." Theo hesitated. The final element of his defense plan would be highly controversial, and he considered keeping it to himself until the thing was done. But the long habit of duty compelled him to speak. "There is one other thing."

"What?"

"Kyrie's airship. The *Grand Edison*."

"What about it?"

Theo swallowed. "I intend to kill her."

At that the Fathers' chorus fragmented into a confused babble. "...impossible... unprecedented... against the Compact..."

"Hear me out!" Theo shouted into the trumpet, his throat tight with rage and anguish. "Even if we prevail in this battle, the Revenants have made it clear that they will not hesitate to summon the zombies again and again until they achieve complete domination. They have bent the Compact nearly to the breaking point already. Killing the *Edison* will only complete a process that the Revenants began. And without her, their strength will be reduced to the point that the other Houses can once again balance them. We can restore the spirit of the Compact only by breaking its letter."

Theo's outburst silenced the Fathers for a long moment. "We cannot officially sanction such an action," they replied at last.

"I understand." The privacy field pressed in on Theo's head like a vise. "Any action I take will be my responsibility alone."

Theo took a moment to compose himself before returning to the floor of the bay, where the zombies were already lining up. The smallest of them was over six feet tall and heavily muscled, and their dead gray skin and lifeless eyes hinted at their incapacity for pain and fatigue while belying the speed of which they were capable. Each wore a poison-green uniform, with Kyrie's Capricorn sigil at the shoulder, and carried a heavy spider-rifle. Theo noted that the rifles' bores and magazines were exactly at the limit prescribed by the Compact.

A company of Musings troops, uniformed in black with Theo's own trident-and-anvil on their shoulders, confronted the zombies with razor-whips at the ready. Theo nodded in approval; standard-issue confusers would be of no use whatsoever against zombies.

The last zombie marched off of the *Edison* and lined up with its fellows. "This is Sergeant Shrive," Theo said to Kyrie. "He and his men will conduct your troops to the gymnasium. Once they are settled, would you do me the honor of joining me for dinner?"

"The honor would be mine," she replied.

"It will be a formal occasion, of course."

They leveled stares at each other like lances at a joust. Under the Compact, a formal dinner was a web of obligations and prescribed courtesies, offering many opportunities for insult. The Revenants' last three battles had all begun over protocol violations at formal dinners -- one of them might even have been justified.

As the invited party, Kyrie had the choice of wine. "I have an Upwelling Iris '623 in my cellars. Would that be appropriate?"

"Delightful," Theo replied. The Revenants always used poisons from the cadenine family with that vintage; he made a mental note to issue the appropriate antidote to his steward. "One of my men will bring you to my quarters at seven bells."

They bowed stiffly to each other, sealing the invitation. But with the formalities concluded, Theo had one more request. "As you may know, I once served aboard the *Edison*. While you are seeing to your troops' comfort, may I come aboard for a visit? An *informal* visit."

Kyrie hesitated. Theo knew she was torn between denying him the intelligence he would gain and granting him the pain and distraction the visit would cause. "Certainly," she said at last. "My captain will escort you."

Theo smiled a grim little smile. As he had expected, Kyrie's sadism had won out over her strategic judgment. His strategem had succeeded, but now he would have to live with the consequences.

The captain was a lean, cadaverous man who seemed half zombie himself. He conducted Theo across the creaking boarding ramp, stretched across infinite blackness from the House of the Guided Musings, and up the *Edison*'s warm and faintly pulsing steps. Once inside, Theo was assaulted by an appalled nostalgia — his old lover's familiar halls, railings, and wainscotings were now covered with a gray coat of fireproof military paint, and oak sideboards had been replaced by racks of laser-guided scramblers.

Theo was led on a circuitous route to the airship's audience chamber. The route itself told him much—clearly something major had been installed on deck three between the fore and mizzen engines, and the captain didn't want him to see it. He thought it might be a bay for boarding-craft, but then the scent of hydrazine in section twenty-five told him it was even worse: guided missiles. Inwardly he trembled, even as he continued counting men at duty stations and analyzing the upgraded fire-fighting systems.

"This is the audience chamber," the captain said unnecessarily. "You may have ten minutes."

"Thank you," Theo said, and slipped down through the opened hatch.

Unlike the rest of the ship, here nothing had changed. It was still close and moist and warm, echoing with the thrum and gurgle of the great zeppelin's life fluids.

"Hello, Theo." The airship's voice was warm and maternal, but still gave Theo an erotic tingle.

"Hello, Edie."

"I'm surprised you came. I thought you wouldn't want to see me."

Tears pinched at the back of Theo's throat, but he refused them. "I... it was a hard choice, Edie. But, the way things have been going lately, I thought it might be my last chance for a while." Maybe forever, he thought.

"I'm sorry, Theo." Warm pseudopods extended from the wall and rubbed his shoulders, and Theo relaxed for a moment into the familiar touch. "Kyrie is keeping me so busy these days."

Theo sat up and brushed the pseudopods away. "Yes, I know. That's what I'm here to talk with you about."

The seat of Theo's chair stiffened and grew cool. "The answer is still no."

"Damn it, Edie!" Now the tears did come, though he sniffed them back. "How could you abandon the Musings—how could you abandon *me*? I loved you!"

"And I loved you too. But the Revenants are the future, Theo. Why can't you see that? The Musings, the Regalia, the Apocrypha... they're trying to hold on to the sky by their fingernails. How many Houses have gone down in the past year?"

"Eight," he replied automatically.

"Eight," she repeated, "and madly flapping the Compact isn't going to keep the rest in the air forever. As long as each House holds its thaumaturgies and technologies close to its vest, each will float or fall on its own... and each one that falls takes all its secrets with it. Only by pooling our best ideas do we have a chance to keep what remains of humanity aloft."

"The Compact has provisions for information sharing."

"The system isn't working, Theo. The lesser Houses — the ones that float lowest and are closest to losing buoyancy — are naturally the most driven to create new techniques. But because of their reduced status, none will trade with them, and so they fail, and so their learnings are lost to us."

"And the Revenants' forced labor and torture are better?"

"We've already learned so much, by combining the work of the Whistlers and the Philosophers and the Radiant Ones. Once all the Houses are united under Revenant guidance, we will surely find the final solution. And then these unfortunate practices can be brought to an end."

"'Unfortunate practices'? 'Final solution'? Edie, what's become of you?"

"Nothing's changed, Theo. I'm still trying to do what I was built to do — keep you all alive, in the best way I know how." The sounds behind the walls changed, as though the great airship's heart were beating more slowly. "Whether you understand it or not."

The hatch opened, sending the harsh military light of the cabin above into Theo's stinging eyes. "Time's up," said the captain, and without a word Theo climbed out of the audience chamber.

He thought he heard "I love you, Theo," as the hatch closed. Perhaps it was only his imagination. But as the captain walked him back to the boarding ramp, he pushed the question out of his mind and focused on the enemy airship's defenses.

Seven bells. Theo paced his dining room, sweating in his dress uniform. Five battalions of the Musings' best troops were hidden in the walls around the lesser gymnasium. Tanks of acid were pressurized and ready to spew, frenzied eagle-cats snarled and battered great wings against the walls of their cages, and trans-dimensional fields strained the vertices of their dark crystals. All was in readiness, but the forms of the Compact must be observed.

As the sound of the seventh bell echoed away down the oak-walled corridor, the door opened and two men in radiation armor escorted Kyrie in. A tiny constellation of five pea-sized diamonds orbited above each of the epaulets of her dress uniform.

"So pleased you could join me, Kyrie." He proffered his arm. "May I show you to your seat?"

"Why, thank you." Her uniform sleeve was lined with ceramic plates, which struck rigidly against the defensive field grid sewn into his own.

He pulled out her chair—the one facing the door, as required—and brushed off the seat with his handkerchief. She sat, and he helped her to push in her chair.

Kyrie peered at the table. All the cutlery was in the proper positions. The napkins were folded appropriately for the time of day and the season. The number and size of servants were within prescribed limits. Theo was certain there was nothing Kyrie could use to provoke an incident. "What a charming table."

Theo bowed, and called for the first course. A serving cart rolled out on silent rubber wheels, parked obediently by the table, and raised its silver dome, revealing fairy shrimp steaming in a glistening brown sauce. The steward carefully ladled out a precise portion on each plate.

Kyrie took a bite... and immediately spat it out. "This tastes like shit!" she said.

"Yes," Theo said, and smiled. "My own, to be precise."

Kyrie sat, mouth open, too stunned to say anything.

"I decided to cut short the agony of waiting and give you your opportunity to attack in the first course."

"You..." Then she snapped her mouth shut and gave him a brief bow of acknowledgement, not taking her eyes off him. "Very well. I, Kyrie Destinia Strommond of the Pulp Revenants, do take the gravest offense at this violation of protocol, and under Article XVII, Section 7 of the Grand Compact of Humanity, I invoke my right to restitution." And then she clapped her hands together and vanished with a blue flash, leaving behind the tingle of thaumaturgical energies and the smell of ozone.

Theo bent down and spoke to the brass trumpet fastened to the arm of his chair. "We are at war."

"Acknowledged," came the voices of the Fathers, and alarms sounded throughout the House.

Throwing his napkin on the floor, Theo hurried up the spiral stair to the library. The bookshelves had already been cleared away, replaced by screens and crystals showing views from throughout the House and the air nearby. On one screen, zombies in pale shimmering armor waded through hip-deep acid, their spider-rifles spitting poisonous metal spiders at the defenders. On another, an enormous zombie, stripped to the waist, mowed through Theo's black-uniformed troops with a broadsword in each hand.

But Theo's attention was riveted to the three-dimensional display in the center of the room, a rotating web of crystal threads that depicted the House and the airships nearby. With the exception of the *Edison*, they were all Musings ships; on Reunion Day, all members of each House would be with their loved ones. And the Musings' best zeppelins were no match even for the *Edison* in which Theo had served, never mind her new configuration.

Nonetheless, Theo ordered his zeppelins into combat. *Tarantella* and *Eagle Scout* immediately slipped their moorings and drove ponderously toward the *Edison*, followed shortly by *Razor* and *Wedgwood*. *Edison* responded smartly, whipping out of her berth with the full power of her seven enormous engines. She began hammering the Musings' airships with missiles, lasers, and black coruscating webs of arcane energy; soon *Razor* and *Eagle Scout* had been reduced to embers, fluttering down into the endless dark, and *Tarantella* was listing badly.

Theo cursed the loss of life, but the attack had achieved the desired effect: it had brought *Edison* out into the range of his zeppelin gun. He ordered his first subcommander to take charge of the aerial defense and clambered up the ladder to the highest point in the House.

Zenobia had done well. The zeppelin gun gleamed, its long brass barrel polished to perfection, its sights precisely aligned, its every nickel-plated wheel and lever gleaming bright. The harpoon was loaded and charged, humming with electricity and shimmering with thaumaturgical energies.

This one harpoon had cost nearly half of Theo's defense budget five years ago. The arguments had gone on for months. Now he was vindicated, and nothing could have made him more miserable.

Theo stepped into the zeppelin gun's shoulder braces and placed his hands on the grips. The dome overhead divided smoothly, letting in a wedge of night and fog. He peered through the gunsight at the *Edison*, heeling hard to the right as it unleashed a flight of missiles at *Wedgwood*. With only the one harpoon, he had to be certain of his aim.

"Commander!" cried his second subcommander from the room below. "The zombies are breaking through into the Blue Star section!"

Theo spat out a curse, then spoke into the trumpet to the House Fathers. "Cut loose the Red Diamond section immediately."

"Acknowledged." A new set of alarms sounded, ear-shattering and urgent. On the displays, those Musings troops not directly engaged with the enemy dropped their weapons and ran; in the library, subcommanders and lieutenants began securing equipment.

The voices of the House Fathers sounded over the public address system. "The Red Diamond sector will be separated in sixty seconds." It was the first time Theo could recall the Fathers speaking to the entire House at once.

"Fifty seconds." In the sight, the *Edison* had finished off the *Wedgwood* and was turning to strafe the House. She would be closer than the gun's minimum range in less than a minute. He engaged the harpoon's tracking, evasion, and anti-thaumaturgical systems.

"Forty seconds." Theo breathed a prayer and pressed the firing stud. The floor shuddered and, with a scream of superheated steam, the harpoon flung itself out of the gun, trailing its cable behind.

"Thirty seconds." Steam obscured Theo's view. The floor thrummed as the cable paid out. Theo cursed, over and over.

"Twenty seconds." The view in the gunsight cleared just as the harpoon pierced *Edison*'s silvery envelope. The great zeppelin twitched all over at the impact, then convulsed as a mighty charge flowed into the harpoon from the alchemical batteries beneath Theo's feet. He could almost hear her scream through the gunsight.

"Ten seconds." *Edison* continued to quiver and shake as though with fever, jerking and twisting, but the harpoon held firm in her envelope. Reluctantly Theo stepped back from the gun and slid down the ladder.

"Five. Four. Three. Two. One." Theo held onto the ladder as though it were his long-lost sister.

A rumble as though the whole House had indigestion vibrated through the floor, the wall, and the ladder, as chemical and magical explosions severed the structural connections between the Red Diamond section and the rest of the House. Half the displays went black; most of the rest showed pandemonium.

In the center of the room, displayed in a tracery of crystalline filaments, a large lobe fell slowly away from the House, while three huge gasbags detached from the top of the structure to compensate for the lost weight.

Meanwhile, *Edison* thrashed at the end of her line. Then, suddenly, she reversed herself and dove toward the House. "No!" someone shouted — Theo realized it was himself.

The ghostly, crystalline *Edison* smashed into the top of the ghostly, crystalline House. The impact drove the House sideways, knocking everyone in the library except Theo, who still clung to the ladder, off their feet. The lights flickered, along with the technological displays; when they cleared, it was plain that two of the House's gasbags had been destroyed by the collision. Above them the *Edison* floated free, still connected by the slack cable but no longer twitching. It was unclear whether she was dead or alive.

Theo dragged himself to the nearest trumpet, as the floor shivered and tilted and a queasy feeling of uncontrolled descent flowed through his stomach. "Deploy emergency lift!" he shouted to the House Fathers.

"We have already done so," came the reply. "It is not sufficient. Too much reserve gas was lost in the detachment of the three gasbags that supported the Red Diamond section."

Theo sagged against the wall. The House of the Guided Musings was doomed. Helpless, he watched the altimeter drop. The room tilted slowly to one side as the crystalline model of the House fell away from the model of the *Edison*.

And then the *Edison* came to the end of the cable. Or perhaps the House did. In either case, there was a sickening jerk and the floor suddenly tilted fifteen further degrees. Theo's head slammed against the wall and he lost consciousness.

When he recovered, probably only a few seconds later, the three-dimensional display showed the *Edison* floating at the top of the cable, docile as a child's balloon. The altimeter was nearly stable; the great zeppelin had just enough lift to compensate for the two destroyed gasbags.

Theo stumbled across the tilted, debris-littered floor to the ladder, then clambered up to the gun room. The cable stretched through a gash in the dome, thrumming like a guitar string, and the whole room groaned with structural stress; there was no telling how long the cable, or the drum to which it was attached, or the structure to which the drum was in turn secured, would hold out.

He climbed up on the zeppelin gun, now bent nearly in half, and put his head next to the cable. Peering along its length, through the broken dome, he saw the *Edison* rotating slowly high above. Gas leaked from the rent where the harpoon pierced her skin.

And he heard his own name.

He looked around, but he was alone in the gun room, and the voice was so soft it could not have come from very far away.

Then he heard his name again, and this time he felt it as well— felt it thrumming under his fingers in the cable that held the House to the *Edison*.

He pressed his ear to the cable.

Theo, came Edie's voice, vibrating down the cable to his ear. Or perhaps it was just his imagination. *Theo, Theo, Theo... I still love you, Theo, though you have killed me.*

"I still love you, too, Edie," he whispered to the cable.

All around him the shadows deepened, as the House's lighting failed and the endless night crept in.

ଔ

The Tale of the Golden Eagle

THIS IS A STORY ABOUT A BIRD. A bird, a ship, a machine, a woman—
she was all these things, and none, but first and fundamentally a
bird.

It is also a story about a man—a gambler, a liar, and a cheat, but
only for the best of reasons.

No doubt you know the famous *Portrait of Denali Eu*, also
called *The Third Decision*, whose eyes have been described as "two
pools of sadness iced over with determination." This is the story
behind that painting.

It is a love story. It is a sad story. And it is true.

ભ

The story begins in a time before shiftspace, before Conner and
Hua, even before the caster people. The beginning of the story lies
in the time of the bird ships.

Before the bird ships, just to go from one star to another, people
either had to give up their whole lives and hope their children's
children would remember why they had come, or freeze themselves
and hope they could be thawed at the other end. Then the man
called Doctor Jay made a great and horrible discovery: he learned
that a living mind could change the shape of space. He found a way
to weld a human brain to the keel of a starship, in such a way that
the ship could travel from star to star in months instead of years.

After the execution of Doctor Jay, people learned that the part of the brain called the visual cortex was the key to changing the shape of space. And so they found a creature whose brain was almost all visual cortex, the *Aquila chrysaetos*, or as it was known in those days the golden eagle. This was a bird that has been lost to us; it had wings broader than a tall man is tall, golden brown feathers long and light as a lover's touch, and eyes black and sharp as a clear winter night. But to the people of this time it was just another animal, and they did not appreciate it while they had it.

They took the egg of a golden eagle, and they hatched it in a warm box, and they let it fly and learn and grow, and then they killed it. And they took its brain and they placed it at the top of a cunning construction of plastic and silicon which gave it the intelligence of a human, and this they welded to the keel of the starship.

It may seem to you that it is as cruel to give a bird the intelligence of a human, only to enslave its brain, as it is to take the brain of a human and enslave that. And so it is. But the people of this time drew a rigid distinction between born-people and made-people, and to them this seemed only just and right.

Now it happens that one golden eagle brain, which was called Nerissa Zeebnen-Fearsig, was installed into a ship of surpassing beauty. It was a great broad shining arrowhead of silver metal, this ship, filigreed and inlaid with gold, and filled with clever and intricate mechanisms of subtle pleasure.

The ship traveled many thousands of light-years in the service of many captains. Love affairs and assassinations were planned and executed within its silver hull; it was used for a time as an emperor's private yacht; it even carried Magister Ai on part of his expedition to the Forgotten Worlds. But Nerissa the shipbrain saw none of these things, for she had been given eyes that saw only outward. She knew her masters only by the sound of their voices and the feel of their hands on her controls.

When the ship was under way, Nerissa felt the joy of flight, a pure unthinking joy she remembered from her time as a creature of muscle and feather. But most of her time was spent contemplating the silent stars or the wall of some dock, awaiting the whim of her owner and master.

Over the years the masters' voices changed. Cultured tones accustomed to command were replaced by harsher, more unforgiving voices, and the ship's rich appointments were removed one by one. In time even basic maintenance was postponed or disregarded, and Nerissa found herself more and more often in places of darkness and decay. She despaired, even feared for her life, but shipbrains had no rights. The strongest protest she was allowed was "Sir and Master, that course of action may be inadvisable."

Finally the last and roughest owner, a man with grating voice and hard unsubtle hands, ran the ship into a docking probe in a foul decrepit port. The tarnished silver hull gave way, the air gushed out, and the man died, leaving a legacy so tattered and filthy that none could bear to touch it. Ownerless, airless, the hulk was towed to a wrecking yard and forgotten. Nerissa wept as the ship's power failed, her vision fading to monochrome and then to black. Reduced to the barest reserves of energy, she fell into a deep uneasy sleep.

While she slept the universe changed. Conner and Hua discovered shiftspace, and travel between planets became something the merely well-off could afford. The Clash of Cultures burst into full flower almost at once, as ten thousand faiths and religions and philosophies collided and mingled. It was a time of violence and strife, but in time a few ideas emerged as points of agreement, and one of these was that what had been done to the golden eagles was wrong. So the hatcheries were closed, the ships retired, and the shipbrains compassionately killed.

All save one. One that slept forgotten in a wrecking yard orbiting an ugly red star known only by a number.

The Clash of Cultures gradually drew to a close as points of agreement grew and coalesced, eventually giving birth to Consensus. But much knowledge was lost, and so when a king's tinker entered the wrecking yard and found the hulk of the great ship he had no idea what a unique treasure he had stumbled upon. He saw only the precious metal of the ship's hull, and it was for this metal he purchased it for his master.

As the ship was broken up, the tinker saved out a few of the most interesting-looking pieces for later use. One of these was the housing containing the sleeping brain of Nerissa Zeebnen-Fearsig. She felt a blinding pain as she was crudely torched from the ship's keel, and she feared her end had come at last, but then the pain receded and she slept once more.

Nerissa sat unconsidered for some years in one of the king's many storerooms, surrounded by a thousand other dismembered devices. But then came a day when the tinker entered the storeroom in search of some wire. He spotted a likely-looking length of wire beneath a pile of dusty components, but when he pulled on it he found himself with a peculiar rounded thing that piqued his curiosity. He took it back to his workbench, where he puzzled out its contacts and connectors, its inputs and outputs, and finally he connected an ancient scavenged power unit and Nerissa returned to awareness.

Waking was far more painful than being cut from the ship's hull. A torrent of discordant colors and textures flooded her senses, but her screams went unheard for the tinker had not connected her voice. Instead, a series of meaningless numbers and letters stepped delicately onto a small display plate. The tinker was fascinated by this, and stayed up all that night, probing and prodding, trying to understand just what manner of machine he had found.

Nerissa was nearly driven mad by the pain and the random sensations, and it was nothing but good fortune that when the tinker happened to hook up a voice unit to the proper outputs she was praying aloud for relief rather than crying incoherently — praying in Nihon, already an ancient language at the time of the bird ships, but still understood in the tinker's time as it is today. He dropped his soldering iron in astonishment.

Soon the tinker found Nerissa an eye and an ear and disconnected the probes that caused her the worst of the pain. They talked all that day, and he listened with apparent fascination to her description of her creation and her tales of her travels; for the first time in many centuries Nerissa allowed herself to hope. But though he professed to believe her, privately he concluded she was merely a machine: a storytelling machine constructed to believe its own fictions. For he was not an educated man, and as he had worked with machines every day of his life he was unable to conceive that she might be anything else.

Though he thought Nerissa was a machine, he recognized her intelligence and charm and decided to present her to his king as a special gift. He called together his apprentices and artisans and together they built a suitable container for her, a humanoid body of the finest and most costly materials. Her structural elements were composite diamond fiber, stronger than her old hull; her skin and hair were pure platinum, glowing with a subtle color deeper and finer than silver; her eyes and her teeth were beryl and opal; and all was assembled with the greatest of care and attention such that it moved as smoothly as any living thing.

The one thing he did not do was to provide the body with any semblance of sexual organs. It may seem to you that this omission is callous and arbitrary, and so it is. But the people of this time thought such a thing would be unseemly.

When the body was finished, Nerissa's brain in its housing was placed gently in its chest and the many connections were made with great care and delicacy. Power was applied then, and Nerissa's beautiful body of precious metals convulsed and twisted, her back arching and a horrible keening wail tearing from her amber lips.

She begged to be deactivated, but the tinker and his assistants probed and prodded, tweaked and adjusted, and gradually the pain ebbed away, leaving Nerissa trembling on its shore.

The king was genuinely delighted with the tinker's gift of "a storytelling machine, built from bits and pieces found here and there." The tinker had warned him that Nerissa seemed to believe her own tales, and so he pretended to believe them too, but Nerissa knew when she was being humored. So she gave him made-up stories, as he expected, though most of them had a kernel of truth drawn from her own life.

Now this king was a kind and wise man, truly appreciative of Nerissa, but he had many political problems and many enemies, so he rarely found time for her stories. After some months he found the sight of her, waiting patiently in his apartments, raised a pang of guilt that overwhelmed his joy at her beauty and grace. So he decided to gift Nerissa to an influential duke. In this way he hoped to put the man in his debt, to broaden the reputation of his tinker, and perhaps to gain Nerissa a more appreciative audience.

So Nerissa joined the household of Duke Vey, in the city of Arica. The king's plan met with great success; the duke, well pleased with the king's gift, spent many hours parading Nerissa before his friends and relations. All were suitably impressed by her stories, her charm, and her gleaming beauty, and the king's tinker received many fine commissions from those who had seen her.

One of those who saw her was Denali Eu.

The son and heir of the famous trader Ranson Eu, Denali appeared but rarely in Arica. When he did visit the city he attended all the finest soirees, displaying his subtle wit and radiant wardrobe, and gambled flamboyantly. All agreed he shared his late father's gambling skill, though lacking his extravagance and bravado. Of his travels, however, he let fall only the vaguest of hints. He liked to say his business dealings were like leri fruits, sensitive to the harsh light of day.

In fact, Ranson Eu had gambled away his fortune, leaving his wife and only child shackled to a mountainous debt. Denali Eu had no ship, no travels, no servants. His time away from Arica was spent in a small and shabby house not far from town, the family's last bit of property, where he and his mother Leona survived on hunting and a small vegetable garden. In the evenings they sewed Denali's outfits for the next expedition to Arica, using refurbished and rearranged pieces from previous seasons. It is a tribute to Leona Eu's talent and taste that Denali was often perceived as a fashion leader.

It pained Denali to maintain this fiction. But he had no alternative, for as long as he was perceived as a prosperous trader his father's creditors were content to circle far from the fire and dine on scraps. His social status also gave him access to useful information, which could sometimes be sold for cash, and gave him entree to high-stakes gambling venues. Ranson Eu had, in fact, been an excellent gambler when sober, and had passed both acumen and techniques on to his son. Denali often wished he could have returned the favor by passing his caution and temperance on to his father.

It was across a spinning gambling wheel that Denali Eu first saw Nerissa Zeebnen-Fearsig. The lamplight glanced off her silver metal shoulder as a cat rubs against a leg, leaving both charged with electricity. Her unclothed body revealed every bit of the expense and quality of her manufacture. She stood with head tilted upward, her amber lips gently parted as she spoke to the taller Duke Vey beside her.

"Who is that?" asked Denali Eu to the woman beside him as he gathered his winnings.

"It is the duke's storytelling machine. Have you not seen it before?"

"No... no, I have not. She's beautiful. She must be worth millions."

"It's priceless. It was a present from the king."

At that moment Eu made the first of three decisions that shaped the rest of his life and set a legend in motion: he determined to win Nerissa from the duke in a game of senec.

Denali Eu was a keen observer of people, as he had to be given his situation, and he had often found himself seated across a senec table from Duke Vey. The duke, like many senec players, had a mathematical system for playing the game. It was a good system; in fact, Eu had to concede it was better than his own... most of the time. For he had noticed a flaw in the system's logic. He had husbanded this knowledge for many months; he knew that once he had exploited the flaw the duke would not fall into the same trap a second time.

Here was the opportunity he had been waiting for. The machine's platinum and jewels alone might fetch enough to retire his father's debt, even at the price (far below their actual value) he could obtain on the black market. It would be a shame to break up such a fine creation, but he could never sell her entire; to do so would attract far too much attention to the Eu family's affairs.

It was two weeks before Denali Eu was able to engineer a game of no-limit senec with the duke, and when he sat down at the table Denali's nerves were already keening with tension. He usually kept his visits to a week, and despite his best efforts he thought some were beginning to suspect he had only two suits of clothing to his name.

Denali knew the duke would not be easily trapped. As he played he extended himself much farther than he usually did, risked much more than he normally would, to engage the duke's attention. His smile grew forced, and trickles of perspiration ran down his sides; he had to restrain himself from nervously tapping his cards against his sweating glass of leri water.

Eyebrows were raised around the table. One of the other players muttered "seems he has a touch of the old man in him after all" behind his cards. Again and again Denali raised the stakes, pushing his system to its own limits. Repeatedly he seized control of the dealer's token, the surest way to maintain his lead but the greatest risk in case of a forfeit. And forfeit he did, not just once but twice, for even the best system must occasionally fail in the face of an improbable run of bad cards. But through aggressive play he beat back from his losses, bankrupting one player after another. And always he kept a weather eye for the run of staves he needed to exploit the flaw in the duke's system.

Finally only Denali Eu and Duke Vey remained, the reflected light from the maroon felt of the senec table turning both their faces into demon masks. The other players watched from the surrounding darkness, most of their stakes now in Denali's possession. He could walk away from the table right now and it would be his most profitable trip since his father's death.

"One last hand," he said, placing his ante, "before we retire? A hand of Dragons' Delight, perhaps?"

"Very well," replied the duke, matching the ante.

Dragons' Delight was a fiendishly complicated form of senec, with round after round of betting and many opportunities for forfeit. Denali trembled beneath his cape as he raised and raised, trying to pull as much money as possible from the duke's hand, but not so much that he would be tempted to fold.

The seven of staves came out, and Denali raised his bet. The duke matched him. Then the prince of staves snapped onto the table. He raised again, substantially, and the duke raised him back. He matched, then dealt another card.

It was the courtesan of staves.

Their eyes met over the red-glowing table, the little pile of colorful cards, the heaps of betting counters. Denali knew the duke's system predicted an end to the run after three staves: a win for the duke. His own system said the odds of a fourth stave at this point, yielding a win for him, were better than eighty percent.

Denali gathered his hand of cards into a tight little bundle, tapped it against the table to square it, laid it carefully on the felt before him. He placed his hands, fingers spread, on either side of the stack for a moment. Then he reached to his left and shoved a huge pile of counters to the middle of the table. It was far more than the duke could match.

The duke placed his cards flat on the table. "It seems I must fold."

"So it seems. Or... you could wager some personal property."

"I think I know what you have in mind."

"Yes. The storytelling machine."

"I'm sorry. That is worth far more than..."

Denali pushed all the rest of his counters forward.

The duke stared levelly into Denali's eyes. Denali stared back a challenge: How much do you trust your system?

The duke dropped his eyes to his cards. Studied them hard for a moment, then looked back. "Very well. I wager the storytelling machine." A ripple of sound ran through the observers. "But I'm afraid that must be considered a raise. What can you offer to match it?"

Denali's heart shrank to a cold hard clinker at the center of his chest. He must match the raise, or fold. "I wager my ship." A man in the crowd gasped audibly.

Denali's ship, the *Crocus*, which had been his father's, was nothing but a worthless hull rusting behind his mother's house. The drive and other fittings had gone to a money lender from Gaspara. If he lost, his deception would be exposed and he would be sold into slavery to pay his father's debts.

"I accept that as a match," said the duke.

Denali stared at the back of the top card of the deck. If it was a stave, he won. Else, he lost. The little boy on the card's back design stared back at him. He could not meet that printed gaze, and dropped his eyes.

His eye lit upon one single counter that had been left by accident on the table before him, and a mad impulse seized him. He placed his index finger upon that counter, slid it across the felt to join the rest.

"I raise by one."

Stunned silence from the observers.

The duke's eyes narrowed. Then widened. Then closed, as he placed his hand across them. He began to chuckle. Then he laughed out loud. He leaned back in his chair, roaring with laughter, and slapped his cards on the table before him. "You fiendish bastard!" he gasped out. "I fold!"

Pandemonium. Denali Eu and the Duke Vey stood, shook hands, then embraced each other. The duke trembled with laughter; Denali just trembled. Servants appeared to gather the counters and process the transfer of property.

Denali could not help himself. He turned over the top card.

It was the five of berries.

ଓଃ

The next morning Denali Eu came to the duke's city house, his bag slung over his shoulder. He found Nerissa waiting in the entry hall, alone except for two guards. "The duke sends his regrets," said one, "but after last night's entertainment he finds himself indisposed to company."

Denali and the guards signed papers acknowledging the transfer of Nerissa to his possession, and he turned to leave, gesturing for her to follow. But as the door opened for them, a ray of morning sunlight touched her body and sent shimmering reflections into all the corners of the room. Denali turned back and was startled by her brilliant beauty.

"You're naked," he blurted out, and immediately felt foolish.

"Sir and Master, I am as I was made," she replied.

"I myself was born naked, but that does not excuse nudity in polite society. Here." He removed his cape and placed it over her shoulders. It was sufficient for propriety. Then, unsure of the proper term of address for a machine, he silently proffered his elbow. She took it, and the two of them walked out the door side by side.

"What shall I call you?" he said as they strolled up toward the docks. Her feet chimed on the hard pathway.

"My name is Nerissa Zeebnen-Fearsig, Sir and Master."

"Yes, but have you any title?"

"No, Sir and Master."

"Your name is a trifle... ungainly. I shall address you as M'zelle." It was a standard term of address for a younger woman, or one of lower status. None of her other owners had ever called her anything of the sort.

"As you wish, Sir and Master."

"You may address me simply as Sir," he said. The repeated use of his full and proper title made Denali uncomfortable, for he was keenly aware of just how close he was to slavery himself. He was all the more discomfited by Nerissa's inhuman beauty and poise. Walking beside her, he felt himself little more than a bag of meat and hair. Worse, he knew that soon he would have to destroy this marvelous machine, though his mind kept trying to escape that fact. "In fact, you need not use the Sir on every statement. M'zelle." And he inclined his head.

"Yes, Sir and Ma.... Yes, Sir.... Oh, goodness." Though her face had only a few movements to it, her confusion and embarrassment were clear from the set of her tourmaline eyebrows and amber lips. "I mean, yes. Just yes."

"Just so," he said, and he laughed.

Nerissa was unsure what to think of this man, whose clothing and bearing indicated great wealth but whose attitude toward her was deferential. She had sometimes seen fear, from unsophisticated or unlettered people, but this was something else. It was as though she held a measure of power over him.

Then she realized what it was she saw in Denali Eu's eyes. It was something she had never before seen directed toward herself.

It was respect.

They reached the docks, a confusion of utilitarian buildings at the top of a hill just outside of town. This was where the shiftspace ships made landfall. "Here we are, M'zelle," he said, and gestured her into a docking shed like all the rest.

It was empty.

"I do not understand, Sir."

He looked at the floor. His original plan had been to deactivate her at this point. But as they had walked together from town, he had come to understand just how heavy she was. There was no way he could smuggle her to his mother's house unassisted, and nobody other than Nerissa herself who could be trusted to assist.

He puffed out his cheeks, not raising his head. "The reason this shed is empty is that I have no ship. We will wait here until after dark, and then we will walk to my home, which is not far from here."

"You have no ship, Sir?"

"No." He turned and took her hands in his. They were warm, and hummed faintly. The fingernails were chips of ruby. He still did not meet her eyes. "No, M'zelle, I have no ship. In fact, I am afraid *you* are my sole possession of any value." Finally he looked up, his eyes pleading. "I must ask that you keep my secret safe."

Nerissa's heart went out to him then. "I am honored by your trust, Sir."

"Thank you, M'zelle." He led her to a small office, where there was a cot and a chair and a small stasis cupboard. "This is my waiting room. Can I offer you something to drink? Oh."

His expression of embarrassment was charming. "No, thank you," she said.

"But please... do take a seat."

263

"I do not tire, Sir."

"Please, M'zelle. I insist. I could not bear to see you stand while I sit, and I do tire and must sit eventually."

"Very well, Sir," she said. The chair creaked beneath her weight, but held.

Denali poured himself a glass of cool water from the cupboard, then sat on the edge of the cot. "Usually I pass the time until dark reading, but since I am now the owner of a fine storytelling machine, it would seem impolite not to make use of your services. Would you please tell me a story?"

"Certainly, Sir. What kind of story would you like to hear?"

"Tell me a story about... yourself."

A thrill went through her then. "Would you like a true story, or a made-up one?"

"True stories are always more interesting."

And so Nerissa told him a story about a golden eagle who lived for many years as the brain of a bird ship, then slept for a long time and finally became a storytelling machine. She did not embellish—the story was fantastic enough as it was—and she did not leave out the sad parts or the embarrassing parts.

When she finished, it was full dark. The glass of water sat, untouched, on the dusty floor beside Denali's cot.

Unlike the tinker, Denali Eu was an educated man. He knew the history of the bird ships, and he understood just what Nerissa was and what she was capable of. He had inherited his father's notes, his contacts, and his trading expertise along with his debts. He knew in his bones that with a bird ship he could not just repay those debts, but rebuild his family's wealth and reputation.

It was then that he made the second of the three decisions that set a legend in motion: he would find a way to refurbish the hull of *Crocus* and refit it as a bird ship.

But all he said to Nerissa was "Thank you for the story, M'zelle." He knew his new plan was nearly as cruel as the old, because it would still mean the end of her existence as a gleaming almost-person. *But at least she will still be alive,* he told himself. *You have the right to do this. She is your property. You owe it to your mother and to your father's memory.*

Still he felt filthy.

Denali dressed Nerissa in a spare suit of his traveling clothes, with gloves and a large floppy hat to hide her platinum skin, and they walked to his mother's house by the light of the moons. They talked as they walked, he of his life and she of hers. Both asked questions; both listened attentively to the answers. They learned about each other and they grew closer. If Nerissa sensed Denali was holding something back, she was not unduly concerned; she had already received far more confidences from him than she could ever have expected.

The house of Leona Eu had been hers before her marriage to Ranson Eu. It was small and patched, but warm and tasteful and genuine. Nerissa had never seen such a place; she loved it immediately.

Denali introduced Nerissa to his mother and explained that he had won Nerissa at gambling. Later, in private, he told his mother he planned to sell Nerissa on his next trip to Arica, but did not want the storyteller to know this because she would feel unwanted.

The life of the household returned to something like its usual routine, and Nerissa did her best to contribute. She proved to be a tireless gardener (her delicate finger joints protected from the dirt by leather gloves), and her ability to sit completely motionless for hours made her an impressive hunter. Nerissa was soon accepted as part of the family. This was something she had never experienced before, and she was honored and delighted. In the evenings, they all entertained each other with stories.

After Leona and Nerissa had gone to bed (for though her body never wearied, Nerissa's brain still required sleep), Denali stayed up late for many nights. He researched the bird ships and hauled out the old plans of *Crocus*, then drew new plans. The refitted ship would be stronger in the keel and lighter in weight; less luxurious, but with more lifesystem and cargo capacity. He sent both sets of plans to his father's chandler. The reply arrived in a few days: the chandler would do the work, though he said the design seemed insane.

The price he quoted was high. But the money Denali had won from the Duke would cover the down payment, and the balance was less than Nerissa's empty body would bring on the black market.

The next week the chandler came by with his delivery dirigible. He hooked chains and cables to *Crocus*'s corroded hull and hauled it away. Denali emptied out his secret personal cache of money and told Leona it was the proceeds of the salvage sale.

"I thought we had sold every part worth salvaging long ago," she said. "Surely the expense of the dirigible was more than the hull was worth?"

"I met the chandler on my last trip to Arica, and persuaded him he owed us a favor."

Leona still seemed unconvinced, but she accepted the money.

In the following weeks Nerissa's sense that Denali was hiding something from her increased. He grew haggard, and she found he would not meet her eyes. She wanted to ask him about his troubles, to repay the concern and respect she had been shown. But her years of servitude had ingrained in her a pattern of silent obedience and she said nothing.

For his part, Denali felt an agony of silence. He could confide neither in his mother, who would berate him for hiring the chandler with money he did not yet have, nor in Nerissa, whose beauty he planned to tear away and sell for his own profit; yet he ached for reassurance. He found himself uninterested in food, and spent long hours of the night staring at his ceiling, unable to sleep.

On one such restless night, he watched a patch of shimmering moonlight, reflected onto his ceiling from a small pond near the house, as it passed slowly from one side of the room to the other. Suddenly, silently, it flared and danced all over the room, then returned to its previous state. Just as he was about to dismiss the phenomenon as an effect of his tired eyes, it happened again. And a third time.

He rose from his bed and looked out the window. What he saw then captured his heart. It was Nerissa, dancing naked on the shore of the pond. He had seen the moonlight reflected from her shining metal body.

Nerissa's dance was a soaring, graceful thing, a poem composed of twirls and leaps and tumbles. The great strength of her legs propelled her high into the air, in defiance of her metallic weight, and brought her to landing as delicately as a faun. Her platinum skin in the moonlight shone silver on silver, black on black; she was a creature of the moonlight, a pirouetting dancing fragment of the night.

She was even more beautiful than he had thought.

His heart was torn in two. Part of it wanted to fly, to leap and dance with her in the night. Part of it sank to the acid pit of his stomach, as though trying to hide from the knowledge of the plan he had laid. How could he destroy this beauty and grace for mere money? But how could he sentence himself, his mother, and his father's memory to a continued life of debt and deceit—a life that must eventually end in discovery and shame—for the sake of a machine?

Perhaps he let out a small sound of despair. Perhaps it was the sight of his white nightshirt in the window. For whatever reason, Nerissa noticed she was being watched. Clumsily she stopped her dance and stared directly at him, her eyes two tiny stars of reflected light.

He descended the stairs and met her in the doorway. The moonlight shining from her cheek was painfully bright, and in the silence of the night he heard the tiny sounds of her eyes as they shifted in their sockets.

"I'm sorry I disturbed your sleep, Sir."

"No, no... I wasn't asleep. You dance beautifully, M'zelle."

"Thank you, Sir. I do enjoy it. It is as close as I can come in this body to the joy of flight between the stars."

The sundered halves of Denali's heart fused together then, for he realized then his plan for Nerissa was exactly what she wanted as well. He would restore her to her former life of sailing the currents of space, which she had described so vividly to him, and at the same time restore his own fortune.

Nerissa saw the smile spreading across his face, and asked what he was thinking.

"I have just thought of the most delightful surprise for you, M'zelle. A gift for you, to express my appreciation of your dance. But it will take some time to prepare, so I must ask you to be patient." He bent and kissed the warm metal of her fingers. "Good night, M'zelle."

"Good night, Sir."

He returned to his bed and fell immediately into a deep and dreamless sleep.

Three days later the chandler's dirigible returned, the refitted *Crocus* hanging from its gondola. The ship's gleaming hull wore vivid stripes of red, yellow, and green, the colors of Ranson Eu's former trading company. Denali, Leona, and Nerissa gathered together and watched as the dirigible lowered it gently to the ground. The pilot waved from the gondola as he flew away.

"This is my surprise to you both," Denali proclaimed. "Behold: *Crocus* is reborn!"

Nerissa stared at the ship in silent rapture, but Leona turned to her son with concern. "I suspected you were hiding something from me. This is a wonderful surprise, to be sure, but I thought we had no secrets from each other."

"Only this one, Mother. And there was a reason. Nerissa, here is my gift to you: this new *Crocus* has been built especially for you. In this new bird ship you will fly the stars once more."

Nerissa's reaction confused and disturbed him. She went rigid, her features drawing together and her eyes widening. "This is... a bird ship?" she said. "But where did you obtain the shipbrain?"

"There is no shipbrain, M'zelle. That position has been reserved for your own sweet self."

Nerissa's metal hands bunched into fists, held tightly against her chin. She seemed to shrink into herself. "No," she whispered. "No, no... please, Sir and Master... I beg you..."

Denali Eu felt his hands grow cold. "But M'zelle, when I saw you dance in the moonlight... I thought to fly the stars was your greatest joy."

"To fly is joy, yes... but to be cut from this body... to be severed... uprooted... the pain, Sir and Master... that pain is something I could never endure again." She crouched, trembling, on the stones of the path. Her eyes were huge. "I would rather die, Sir and Master. I would find a way, Sir and Master. Please, Sir and Master, please... I know you are my owner, I know I must obey your wishes without question or hesitation, but I beg you... do not ask me to do this." And she fell at his feet, her hands raised as though to ward off a blow.

All the color ran out of Denali Eu's world. He turned from Nerissa and Leona and marched clumsily into the woods behind the house. They did not follow.

Some time later he found himself seated on a fallen log. The sun was low in the sky and his clothes and skin were torn from thorns and brambles.

How could he have been so stupid? He had lied to his mother, lied to Nerissa, made unwarranted assumptions, and promised money he did not have. Soon the chandler's bill would arrive and he had nothing with which to pay it.

He considered his options. He could follow through with his plan—and Nerissa would find some way to end her life, or else would serve in unwilling misery. Even if he were heartless enough to force her to do this, he did not relish the idea of trusting his life to a ship he had betrayed.

He could break up Nerissa, sell her platinum and precious stones to pay the chandler—and she would be gone completely, and he would have only a worthless hull without a drive.

He could sell Nerissa in one piece—and it would be the same, only with more money. Nerissa would still be lost to him, and subject to the whim of some other master who might treat her still more cruelly.

He could repudiate the chandler's bill, declare bankruptcy— and see Nerissa sold off, along with his mother's house, and himself sold into slavery.

But there was one more option. Denali Eu was an educated man, and he knew the history of the bird ships. He also knew Nerissa's story. And because of this knowledge, and despite this knowledge, he made the final, fateful decision that set a legend in motion.

He spent a long time sitting on the log, his head in his hands, but he could think of no other alternative. Then he stood and walked back to his mother's house. There, as the sun set, he told Nerissa and Leona of his decision. His mother cried and shouted and beat her hands upon the kitchen table; Nerissa sat upon a chair with her head bowed, but did not speak. Neither of them could change his mind.

The next day Nerissa and Leona took Denali Eu for a walk in the forest. He listened to the birds and the rustling of the leaves, and he felt the cool wind brush gently against his skin. He smelled the green of the leaves and the damp of the earth, and as many flowers as they could find. In the evening they prepared for him a fine meal, with pungent spices and fresh vegetables, and succulent fruits new-gathered and sweet. Nerissa massaged his back with her strong warm fingers, and his mother cried as she brushed his cheek with pieces of silk and fur.

On the following morning he went into the city and gave himself to the doctors. He told them what he wanted, and he swore three times that this was his will.

And so they killed him, and they took his brain and welded it to the keel of the *Crocus*. For the techniques of Doctor Jay were legal, as long as the donation was voluntary and sworn to three times, and the organs of a young man in the best of health could be sold for enough money to pacify the chandler.

The operation was every bit as painful as Nerissa had said. But Denali found sailing the stars was even more delightful than dancing in the moonlight: a symphony of colors and textures beyond his human experience. And this ship was equipped with eyes and ears and hands within its hull as well as without.

The ship, renamed the *Golden Eagle*, became a hugely successful trader. Denali Eu's knowledge and skill, combined with Nerissa Zeebnen-Fearsig's beauty and charm, were something no seller or buyer could resist and no other trader could surpass. The ship with a human mind and a metal captain was famed in song and story, and when after many years Leona Eu died she left one of the greatest fortunes in the Consensus.

Denali Eu and Nerissa the Silver Captain have not been seen for many, many years. Some say they sought new challenges in the Magellanic Clouds or even beyond. Some say they settled down to a contented existence on an obscure planet. But no one doubts that, wherever they are, they are together still.

‍‌‍‌‌‍‌‌ϋ

About the Author

David D. Levine's "Tk'Tk'Tk'" won the 2006 Hugo Award for Best Short Story. "The Tale of the Golden Eagle" was a previous Hugo nominee; it also appeared on the Nebula preliminary ballot and was a finalist for the Sturgeon Award and Locus Award. Levine was a John W. Campbell Award nominee (2004 and 2003), Writers of the Future Contest winner (2002), James White Award winner (2001), and Clarion West graduate (2000). His stories have appeared in *F&SF*, *Asimov's*, *Realms of Fantasy*, and anthologies including Mike Resnick's *New Voices in SF* and four Year's Best volumes (two Fantasy, two SF). David lives in Portland, Oregon with his wife Kate Yule.

Coming From Wheatland Press 2008

Can't Buy Me Faded Love
Stories by Josh Rountree

A collection of Josh Rountree's unique brand of alt history and other brands of speculative rock 'n' roll stories. May 1, 2008

Laughin' Boy
By Bradley Denton

This amazing novel was written well in advance of the September 11 attacks, but was rendered unpublishable for some time after. It was published in 2006 in a collectors limited edition by Subterranean Press. WP will be doing the trade paperback. May 25, 2008

Polyphony 7
Edited by Deborah Layne and Forrest Aguirre

The multi-award nominated cross-genre anthology series continues with a new editorial team. August 15, 2008

The Moone World
By Howard Waldrop

A novella from the most unique voice in science fiction and fantasy. Twenty-eight years in the making. August 15, 2008

About a Duck
Stories by Ray Vukcevich

The second collection from the critically acclaimed author of *Meet Me in the Moon Room* and *The Man of About a Half-Dozen Faces.* August 15, 2008

For ordering information visit:
http://www.wheatlandpress.com

www.ingramcontent.com/pod-product-compliance
Lightning Source LLC
Chambersburg PA
CBHW030353020726
47493CB00003B/797